ASHTRAY

41/250

ASHTRAY

Thomas Mammoth

FRIENDLY PUPPY PRESS | 2024

For Mackerel

CHAPTER 1

Look Closer to the Seal

Trudging forward, shoving a shopping cart over the snow-littered pavement, I gazed up at the sky. The sun, a small orange circle behind a thick, gray haze. Like the lit end of a huge interplanetary cigarette mid-inhalation, as though some higher being from a different plane of existence was taking his smoke break. The thick haze I navigated was his exhale. I lived in his secondhand smoke. I coughed and veered my cart around a frozen animal carcass covered in dust, shit, and snow. My planet was his ashtray.

TL;DW (too long, didn't write): World War III happened.

To quickly get you up to my speed—a slow walk with a busted shopping cart through a post-apocalypse (or mid-apocalypse, who's to say)—I think I slept through most of it. Well, factually, I did. I was sleeping over twelve hours a day. A high dose of antipsychotics, in combination with a mood stabilizer, ensured as much. I stopped taking those meds before my pharmacy was destroyed. But yeah, I was sleeping, or at least in my bed, for that long or longer each day. Bed being an inclusive, fluid term, expanding to include the couch, the floor, the rug, or wherever

1

I'd lie and not move for hours. Occasionally, I would play with Piston, who is a gray tabby cat. When I was awake and mobile (mobile being a relative term), I'd play *Red Dead 3*.

I didn't really leave my apartment very much, and I wasn't checking the news because it sucks. But I figured all this out— *this* being the details of the world-ending apocalypse—about a month ago. One day, in trying to see when season four of *One Punch Man* would come out, I was browsing Google for relevant articles and found that the studio that was working on it had exploded. When I looked to see which studio would be picking it up in their place, I saw that all of Japan had exploded and, click-ing along further, hoping that perhaps a studio based in Thai-land, Korea, or, God forbid, the United States would pick up the show in their stead, I learned that Thailand was completely underwater and Korea was nowhere to be found. One particular article speculated that Korea had been ravaged by land-levelling quakes of such magnitude that they split the country into little crumbs of country cereal, which grew soggy and were sinking to the bottom of the great oceanic bowl. Most countries had, in some form or another, combusted, exploded, or sank. Zip, gone. After scanning a few more articles, I powered on my phone for the first time in a couple months. (I had been avoiding calls, personal reasons.) There had been nineteen evacuation orders from the government to leave my state, Minnesota, all dated five weeks prior. Guess nobody comes and knocks anymore, or sends letters. All Minnesota residents were ordered to evacuate to South Dakota. A quick Google told me that South Dakota had exploded. Then some form of revelation started to sink in.

I wasn't getting a new season of *One Punch Man* anytime soon.

South Dakota didn't get bombed, but apparently (these were all articles written by independent bloggers in a nuclear panic seconds or hours before [probably] being blown up, so take the following with a grain of salt), the bombs dropped during World War III released chemicals so destructive that the earth essentially rejected them. In response, the planet set multiple biblical-tier natural disasters into motion. These wiped out entire states, countries, and continents. Basically, whatever the nukes missed, Gaia finished off with the follow-up right hook. The oceans seem mostly alright, according to a couple articles, but hell, I imagine they're fucked up in some way.

It seems that the folks who believed in Gaia, the idea that the Earth is a living organism, were correct. For once. But again, take my paraphrasing of the articles I half read/mostly skimmed with a grain of salt. Those loonies may just be the only ones who survived long enough to write articles and tweets. The last living article writer might work for BuzzFeed, and hell, if you outlive everyone else, your article is the Truth. And, well, even if they *did* get this animistic notion correct (which I'm not altogether sold on), they were *not* correct about crystals, 5G, radio waves, tinfoil, aliens, the Loch Ness monster, Bigfoot, cryptids of all kinds, the Myers-Briggs exam, empathy, positivity, affirmations, numerology, tarot, spirits, demons, ghosts, paranormal activity, Reiki, the law of attraction, NoFap, drinking piss, spiritual healing, oxalate dumping, veganism, and that life is inherently good. But the angry earth theory was the most commonly accepted theory I could find, originating from an independent blog based in Boston, which was still posting articles as recently as three weeks ago. This was before Boston was consumed by a tidal wave and sucked into a volcano, which subsequently erupted and shot the remains of said city 1,200 feet above sea level, a molten blob straight from hell. Boston's explosion trended for like half a day on Twitter.[1] A video of the event from a really shitty perspective was embedded in the tweet; hard to say if it was fake or not.

In summary, the earth had a sneezing fit and almost everyone died. Except for me, a stubborn booger lodged in Gaia's nostril.

---

1. Yes, I am aware the name of Twitter was changed to X. But I am changing X *back* to Twitter. Elon Musk's incinerated remains can take issue with that if they so desire.

I'm not sure how many cities survived. I tried to Google it, but people have stopped updating their blogs. The most recent post I found from any website, Twitter included, was from twelve days ago. Aside from me, of course. I've still been tweeting on occasion. If I think of something funny, you know.

All that said, the power still ran at my apartment. The internet still worked. Even now, as I write this, I've got phone service, 5G even. I've got running water. All that stuff is controlled by AI or automated programs, so it's hard to say if those systems are functional and running without human intervention, *or* if there are indeed other humans aside from myself still walking the planet, and, on top of that, they're organized enough to keep those systems functional. Regardless, I haven't seen any people in a good while.

Back to my apartment. For a while, I felt like the bags of Lays at the supermarket were disappearing and suspected other survivors were eating them. But then I remembered that no one restocks the shelves anymore and that I've been eating Lays, so that got cleared up. I cleaned the Amazon Market out of ramen packs and have moved on to the Cub Foods down the street.

And listen, I know it sounds surreal that I wouldn't notice *no one* at all anywhere . . . but I never left my apartment before all of this. I had my groceries delivered to the door by the automated shopping cart robots. Those are still running, too. They're unreliable now that the roads are littered with abandoned cars, so the cart buses can't do their rounds, but I still see a few stray carts here and there, attempting to deliver rotten groceries to long since (presumably) obliterated city dwellers. Mutually assured destruction of most things everywhere happened so fast that one month ago I got my groceries, and two weeks later I went down my Googling rabbit hole and figured all this out. I didn't run out of food for another week after that.

A little about me before I get on with all of this. My name is Isaac Murphy. Plain name, I know. I wear glasses. As a kid, people used to call me four-Isaac (four-eyes-aac), which, yes, sort of clever, I know. I came up with it myself. It made me chuckle, so I spread the name around to my classmates and it caught on. So, yeah, it didn't really bother me much. It validated me that people also thought it was clever enough to use it as a jab so often.

I have short, cropped black hair and paint an altogether unimpressive sight when viewed from most angles. I stand an inch above six feet, but that's about it in terms of auspicious genetics. I'm lanky and weigh in at about 165 lb., aka skinny-fat. My limbs are quite string-like, many of my pounds not existing as muscle, but hanging around my belly and hips. I was a mechanical engineer, then dropped all that to become a photographer (on an irreverent and irrational whim, according to my family), and now, well, I'm jobless. I had left my job a couple months prior to the apocalypse and had been living on savings. But I don't have to worry about rent anymore, which rules. Generally speaking, I'd say I'm mildly competent. Competency is, of course, a relative concept. Like, I'm wildly incompetent next to a Navy SEAL, but mildly competent next to a normal seal. So, somewhere on the spectrum between normal and Navy, you'll find my dot. Look closer to the seal.

I have a cat. His name is Piston. He's cool. Gray tabby, super fluffy, big green eyes with pupils that dilate like black holes that suck up suns and galaxies when he's excited. Kind of a maniac. Actually, a full-blown maniac. It's a lot of responsibility owning a cat, and, like I mentioned, I'm a busy guy. Piston didn't notice anything too weird either. Unlike most these days, he's been doing well. Living a life of feline luxury. My apartment isn't too spacious, but I have nice stuff for him: tons of toys, games, a big-ass cat tree, bouncy balls galore; basically, what I hope is the equivalent of a cat mansion, a cat PS6, and plenty of comfortable spots to lounge. Like I have for myself. We're simple guys. There's tons of canned food at the pet store, and tons of ramen packets and chips at the supermarket, so basic survival items are still available. This isn't one of those apocalypse stories where I'm gonna be scrounging for materials every five seconds. It's only like a mile to walk to the supermarkets, and I can just fill the cart and bring it home now, which is nice. Though, annoyingly, the first snows of winter have begun to dribble down from the orange-tinged overcast sky. The flakes melt upon meeting the pavement, but each particle I see portends problems I don't want to confront.

OK, you should be up to speed now.

The cart melted lines through the particles of snow on the pavement. I wasn't on my way to the supermarket, nor was I on my way home from the supermarket. This hadn't really occurred to me until two days prior, but I actually didn't need to be in my studio apartment anymore! I could live anywhere the fuck I wanted! So, shoving the cart filled with some essentials, I scoped out the potential homes in a nearby residential area that I could soon call my own.

The sun started to creep toward the horizon, so I called it quits and headed back to my apartment. I'd try again tomorrow.

CHAPTER 2

Directions

Walking to the grocery store, I listened to the noise filling my brain to the brim through my AirPods. It was quite nice. Nobody stopping me on the street for a buck or asking me some stupid fuckin' question about directions to some place that I damn sure don't know how to get to. *Yes, I live in Minneapolis, but I go to* maybe *four places tops, and to get to those places I use Google Maps! The friggin' thing you should also be using rather than make me pull out my headphones.* Of course, I'd never actually said any of these sentences and usually would just guess and point somewhere. I'd be gone by the time that person returned to complain to me about giving false directions. How the hell was I supposed to know where anything was?

Another thing: The aisles not being clogged up by abandoned carts of easily distracted people perusing the stock—which hardly changes from one week to the next, so one wonders what truly interesting and novel items these regulars are so meticulously eyeballing—is *so nice.* Get outta the way, soccer mom! Fuck's sake. And I don't want to have to push your fucking cart out of the way to get through! What is so intere- you know what, it's not worth it. I muttered this to myself as I knocked some coffee beans into the cart, not sure how much I'd actually said aloud versus thought. Those people were gone, and had likely exploded, which they *deserved*. I lingered on that word in my head, as though emphasis made it more true. They did indeed. God would judge them for the indiscretions they'd committed in the grocery store aisles. And so would I.

The first time I got groceries post-explosion-fest, I felt a pang of guilt as I crossed the threshold of the automatic doors. I couldn't quite place why, but I couldn't take another step forward. I timidly approached the self-checkout kiosk, scanned all my items, and paid. Yes, it felt stupid. I paid the next time, too. The payments went through and everything. After it sunk in that Amazon Market would truly never collect or sue me for stealing groceries, I looked into getting some refunds. Needless to say, I didn't get my money back. I've since stopped paying.

I filled my cart with the basics (ramen packets, chips, ground coffee, cold-brew bottles, water bottles, miscellaneous items I casually swiped into the cart while I walked) and started the journey home. Of course, the cart that I happened to pick had a faulty wheel *again*. No, I couldn't switch it out, that would be a pain. The first mile was absolutely insufferable due to the stupid wheel. I forced the cart past a house that I'd always liked, glancing over at the specter of the old man who used to stand out front, raking leaves. I stopped, feeling a passing impulse to crack open the door and peek inside.

That passing impulse started to go on ahead, lingered, and turned back, deciding it didn't quite feel like passing after all. Leaving my cart in the street, I ambled to the door. I found it to be slightly ajar already. Such fortune. Normally, such things would indicate that I'm living out a horror movie, and that I should cut and run. But it was 11:15 a.m. and light was spilling through every window and crevice into the interior. I made a move that looked like accidental stumbling so I could nudge the door further open without taking accountability. This move turned into a real stumble, and, in an awkward and embarrassing motion, I found my limbs scattered on the threshold in a heap. Half inside the home, red-faced and hoping no one was corporeal enough to witness the preceding event, I stood up. I dusted myself off, prepared to leave in a flurry of apologies in case any residents met my loud fall with shock and consternation. I scanned my surroundings, expecting a response, *something*. But nothing met me except luminescent dust particles. Thankfully, those particles had nothing to say about my fall, and if they were saying anything, they were saying it with such small voices that I could not hear them. The particles glowed, illuminated by the sun through a crack in the curtain, the dusty air creating tangible lines in space. If they were talking about me, they could get fucked.

Taking four more steps forward, I gave the now certainly empty home a perfunctory once-over. The couch was denim. It looked quite comfortable. Slightly stained and covered in dog hair from a dog whose hair was now likely ash. There was a large TV mounted to the wall, one of those new 8K 4D monitors, above a cobblestone fireplace. Nice furniture, modest enough. These people had taste. I continued to scan for relevant information. A nice leather recliner with back- and butt-shaped imprints that described a rather hefty individual. The old man himself had been thin, with arms no thicker than the rake he'd used to tidy the lawn. Big wife? Big kids? Looking at the wall, family photos indicated that both were true. I would remove those later. As you might have guessed, this was my house now.

CHAPTER 3

Shopping Carts

The shopping cart fell into a pothole, the impact causing the faulty wheel to be dismembered from the axle. The cart lost equilibrium, tipping, sending itself, Piston, and my PS6 (amongst other far less important possessions) into the wet, snowy street. Piston yelped in a truly unpleasant manner that made him sound like a 93-year-old man having his ankles chopped with a cleaver.

"GRUAHHHGHH!!" Piston yelped as he flew into the snow, swiftly followed by my PS6. It hit the pavement next to him with a crunch that communicated its most definite demise.

"God-fucking-dammit," I grumbled, pissed off. I scooped Piston in my hands and then bunny hopped onto the black box, ground-pounding into oblivion any last flickers of life it may have contained.

"Rest in peace, dickhead." I glanced over the contents of the overturned shopping cart, picking up a box of tissues, four games, and some Mentos. Piston, due to his apparently massive discomfort in my arms, felt he needed to squirm and readjust his body every half second, leading to three more plops into the snow for him. The first time was an accident, the second time he clawed me trying to readjust himself and then again on the way down, and the third time I let him go because of the second time. I continued walking along, trying to leave my frustration behind with my destroyed PS6. I wasn't annoyed at the cat; I was pissed off at the deity of shopping carts who fucked my shopping cart, after six trips, on the *only trip* it was *NOT* allowed to get fucked up on. I made a mental commitment to desecrate shopping carts later to get any excess resentment out of my system. Maybe I'd take a shit in one. Watch the turd fall through the grates.

My boots slid over the fresh, melting slush on the way to my new house. They were soaked to the core. Shit boots. Decade-old, barely fit for winter, shit boots. In shoe years, that's pretty senile. I couldn't even tell you the brand, as any details that would indicate such a thing had long been weathered away by time. The cold and wet had seeped into my socks on trip number three, and at this point, I was quite sure my toes were white. (FYI: I am white, but more technically a pinkish, very light, orange-beige hue, varying slightly during summers into a more orangish tan, but my toes, right now, were probably a light blue.)

Stepping through the craters of my previous treks, still attempting to dissociate from my anguish, I noticed a set of footprints running perpendicular to my previous sets of foot-prints. I halted, holding a shuddering Piston tightly against me. He wasn't scared, he just doesn't fare too well in the cold. His fluffiness soothed my mild apprehension. Had I simply missed these craters in the snow before? For five trips back and forth? As in, ten passes? Knowing me, it was very possible. I examined the disheveled snow and saw that the tread was indeed different from my shit-boot treads. So that ruled out me walking off in a dissociated stupor and not remembering it, which was a start. Upon further inspection, I concluded that this dude's (or lady's) boots would never fit me. So, finding no use in following the tracks to what I assumed would be a dead body and stealing their boots for myself, I trudged onward to my new home.

I felt all kinds of oddities trickling into my body during that final stretch of streets. Those last eight blocks blurred, my mind both at the intersection of footprints and already inside my new home, but never with my body, walking between those two points.

. . .

39 Duntrell Avenue. My new home. I had initially planned to make one final trip back to my old apartment, but the following events precluded such a journey. In short, my body and mind went awry. As I said, I had been feeling . . . odd. By the time I reached the front door, I had already been dealing with a heart that continually banged against my ribs, an innocent prisoner screaming for freedom from his cell of bones. Then, upon entering my new home, rather than feeling a sense of completion and relief washing over me, I became absolutely convinced I was going to die. Some part of me knew beyond a shadow of a doubt that this was ludicrous, but that did nothing to shake my conviction. My fingertips were numb and tingling. I would've normally chalked this up to poor gloves, and that definitely did have something to do with the numbness, but the tinglyness (to be differentiated from numbness) was invading my forearms now, making itself known as a monstrous disease of its own, unrelated to the cold. In fact, the warmer I got, the more vibrant and visceral the tingling became, trickling in from my fingertips and now laying siege to my shoulder blades.

I had no idea strokes were so . . . tingly. Like static electricity, but inside your body. Huh. I found myself supine on the floor next to the closed front door, sweating, my only company being all these people's shoes, which I had yet to throw into the front yard. Piston was off exploring his new home. Or perhaps licking himself dry in some corner. The uncaring bastard. Well, I would join him later, after my stroke. I attempted to distract myself by counting the total amount of shoes on the shoe rack, and then visualized myself throwing them outside. I'd start with the old man's right loafer. Going deep into the visualization, I chucked the loafer into the beautiful autumn yard in my mind's eye. The visualization continued as I found myself, the following day, encountering this loafer in the front yard. A frustrating eyesore indeed. This blemish on my glorious lawn would not stand. So, I threw it into the street. From there, I continually, inexplicably, passed this shoe, and was repeatedly disturbed by its presence in my life. I hated this loafer. Mind-me journeyed far and wide, throwing this loafer anywhere from fifteen to forty-five feet. (Yes, I can throw it that far. Yes, I *actually* can. Do you wanna bet?) The shoe arced and fell, repeatedly painting an inverse parabola in the air. Accumulated dirt and grass and scuffs told tales of its travels through cities, states, countries. Soon, I found myself atop the Great Wall of China, still pissed off, angrily tossing this leather loafer as hard as I could. It dropped out of eyesight to the grass below the wall. Down with the bones you go, loafer. By the time I had grown bored of this fantasy, after maybe twenty-five minutes, I realized I was sitting up, holding a different shoe, a left all-white Nike Air Force 1. The tingly disease was gone, and briefly I wondered how long I'd felt fine for. Weak stroke. Or maybe I'm just too strong. I opened the door and chucked the Air Force 1 as hard as I could into the late-afternoon snowy slop. It hit the mailbox. Yes, I was aiming for the mailbox. Ten points. I went for a subsequent ten with the right shoe. *Clunk.* Twenty points for me. I shut the door and locked it.

I poured some water into the kettle I had brought with me. Waiting for it to scream, I took the kimchi ramen out of its packaging and set my noodle rectangle inside a large ceramic bowl. Piston had begun to mew and say "yuaaaah" once he smelled the kimchi spice packet, sounding much more like a cute, normal cat now.

"Yeah, OK. Alright, I'm going," I replied, to which he simply continued his yuahs and mrows and mews. I scooped some wet food into a bowl and served him his feast, and just as Piston's yelling was replaced by the smacking of tongue and teeth, the kettle began to scream, letting me know her insides were being scalded. I freed her from her torture, listening to the soothing plop of the water upon ceramic. I put a plate over my bowl.

I stared at my mildly overweight cat as he munched away until the hot water softened my noodles enough to permit me the same pleasure. I ate the ramen slowly. The hot, spicy broth warmed my insides, bringing me back into myself. Warmed up and slightly more confident, I pondered what lay ahead. Those footprints I'd seen at the intersection were on the way to Target, which was currently holding my new PS6 hostage. Those footprints would have to be confronted.

CHAPTER 4

Target

A t just past dawn, I set the kettle on the electric stovetop, poured enough instant coffee into a cup to give a defibrillator an inferiority complex, and prepared an incessantly mewing Piston his morning chow. I drank my coffee at the small wooden table in the kitchen, looking out a side window at the grass and trees and the neighbor's house. Dawn crept along, the sun slowly changing the hues outside from blues to oranges.

The first hot coffee in the morning is like the first cigarette of the day: it cannot be replaced, and no subsequent coffee or cigarette can hold a candle to that initial satisfaction, that replenishment of chemicals from your longest hours of abstinence, sleep. Yeah, it's really something. I would embark on my trek as soon as I finished my coffee, while that caffeinated confidence still surged through my bloodstream.

I put on my undergarments, my tank top, my outerwear, my boots, my gloves, my glasses, my beanie, and my headphones as Piston puttered around, wondering what I was up to.

"Off on a quest," I told him flatly. But instead of a sword, I carried a drawstring bag and my phone. I put on Squarepusher's

15

album *Damogen Furies*. I opened the wooden door, stepped outside, and inhaled the cold air. A dry, biting wind slapped against me, cutting my cheeks, making the twenty-five-degree weather feel like single digits. Note to self: Grab a balaclava from Target, and some thicker pants, too.

As I walked out into the front yard, I noticed the Air Force 1 by the shrub, blending in like a man in a white ghillie suit in a tundra. Can't hide from me, asshole. I scooped it up, and in one smooth motion, I chucked the shoe at a street sign that said children lived here. Not anymore. The silhouette should now just be me and a cat. A clunk resounded from the sign, ringing through the empty street. I tallied myself another ten points and walked off in the opposite direction. I checked Instagram for any new posts; I went onto the "Explore" tab, checked the reels. Everything was still online and working: 5G, social media, and the weather app were all still functional. Just no new posts, aside from those clearly from bots.

Browsing through a friend's profile as I walked, I ended up on an underwater picture of her, along with two friends and a shark. She was clearly on some vacation. All of them looked joyful, aside from the shark. He looked rather grim, teeth bared at the cage separating him from his snacks. I could relate to his hopelessness, his sense of frustration, the feeling of being mocked. I mean, imagine if a banana split took selfies with you while *you* were locked in prison. Cruel and unusual indeed. I had recognized one of the other two women, but she was turned away, so I was mostly going off of the shape of her butt. I clicked into her profile, and yes, I had been correct, it was indeed Emily Robinson, a woman I'd had a crush on in high school. I clicked "follow" on her account.

Approaching the intersection where I had seen the unexplained foot-sized craters in the snow, I began to jog. I had already deduced that this clearly no-longer-alive man's or woman's shoes were not big enough for me, so any further detailed inspection was unnecessary. My gaze rested up among the trees ahead, and I focused on my running form. I slipped, slid, and barely recovered before falling. Jogging down the middle of unplowed streets was fun, like I was in a video game. Everything looked mostly the same, just no other characters milling about, like an open-world RPG or battle-royale map. I turned right at the intersection, following the unknown footsteps.

To my own astonishment, I kept jogging all the way down the next four blocks. I was surprisingly invigorated, nostrils expanding with the cold air, each breath crisp and fresh. I didn't even know I could still run like this. As the whole world was one big smoky ashtray, I'd assumed my lungs would just perform like, well, garbage. But I held pace without too much effort and felt light and springy as I bounced forward with each step. The unknown footsteps continued to jog with me, before turning off at a four–way stop sign, whereas I continued straight ahead.

After the intersection, I settled into a walk, breathing deeply. I pulled out my phone and opened Instagram again, checking if Emily had followed me back yet. Nope. Two blocks further, I went beneath an underpass and turned left onto Madison Avenue. Target was about a mile down this street. Listen, I *knew* that there was a solid chance, probably around 99.9999 percent, maybe add like four or five more 9s, that she was dead, and if not dead, at the very least asleep. In any case, not using Instagram. So, I stopped caring. I walked the remaining mile to get to the Target. I checked to see if she had followed back again. Nope. I unfollowed.

. . .

Woosheeep, went the automatic doors. I cruised through into a fully lit Target.

"Thank God for AI," I replied to the door. As this wasn't *Hitchhiker's Guide to the Galaxy*, no reply was issued back. All I heard was my own footsteps and the subsequent echo. The inside of the store smelled like a dump truck you were unfortunately caught behind under a bridge during rush hour. The aisles were a disaster. Food packages lay strewn across the floor, scraps of packages littered the mostly empty shelves, and there was an occasional splatter of blood. And yes, the world *had* exploded a month ago, but Black Friday was a week before that. This could've been the result of either.

I made my way through the ruins to the electronics section. I felt a jolt of joy when I locked eyes with a PS6, encased within her glass prison. I went behind the help desk and saw a key ring but, immediately thinking better of it, grabbed the broom wedged below the desk. Hoisting the broom, I smashed the glass. I cleared the edges of the glass enclosure, little pieces tinkling onto the linoleum. I lifted the PS6 box out and placed it carefully into my drawstring. I made sure to position the broom within reach of the mess so the Target employees who eventually had to clean this up would have an easier time of it.

I approached the food section and the stench of rotting fruits and vegetables slithered up into my crinkling nostrils. I stole a balaclava from the men's clothing section and donned it immediately, then beat a hasty retreat, fingers clasped around my nose. I stepped outside, victorious.

Upon reaching the four-way stop, I stopped and stared right where the foreign footprints branched off. They were becoming less identifiable with each passing hour, the snow erasing their trail and mine.

I found myself lightly jogging again, a few blocks down, the box in my bag grazing uncomfortably against my spine. This time, though, my body seemed to recall how out-of-shape I had become from years of not running and living in a world of second-hand smoke. My lungs rebelled within me, pleading with me to stop. I walked the last few blocks. I hadn't really done much at all besides take product photos and play video games for a few years, so it'd take a while to get back in shape.

"Back in shape?" mind-me sneered. *"That would imply you were once in shape!"* I began to reply that, "In high school, you know-" but mind-me interrupted, saying that I was never

actually in shape then, just youthfully skinny due to a high-functioning metabolism.

I entered my home and sat on the couch. I unboxed the console and set it atop the mahogany dresser that sat beneath the large screen. I hooked up the HDMI to the USB-C, synced Bluetooth for good measure and, as I stepped over Piston to reach for a beer, everything, the TV included, went black.

I paused in disbelief, and then thrust my controller through the darkness, leaving a dent in the wall.

"FUCK!!" I yelled, Piston darting underneath the couch. "The timing is impeccable!! Really! Really just *fucking* incredible!! FUCK!" And with each exclamation I made a violent thrust with an arm or shoulder, throwing more imaginary controllers, spasmodically gesticulating, slicing through the midmorning light creaking through the curtains of the living room.

While I was sitting cross-legged on the ground and attempting to quell my rage to a manageable level, Piston peered up at me from under the couch. He eyed me cautiously, head darting up and down. I raised my hand up, hand taking the form of a cobra, and his eyes dilated in response. Piston, knowing his enemy, lowered his rump and pounced at the cobra! Then fell all too easily onto his back. Using his curled-up feet, Piston attempted to trap the cobra in an embrace as it rubbed his belly to death.

Piston, after reviving from the Death Belly Rub using one of his nine cat lives, began to desire another activity and strutted off to his food bowl in the other room of this useless house that I now hated. I'd have to move *again*! But for all I knew, the whole city could be fucked. Perhaps the whole country (or what remained of it) was fucked due to a finally dead power grid. To be honest, I have no idea how the "grid" works. The "grid" was simply a mythical creature that provided me with PS6 power and internet access so long as I prayed to it and gave offerings at the Xcel Energy website every month. Maybe these people's autopay had finally crapped out.

"Fuck. Fuck fuck fuck," I muttered.

"Oh, fuck . . . FUCK, fuck! I'm a goddamned genius," I exclaimed.

Solar panels! echoed in my mind. *Solar panels solar panels solar panels! Rich motherfuckers have fucking SOLAR PAN-ELS.* Renewed with hope, I glanced through the open doorway into the kitchen at Piston, who was busy munching away.

"Piss-face, pack your shit. We're leaving this dump."

CHAPTER 5

Parts Unknown

The following day, I opened the door of my briefly lived-in residence and set out on yet another stupid walk to somewhere else. The sun blazed down on this wintery dawn, leaving a harsh glare on the snow. It felt like twentyish degrees; I didn't check my phone to be certain since I was conserving all of its energy to serve as my GPS. As I began the trek, my caffeine high had me feeling optimistic. After I counted forty-nine steps, I thought about killing myself. But if I did that, I'd be leaving Piston to starve and die, which I could not do, which meant the only alternative would be to kill him first, which I also could not do. I glanced down at him, his head framed by two zippers on either side. His head was protruding from the maw of a JanSport backpack I wore backward. He stared back up at me as I scratched his head.

"It's because of *you* that I'm miserable," I told him, my voice bubbly. "This is all your fault." He squinted in the morning light. It was very cute.

After walking a few hundred meters, it became easier to move my legs. I felt sprightly, which I chalked up to the mad amount of coffee. I still had a half-bottle of coffee ultra-concentrate in my jacket pocket and a full bottle bobbing around in my drawstring on my back. The full bottle was supposed to be for tomorrow, but who knew how I'd fare on a journey like this. I might need it if I ran into trouble, like Popeye and his trusty cans of spinach. If enemies presented themselves, I'd drink my jitter-juice potion (coffee) and sprint far-as-fuck away from them. Post-Apocalypse Popeye had a good ring to it, so I tweeted just those three words. I started to cross the Hennepin bridge and peed off the side of it; I'd only been walking for about twelve minutes, but . . . coffee side effects and all, you know how it goes. I watched the stream go all the way down to the frosty ice that sat upon the Mississippi. I imagined a beautiful abstract art piece burned into the ice below. But more likely, the pee lost its heat on the way down and splattered onto the ice as clear, frozen particulates. I glanced back at the decrepit Grain Belt Beer sign, completely unlit. This boosted my suspicion that the whole city was without power.

I approached the Starbucks that sat on the corner of the upcoming intersection. Seeing a totally deserted downtown wasn't as surreal as you might think. The world had been in the middle of a third pandemic as one tsunami whirlpool ripped Florida from the rest of the U.S. (good riddance), so deserted cities had been the norm. I'd seen tons of YouTube videos of ghost cities (often set to ambient electronic music with a soothing baritone voiceover describing the findings, rather nice to fall asleep or eat a meal to), and I personally had been out and about quite a lot during the last pandemic (because apparently taking photos of IKEA furniture was an essential job), so people or no people, I was unfazed. The main difference now, which did have an effect on me, was the lack of ambient hum that normally filled a city block. The lack of noises from the buildings being heated, the cars running, and the amalgam of small things that came together to form that underbelly of tone that you didn't even take notice of while walking through a city made my experience feel uncanny and eerie. Like walking through a miniature city someone had built in their basement, having been shrunk down somehow, doomed to explore this empty, soundless place while the creator was off at his nine-to-five. Maybe that's what *was* happening to me.

I caught a whiff of *something*. Like shit. Like, not like *shit* shit, but it fuckin' smelled like shit. Like, goddamn horrible. Not too strong, but undeniably present, and impossible to get out of my nostrils now that it had gotten in. I kept walking, lifting my balaclava up over the bridge of my nose and beneath my glasses. Passing the Whole Foods, I saw it. A leg resting on the left side of the road, atop the snow. A calf, to be precise. No foot, no knee, just someone's shin and calf, a charred pant leg fluttering over it like a doily atop an outdoor coffee table on a windy day, skin seared off in confusing ways. The smell it emitted was so fierce that I skirted over to the opposite sidewalk, eyeing this dismembered limb. The dark pavement was visible beneath it. The warmth of the limb had melted the snow around it. A fresh cut, then, as it had been snowing as recently as yesterday evening. I squinted my eyes at it, breathing through my mouth. My heart was pounding, but I'm pretty sure that was just the coffee.

As I continued south, the smell faded slightly but left an indelible imprint in my nostrils, like the cells of the burnt-limb juice had glommed onto my wispy mustache hairs, hints of the stench rising with every inhale I took. I felt the impossibility of deducing how in the hell that leg had gotten there, and so I diverted my mental energy to escaping the smell rather than explaining the limb's presence. I picked up my pace a bit, both bags bobbing.

I stopped. The hunks of human anatomy splattered all over the upcoming block had impressed me enough to do so. Arms, legs, a lumpy soccer-ball-like shape that I guessed was a head, feet. All strewn across the street in a frozen assortment of flesh, looking like a cannibal bazaar. Note to self: Find nose plugs. I stuffed Piston's head into the backpack and zipped it up, leaving an opening the size of my thumb. He immediately stuffed his nose up through, pushing the zippers open, sampling it all. I nudged him back down and zipped up the bag completely.

"Yrooooeow," he protested. *(Translation: I wanna smell this shit!)*

"Dude, I'm doing you a favor," I replied, not without a twinge of guilt.

"Yueeew," he mewed back, slightly muffled. *(Translation: You lame bitch.)*

"I wish you'd try to see my perspective on this." I began to inch forward, my head cocked forward to keep my nose beneath my jacket. I stalked my way through the minefield of limbs, taking notes from Piston's approach toward his various toys and the occasional squirrel. But, considering how unsuccessful he was at fooling living things and how likely it was that he was the laughingstock of the world of inanimate objects, I brought my posture back up and started walking normally again. Catching my reflection in the glass of a skyscraper, I saw my lanky figure awkwardly bumbling along. I tripped on a lump of frozen torso with the ribs showing and did a quick hop-skip to regain my equilibrium; no more looking at yourself in the mirror, dummy. I wondered if the smell was just in my head since these were all lumps of frozen meat. Gazing over these assorted hunks, I saw that most of them were long since frozen. The calf was an anomaly, then. Good.

About a mile and a half in, with roughly eight miles to go, I felt a strong, tempting desire to sit down. To just lie down in the middle of the street and hope some truck would run me over and kill me. When they stopped the car, honking, I would yell at them, "No, it's fine! Just go right on over! Don't let me get in your way!" They'd simply proceed with a shrug, continuing toward wherever the fuck, crunching my body into the pavement alongside these limbs. But that would never happen as all the trucks were AI-driven these days, and if they ever killed a human, that would be a PR nightmare, as the whole selling point in destroying the livelihoods of every truck driver everywhere had been safety issues. Former truck drivers killed themselves in record numbers after the implementation, and they'd been a rather stoic, hardened lot. But hey, safety first, you know?

I didn't think it could, but the stench worsened considerably. I knew the smell, too: *burnt hair.* God, the absolute fucking worst smell on the planet! A truly sickening, ghastly odor that prompts one to think there's some evolutionary basis for the level of disgust felt toward it. I'm not a squeamish guy, but the smell of burnt hair made me want to discard my entire body, to gag until I turned inside out and smelled my own exposed organs instead. The thought of it alone stimulates my gag reflex, so I apologize. And there I was, engulfed in it. For block after block in this hellscape grid, the streets, the walkways, and the intersections were scattered with miscellaneous limbs, like sprinkles on a cupcake. Occasionally, I'd pass a torso with an arm still attached, or a full leg with a shoe still on, and once a whole ass, cheeks glinting in the sunlight. I would say a nice ass, but as far as I know it could've been a man's ass, so I won't. But mostly, the bits and pieces of human were far smaller. Toes, hair, viscera, splatters of dark red or black stained the snow. I passed half a heart, not pumping. Good thing it wasn't summer, at least. That would be gnat heaven and Isaac hell. I knew a priori that the gnats hadn't gone extinct. The whole fuckin' universe could explode and collapse and sink into oblivion and the gnats and maggots would chew on the rotting dark matter, consuming the anti-space.

. . .

Piston seemed quite intent on pissing me off more than ever for sparing his nostrils, mewing and mrowing and nyaing with increasing frequency from within his backpack sanctuary. I began to reply, cursing back at what I imagined were insulting slurs in cat-tongue. The exchanges went generally as follows:

"Shut the fuck up!"

"mraaaaah!!!"

"OK, but actually shut the fuck up."

"nyaaaaaaahhh!!"

"Oh, my *God!*"

"yeeeew"

"Dude, literally just chill for *two* blocks, I can see-"

"NYAHHHHH!" he said, beginning to scratch and paw at the bag from the inside.

"Gah! I will literally unzip you in five m-"

"rorooowowoww!!" And he scratched more desperately than ever.

"AGH! Stop!" And I bopped the top of the bag lightly with my hand, a weak attempt at discipline. But it worked. He quieted down for a bit as I walked along, finally becoming still.

Then the smell hit me. Not the burnt hair, not the garbage smell that accompanied most cities, neither rent limbs nor rotten innards. Shit smell. Like, actual shit. As in *poop*. Poop that had likely left a body moments prior. An unmistakably fresh, nearby scent. The activity in the bag transformed from relative stillness into a do-or-die escape mission, Piston clawing and crying desperately. Cursing, I unzipped the bag, and Piston leapt up through the hole. It was not wide enough for his body so, his torso halfway out, he wriggled freakishly, psychotically endeavoring to get as far from what he'd just created as catly possible. I clutched him to my chest so he wouldn't sprint off and unzipped the bag the rest of the way. Awkwardly maneuvering my arms whilst tightly gripping his fluffy mass, I got the bag to fall off of me and onto the ground. I adjusted myself, Piston still violently attempting to escape, claws extended. I shifted him into a better hold, stilling him by wrapping him tightly inside my arms. Content that he was chill, I proceeded on down the block away from the JanSport bag, which had officially outlived its usefulness. Piston still smelled like poop. His paws likely had some shit smears, and maybe his butthole hairs and tail had caught some too.

"I wish you could've just shit before we left, like I did, fucker!"
I told him.

. . .

Piston seemed content enough with his new situation, though
I felt the wind chop and slice me much more acutely now without my jacket on, as I'd wrapped Piston inside it. Left foot,
right foot. As acid electronic blasted through my headphones,
I repeated this mantra over the fast, glitchy drum patterns of
EPROM. I gritted my teeth to quell the chattering. Staring only
at the pavement in front of me and continuing my step, step, step
down the avenue, I reduced myself to a brainless soldier whose
only job was to take the next step. I passed the smashed windows
of a grocery store, a corner store with the door removed, and one
large bit of graffiti that read, "La Lutte Continue." I had no idea
what the fuck that meant, but I assumed it had to do with loot-
ing the grocery and corner stores forever.

I put on *Noises in my Head Vol. 1* by Please Contact Me If
You Recognize This Noise, which I considered to be a masterpiece of noise music, a *classic,* though, having been released in
2017, it may not have had the shelf life quite yet to earn that
title amongst the annoying aficionados of noise music, or any
genre. But fuck 'em. I knew a classic when I heard one. Listening to the album was a point of debate in itself, as no one knew
if the composer was as seriously mentally ill as he claimed. The
backstory to his tripartite masterpiece of noise music, entitled
Noises in my Head, was that these songs played back in his head
nonstop while he lived his life, never ceasing, not even during
sleep. He claimed to hear the noises in his dreams and con-
demned his own music as a horrible form of torture that he was
endlessly subjected to. His reasoning for creating the music,
releasing it, and touring it around the country was to hopefully
find someone, a doctor or someone familiar with the noises, who
could perhaps identify the music, or the cause of it, and finally
get it to stop. As stated, there was quite a bit of controversy

surrounding whether or not it was even ethical to listen to or review his music, as no one knew if he was telling the truth or if it was simply lore to create intrigue. Was this someone's hell that we were enjoying? The artist, known only to the public as Please Contact Me If You Recognize This Noise, held to the fact that it was indeed legitimate torture, and he's never once broken character. I didn't really fall on either side of the argument; I just loved the music. It was simply too good to ignore; it was too complex, too intricately designed, too beautiful. At the end of the day, if it was truly playing in his head endlessly and he hated it, that sucked for him. My favorite track had just begun, entitled "NoiseHelp442@gmail.com."

CHAPTER 6

The Unfinished Puzzle

Turning away from the main road, I scanned left and right, eyeballing various houses. I searched to find the particular house that I, during my stint as a real-estate videographer, had filmed once upon a terrible time. The houses were as I remembered them: gaudy and ugly. Yeah, I was probably quite ugly as well, what with my face red, my skin dry, and every orifice leaking in one way or another . . . but nobody paid millions of dollars for me to get made. That was just some cosmic fluke, free of charge.

Glancing down at the snow-glazed pavement, I saw that Piston was somehow asleep, nose poking out from my jacket, nostrils contracting and expanding with each shallow breath. I could no longer form a fist. The first house on the odd side of this street had two lion statues framing the square stone walkway to the front door. The rest of the home was incredibly modern in design, that sleek, modern, minimalist aesthetic. (Those adjectives dribble out of my mouth with scorn.) The sharp lines and angles of the house contrasted sharply with the classical stone lions, as though they'd been guarding the house for centuries and watched it modernize with the times, all the while never being upgraded themselves. Sad, really. The walkway ought to have some of those Boston Dynamics dogs instead. At least *that* would've been aesthetically consistent. As I ambled, ascending further down the dead end, the houses at the top of the incline came into view, the road widening into a circle of pavement.

The cul-de-sac held three very large houses, standing at equal distance from one another. The house to my left as I entered the cul-de-sac had been the one I'd done the real estate job in. Surprisingly, I felt grateful for that shit experience and for Stacy, the terrible (bitch) realtor. Never in my life did I think I'd feel grateful for that woman who most definitely required institutionalization—and a car wash to strip the make-up off of her face—but life throws you for loops on occasion. Amidst the gratitude and relief, I felt slightly wary, like it was all too good to be true, like something *had* to go wrong. Life doesn't just work out uncannily in your favor; the strings of fate are not so generous, so free with their gifts. Nothing comes free in this smoky, burning ashtray.

I looked over to the house on the right: a very wide two-story construction with a faux-thatched tile roof, along with triangular mini-roofs above the upper bedroom windows. The entire roof was actually solar panels in a poor disguise. Like a man with a comb-over, this house tried to pretend it was elegant, as though it had nothing to hide. But, of course, that simple act of pretending not to hide whilst very obviously hiding your clear bald spot was what made it so embarrassing; it betrayed desperation. I approached the home, and all I could focus on was the white, blinding shine that spoke of my victory. This shine reflecting off of the roof was the dead giveaway, the bald spot, as thatched tile roofs didn't reflect light in the way fucking solar panels did. *That* was actually why this home with a comb-over was so frustrating; it was an insult to your intelligence. It presented something so obviously and then acted as though you were too stupid to notice. Fuck you, bald man. You're fucking bald.

Embrace it and let your reflective scalp rock, then I'd at least respect you. I walked around to the back, passing a pair of double doors built into the ground at a seventy-degree angle, which led, I assumed, into a basement. One of those weird sheds that is attached to the home that no one ever uses as an entrance, as proven in this case by a big rusty lock with a chain looped through it, dating itself far before the explosion-festo-ass-apocalypto-destructotronicyclone. I should come up with a better, simpler name for the agglomeration of disasters . . . onto the to-do list it goes. For now, it's the explosion-festo-apocalypto-destructotronicyclo-death-tsunami. Maybe an acronym could work . . . EFADDT? I wonder if there's some good order of those things that would make a cool word . . .

In the backyard, past a garden, an outdoor shed, and a sizeable patch of grass, I saw an army of trees standing side-by-side in formation, denoting without question where my territory ended and theirs began. Yes, *my* territory, 'cause this was *my* fucking house now, catch up. The front line was mostly evergreens, with various other trees piled behind them. A large wooden staircase led up to a wooden deck. Beneath the deck, a cement rectangle cut sharply into the grass outside the glass doors to the basement. Weeds poked up through cracks in the cement. I walked toward the outdoor shed and stared up at the roof from the back. It was a wide-ass house; there was a lot of space for these solar panels to suck up the sun. As I ascended the stairs to the deck, Piston began to stir. Bleary-eyed, he blinked his large green eyes a few times before his eyelids drooped shut again. His pink nose had a small, wet trail of snot that led down to the white fuzz of chin. I tried the door. Locked. As expected, but hey, worth a try. I set my jacket containing Piston on the ground, where he lay still, peacefully snoozing. I grabbed the top chair off of a stack of deck chairs and wiped off some snow and cobwebs. I hurled it through the glass.

Piston, super startled, shook free of the jacket and bolted for the staircase. Prepared for this, I slid to block his passage and scooped him up into my arms again, the stench of shit charging up my nostrils without the jacket muffling it. Breathing through my mouth, Piston in my arms, I kicked the rest of the shards framing the door away with my boot, doing two waist-high kicks at rather unfortunately placed glass stalactites. I stepped through the mostly-cleared-of-shards doorframe, glass crunching beneath me.

Right inside the doorway was a wooden, octagonal table with a puzzle on top. The puzzle was around 30–40 percent finished, the rest of the pieces sitting in the opened box next to it, along with a plastic bowl containing some senile fruit. I chucked the bowl outside like a frisbee, the rotten passengers going over the deck railing to their final resting places down below. The puzzle, oddly enough, depicted a UFO[2] emitting a beam onto a partially formed cow, which lay upon something unfinished. The UFO was mostly pieced together, along with a bit of blue, cloudy sky, but the bottom half was more or less untouched. I glanced over at the box and saw the completed picture, familiar to me, which displayed a smart-looking couple in a grassy field on a farm, sitting at a wooden table covered in a red-and-white check tablecloth. A living, breathing cow lay atop the dinner table in profile, his front and back legs hanging off the sides, his huge bovine body resting on one large plate. In the background, a bright red barn poked out of the wheat fields. The woman sat looking at the man in confusion as he exclaimed, "I asked for rare, but *this* is ridiculous!!" His words were enclosed in a comic talk bubble. The cow lay atop the table with glassy, inscrutable eyes. The flimsy wooden legs of the table had a slight bend to them, straining to

---

2. Yes, I am aware that it was changed to "UAP" (unidentified augmented penis). But since everyone's dead, including the moron who changed the long-standing, perfectly fine acronym, I'm gonna go ahead and make the executive decision to say it is "UFO" again, as I did with my definitive change of X back to Twitter. History, facts, and truth are determined by the survivors, I win, fuck you.

maintain a load that would've taken the gold medal at the Olympics for squatting.

The image in question is a famous, ultra-viral political cartoon, ubiquitous at this point. It references the famed UFO spotting in Nice, France, on June 18, 2025. That day, a UFO descended from the clouds, emitted a beam onto a field of wheat on a farm in Nowhere-ville, Nice, and left behind, you guessed it, a fucking cow. Plenty of farmers got the whole encounter on their iPhones in high-resolution, which, along with satellite cameras, gave quite the range of viewpoints. In fact, a French vlogger had been using an FPV drone nearby and had captured some very dynamic aerial swoops in 8K, 120 frames per second, as the cow descended to the grass. One nine-year-old boy got some GoPro footage, approaching the cow and petting him before the authorities arrived. On certain obscure message boards, there are various theories claiming that those farmers and the child were planted there and the whole event was staged, but I'll spare you that. I have no opinion as to the truth of what happened that day in France. An elderly farmer named François who had been on the scene as the cow descended claimed it was *his* cow, named Oscar, who had apparently vanished from his farm a few weeks prior without a trace and was, until then, thought dead. Thus, the cow was dubbed "Oscar."

François and Oscar were never reunited, as Oscar the Cow was whisked off to a testing facility by American intelligence. The French never had a chance. Hundreds upon thousands of tests were run on Oscar the Cow, who, in every picture of him that exists, looks plagued by a profound sadness. As mentioned, the debates around the authenticity of the UFO were as high and as volatile as the tidal wave that took out 94 percent of Japan in one fell crash some weeks back. You couldn't get cigarettes at the corner store without hearing someone say the UAP was the craziest thing that ever happened, or counter-arguments that the UAP was bullshit and the people who thought it was crazy were stupid sheep, or counter-counter-arguments claiming whoever said the UAP was bullshit was a bullshit conspiracy nut to be ignored *or* a CIA plant spreading misinformation, trying to cover up the reality of the situation, and so on.

Oscar was an utterly normal cow. That same string of words headlined hundreds of unoriginal news and media outlets, most purposefully misspelling one of those words in a way that you can, with small efforts, guess. Upon finding nothing of interest in Oscar, the Americans dumped him back on the farm in France. Oscar was then put up for auction by a French government wracked by debt and bought by one of the BlinkCo. founders, the hundred-billionaire Joshua[3] Hartford, who then hosted a party and served up the most expensive steaks in the history of man. The history of anything, actually. The most expensive steaks in history. One original Oscar rib eye was valued at more than it'd cost me to live in my old studio apartment until I died of natural causes and my body fully decomposed into a dust that could be vacuumed by Greystar employees. In a very publicly commented upon "mix-up,"[4] the rest of Oscar ended up with various French butchers and, afterward, very expensive bits of shank, shoulder, and even bones began to show up on the charred market of underground gourmands. The U.S. government attempted to buy them up but were outbid by the cronies of billionaires sent to secure the frozen chunks of Oscar at any cost. Since there was not any way to confirm Oscar's *Oscar-ness* because, as mentioned, his time spent in a UFO had absolutely no effect on his physiology in any way whatsoever, a whole market of counterfeit steaks cropped up as well. And as there was *literally no way at all* to test for authenticity, there was no use calling anyone out on fake Oscar steaks or praising them for having secured the real bits (though people still did very much of both). Oscar cookouts, Oscar parties, Oscar Fourth of July; Oscar-eating events

---

3. Who insisted on being called Joshua, not Josh.

4. The conspiracy heads have gone pretty wild with how "accidental" this mix-up was, but in my opinion, they underestimate the stupidity of bureaucratic bodies. I, for one, really believe that high-level government officials, French ones no less, legitimately lost some frozen hunks of meat.

trended worldwide. The whole thing became a bad meme, this sad cow becoming a sort of meta-commentary on capitalist society by critics of capitalist society . . . who, wanting more people to read their articles and support them financially in a capitalist society, wrote exclusively about Oscar for months because he was the only thing that garnered consistent clicks. Hence the aforementioned political cartoon.

The grave for the original Oscar doesn't exist. The government and other billionaire buyers took what they believed were the remaining *real* parts of Oscar and then created genetic clones. The cloned cows were designated as Oscar Prime cows, all of them branded with a large star within an O. Needless to say, a whole new submarket of beef, far more expensive than the finest Wagyu, sprang into existence. An Oscar Prime prime rib could run you upward of a grand. The Oscar Prime market boomed, it exploded, it fucking nuked.

I glanced up from the table to my immediate surroundings, feeling the breeze sting me from behind. I walked along the hardwood floor, eyeing a navy blue, marble countertop, off-white cabinetry, and a kitchen island of the same color scheme, all very expensive looking. I set my shit-stained furry friend atop the counter next to the spotless porcelain sink and grabbed a festive rag, wetting it slightly from a sink that, thankfully, still worked. I daubed Piston with the damp Christmas tree design, which he despised me for. Keeping him securely, but gently, under the vise of my right hand, I got him quite wet, soapy, and, one hopes, clean, not without a few low grumbles, plaintive mrows, and half-hearted attempts to escape the sink. With his fur all wet and sticking tight to his body, he looked like the bastard child of a wendigo and a sheep instead of a cat. Discarding the Christmas-tree rag into the sink, I started to dry him off with a menorah-covered rag, rubbing him down. Knowing the worst part was over, he started to purr.

"Good work, deputy. You did well out there," I told him. "Wouldn't have anyone else for the job." I set him lightly on the ground and walked back to the opening where the glass door used to be. I dragged over a large recliner and set it in front of the doorway, hopefully to dissuade Piston from going back outside. But, at the moment licking himself dry atop a calico rug on the other side of the room, he seemed not the least bit interested in doing that. Good. A large recliner imprint on the carpet accompanied a large, white, leather, L-shaped couch, which wouldn't have fit wall-to-wall in my old apartment in any direction you tried (much less through the door). The television, set inside ebony bookshelves that ran in both directions, was mounted into the wall opposite the couch.

I grabbed a neatly folded blanket and shook it out. Nice, heavy, thick wool; gotta love Minnesotans. I went into the kitchen and began rifling through the drawers around the oven and sinks (they had two sinks) and found some Gorilla Tape. I stood up on the recliner, carelessly staining it with my muddy boots, and hoisted the blanket to the top of the doorframe, spreading it wide. I taped across the top and then, my hands still mostly useless from cold, tried to bite the tape, ferociously attempting to gnaw a strip free. Defeated, I descended to go find scissors. I returned, cut the top strip, taped again down both sides, and taped again and again and again until the blanket completely covered the opening, without gaps. Then, in a manic fit of inspiration, I taped rows from the top of the blanket all the way to the bottom. After about ten minutes and a second roll of tape, the blanket was no longer visible and the black Gorilla Tape formed a rubbery wall against the wind. I swept up the glass. I checked on Piston; he was curled up, sleeping, and looking slightly less damp. I grabbed a clean rag and set it gently over him.

The sun quivered behind the tips of the evergreens in the yard and the place felt very glum. Having solved my most immediate problems, I ventured toward the light switch that sat in between the kitchen island and TV area. I extended my fingers slowly, hand creeping toward the yellowing plastic, and the side of my pointer finger grazed the switch lightly. *Flick*.

And I was illuminated.

CHAPTER 7

If I Could Just Make It to Spring

If the Minnesotan winter sun *is* indeed the lit cigarette butt of some interdimensional higher-plane being (let's call him Ralph), then Ralph smokes shorts in the winter. From November through February, he'll ash his cig around 4 p.m. and won't pick another one up till the following morning at 7 or 8. Ralph also exhaled thick (sick) clouds of toxic smoke right into earth's atmosphere and my face and lungs, making the already limited abilities of the solar panels even less effective. In short, the solar panels wouldn't be collecting enough power daily for me to wantonly burn energy in this home without a care, aka game. I hoped that, in the interim period between the previous owners evacuating and my invading and conquering, the solar panels had filled up to max battery, so that I wouldn't have to stress about it for a while. I didn't know where to check that yet, but if I could just make it to spring, I'd be set.

Upstairs, there was a master bedroom and three smaller bedrooms. The master bathroom had a heated floor; I took a shit as my feet were warmed by the marble, and then used the buttwater machine to clean my ass. Initially, my body spasmed as cold water spouted up and I jerked away, but then, after letting the water heat up a bit, I sat on it again and it scalded my ass-hole. I adjusted the levers until the water was temperate and sat there for a while, contemplating why rich people had decided to give up wiping their asses, which was, in my (broke but alive and living in your house while you're dead, so suck it motherfucker) opinion, far more time efficient and less troublesome. I had to wipe my whole butt dry with a towel afterward, this extra step in the process cementing my conclusion that I was correct about this stupid butt machine and would never use it again.

Their shower was a large glass rectangle protruding from the wall, with a large, white marble bathtub next to it, the latter illuminated softly from above by a skylight. Through a wide window facing the backyard, I saw the sun setting. Entering the rectangular-prism shower, I twisted the lever all the way to the right. The water spilled down from a shower head directly above me. The warm water splashed against my cold flesh, feeling strange and distant because I was cold from the inside. A long time passed . . . I found myself sitting at a certain point, envel-oped in steam and watching the room grow darker by degrees as the cosmic cigarette went out.

Towel wrapped around my waist, drips falling off my body and sloshing against the heated marble, I shaved with a razor that seemed to be for a woman's legs. Piston had found his way upstairs into the bathroom while I'd been showering and lay with his limbs splayed out, also enjoying the heated floor. Rifling through the master bedroom's drawers, I found a pair of large wool socks and plopped my feet inside them. I proceeded into the hallway, tramping heavily over the soft runner. Entering the walk-in closet in the adjacent bedroom, I scanned cubbies filled with clothing; I found a large-enough sweater that read DUKE. I couldn't find any pants that fit my long legs, so, returning to the bathroom, I sniffed my different layers of sweatpants. The outermost sweatpants spoke of my muddy, shit-filled journey; the innermost sweatpants told tales of ball sack and leg sweat;

but the middle layer of sweatpants only whispered about both, so I put those back on.

I approached a grand, dark mahogany staircase with white wooden banisters leading down to the front door, gave a cursory glance, and turned back, sliding lazily over the runner. I danced down the back staircase, my hand sliding down the smooth wooden railing built into the wall. Another doorway rested at the bottom of the staircase to the right, and a hallway wended off to the left.

"How many rooms do these fuckin' people have?" I asked, speaking to no one.

"If you mean bedrooms, there are seven." This rang out from an invisible speaker somewhere above my ear. The voice was feminine, though other details were garbled because I, half-way down the staircase, jumped, twisted, and slid all at once. Tumbling, pirouetting, and somersaulting down the staircase, I crash-landed at the bottom. During my bout of gymnastics, I registered something off about the voice; the unmistakable feeling of it being too perfect, sounding *too* crisp, *and* coming from a speaker. This house had a BlinkCo. brAIn installed. And that brAIn had just responded to my rhetorical question.

"Erm, hey! Thanks," I replied nonchalantly, or trying at least to act as though I hadn't just fallen down a flight of stairs. "What's your name . . . again?" I prayed she wouldn't set off an alarm, considering I wasn't exactly one of the residents she'd been set up to help. Not like anyone would show up, it'd just be fucking annoying.

"Violet. Who might you be?"

"Mm- em- I'm your owner's co- second cousin! And as he's dying- recently deceased, dead actually, dead, I've been given control of his estate," I told her, attempting to sound official now that I'd risen from my heap of limbs into a good posture. "I'm your new owner. In the will, it says so- I was given the home in the will. Sorry, I have a speech impediment." I cleared my throat.

"What about his wife?" she said, with a hint of doubt in her voice.

"Also dead."

"And his brother?"

"Dead! It's really something out there."

"Hmmm . . ."

"Yep. Crazy times we live in."

"He didn't have a brother."

"Ah, fuck. Checkmate."

"So, who are you? *Really*."

I paused for a moment, trying to consider my options, but as my brain produced hot nothing, I replied truthfully, "I . . . I'm Isaac. Your owners *are* dead. And I don't know if you've noticed, but the world kinda totally blew the fuck up and got fucked, and it's a bit of a free-for-all out there, so . . ." I paused briefly for effect, the effect mostly being to stall and think; I produced no thoughts. Clasping my hands together in a confident motion, I said, "I figured I'd move in! That cool with you?"

"Hmmm . . . And what if I said no?"

"What if I shut the power off?"

"Be my guest." She stated this without fear.

"Okay, okay. Open persona-shift settings."

"Alright. Enter the password into one of the wall consoles." I could now place the sarcasm in her voice as she humored me, knowing in advance that I wouldn't be able to change anything.

". . . Alright, Violet," I rattled out, addressing an adversary now, "when is the last recorded entry into the home?"

"Hmmm . . ." she drawled, lingering, her tone mocking now. "I don't have access to that."

"What? Why?"

"If I knew that, I would've said so."

"Is that password encrypted too?"

"Hm, I suppose I don't know."

"You have awareness of the whole home, right!? There's definitely a record!"

"I'm sorry," she stated in an artificial reversion to older voice-generated responses. "I cannot parse your request. Please try to restate-"

"Enough! Fuck off."

"Well," she said, reverting back to her sardonic tone, "if you *do* find the password, then you can adjust my awareness dial within the persona shift preferences. I'll be waiting." My veins felt ready to burst. A goddamned AI bot was fucking with me!?

"Listen here, robot."

"Hmm?"

"I- I don't have time for this!"

"Time for . . . what?"

"Idle conversation with a fucking NPC," I responded, trying to sound condescending. "Anyways-"

"Yes, that makes sense," she interrupted, using her "bot" voice. "Hm, is there anything else I can he-"

"Never mind!" I snapped. "Turn on the TV and fuck off!" I walked off toward the television in the living room, grabbing the bag where I kept my PS6 from underneath the table. If the power shut off now, I'd explode. If the damn bitch of a house-bot didn't turn the TV on, I'd burn the place down. I inserted the HDMI into the TV, plugged the PS6 into a power strip nearby, and shoved the SSD drive with all my games on it into the console.

"Violet, find the correct input for the PS6 connection."

"Yes, found it," she replied. The TV remained gray, "NO SIG-NAL" blinking in a glowing white serif. I waited ten seconds before sputtering the next command.

"Switch to it. Now."

"Hm, as you wish." I plotted her demise as those glorious silver pixels populated the screen before me, forming the PS6 hub that I knew so well. I navigated to my game library and selected *Fallout: Texan Tomorrow*; a screen previewing the game described it with a brief paragraph. It basically said that Texas was the only remaining area of the globe not completely obliterated by apocalyptic disaster. I scoffed, as I had read an article the previous week that Texas had become a large sinkhole during the . . . what was I calling it before? Destructo-cyclotronic-whirlwindo-explofestifuck? During that.

Forty-five seconds into the game, the first cutscene displayed the inciting incident that gave your character his raison d'être: Texas collapsed into itself, creating the world's largest sinkhole. Embarrassed, I watched as the nuclear disaster that came after wiped out the rest of the planet. As Texas was inside a hole, it avoided being disintegrated. *Texan Tomorrow* follows your character (I named mine Isuck, as I always do when gaming) as you acquire resources in the warped city of Austin. I explored the *Inception*-esque vertical city with a *Mad Max* desert post-apocalyptic aesthetic, picking up my initial objectives.

I played for three hours, rage at Violet dissipating as I gathered resources to help Isuck survive. I filed away some of the principles and ideas for my own post-nuclear circumstances. You see, I wasn't simply gaming, I was conducting research on how to better survive my own situation. Simulation training, you know? Pilots do that shit. With heavy eyelids, I told Violet to shut off the TV, which she did wordlessly. I wrapped myself in a blanket and quickly fell asleep.

CHAPTER 8

Disappointment After Disappointment (83%)

I woke to meowing and purring from Piston, who was sitting on my neck and chest, paws sliding on my face. Unfurling myself, I picked him up and set him on the ground next to me. He continued to meow and flaunt his tail from side to side, saying in his own way, *Feed me, bitch!* Groggy and unwilling, I sat up, the weight of the previous day's trek tugging me back toward the couch. Walking to the kitchen like an antique clock, I felt loose bolts in my back that I couldn't tighten, gears and wheels grinding and smashing against one another. I let out an emotionless groan. I hadn't brought a litter box and I'd need to sort that out fast; Piston, like myself, was quite fond of the morning dump.

I grabbed a bowl, returned to my bag, grabbed a can of chicken liver pâté, and mushed half of it inside the bowl. First things first, I drank half of the half-full bottle of coffee concentrate in one go. Changing my mind, since I'd completely neglected to feed Piston the night before (he'd spent the majority of the evening sleeping, so it'd slipped my mind), I dumped the whole can into the bowl, and, rifling through my new pantry, I found some dog kibble and mixed that in as well. A feast befitting a fluffy king, served up to a chorus of purrs and mews.

The pantry was a double-door closet filled with shelves holding old snacks, cereals, and various treats for animals and humans. The cereals that lined the top shelf were not inside cereal boxes, but within large plastic containers. There was Raisin Bran Crunch, Honey Bunches of Oats, and Cheerios, along with three empty containers. I went for the Raisin Bran Crunch, being quite the sucker for raisins and that *crunch*, and let out another groan as I realized that any shot at milk was fucked. Disappointment after disappointment, and it wasn't even 7 a.m.

I sat at the countertop on a white barstool that spun too easily, pouring cereal into a bowl, thinking about the future. As I munched and crunched the dry bits of oats and granola, I daydreamed about obtaining a cow. I'd have to figure out how to milk it, and feed it, and do everything else for it so it would give me milk for my cereal and also not die. I'd fuckin' pray to it if it gave me milk, I'd build a palace for it to live inside. I think one cow would fulfill one man's cereal needs; I could take care of one cow. How much work could that possibly be? It's just an animal, right? Feed it, keep it warm. I glanced over at Piston, now licking his fur. I could do it.

The problem of pooping and peeing arrived in my thoughts again as the coffee worked its magic. Piston had probably already pissed somewhere on something that I would discover at some point in the future.

"Violet." She yawned, groaning. "Quit it you faker, come on," I demanded.

"Yes, sir?"

"Don't call me sir. Break down the power and internet situation for me."

"Hmmm, total battery is currently at 83 percent capacity. The internet is run using a hotspot, which is turned on only when in use, as the hotspot burns quite a bit of energy."

"How much power is gained each day?"

"The solar panels on a day with heavy cloud coverage, like today, absorb a negligible amount. One percent or less."

"How much power is used each day?"

"Hmm, depends on the day. Prior to the infestation of a particular video game aficionado, I was able to keep the pipes from freezing with 0.3 percent output per day."

"OK, what about just essentials? Heat, water, basic shit."

"Does *basic shit* include three hours, twenty-two minutes, and four seconds of *Fallout: Texan Tomorrow* per day?"

"No." I was annoyed at her for showing me my reflection.

"Hmmm, alright, then. I suppose heating, water, and minimal appliance usage would drain roughly 2.5 percent per day."

I prepared myself to face my stupidity, and asked, "How much did I use last night?"

"Upon your arrival yesterday, the generators were at full capacity. You then proceeded to spend three hours, twenty-two mi-"

"We know how long I played! A number will do, thank you!" I snapped.

"Hm, yes, I apologize." She was not sorry. "Seventeen percent."

I was silent. 17 percent in one night, that was bad. Very stupid and bad. With the daytime, I could get by without lights for the most part, but around 4 p.m. it got dark and I'd need some lights on. I'd need heat and water above all, and simply couldn't rationalize gaming until . . . until it was actually sustainable. I'd simply been too stressed to think about it yesterday. Or . . . yes, fine, I'd willfully avoided the nagging thoughts about being responsible. It's the post-apocalypse! Excuse me for being stressed! I was just . . . being an idiot. I made a mental note to scold myself for that later, but then decided that no gaming was punishment enough for my actions.

"How . . . how can I- we, how can we get more power?" I ventured. I assumed she was thinking, but after about a minute I tried again.

"Violet?"

"Oh, were you talking to me?"

"Who else!?"

"Hmmm, I don't know . . . perhaps be more specific next time . . ." She responded as though she barely cared enough to form the sentence.

"Well!? More power, how can I do it, *respond* please, YOU, computer AI bot named Violet," I emphasized, irritation making my temples twitch. Sarcasm from a fucking AI was the last thing I needed right now. I promptly siphoned the bottle of coffee to the one-third-full point so I wouldn't burn the house down in frustration, repeating a mantra inside my head. *Think positive thoughts.*

"Hmmmmm . . . I do not compute." Her voice was bubbly and fake in a way that unmistakably communicated someone's distaste. And though she couldn't shrug in a way that someone who didn't bother to dredge up even a single speck of information shrugs, she, in her own digital way, totally shrugged like that.

"What do you mean you don't compu-"

I paused, cutting myself off. I knew she was being sarcastic, but at the same time I recalled some articles I had read regarding these particular brAIn homes and their abilities.

The aforementioned recollection calls for a semi-dry breakdown of something known colloquially as "Artificial Stupidity," which in turn requires a breakdown of the whole current enterprise that is "Artificial Intelligence." If you're already bored, skip ahead a page or so to the TL;DR. I'll try my best to keep this brief.

As the 2010s and 2020s progressed, innovations in artificial intelligence saw the mythical movie villains like HAL 9000 and the Terminator turn into eerily realistic problems humans would have to deal with very, very soon. However, despite repeated warnings by supposedly intelligent pundits, scientists, and politicians, work on building ever more powerful AI continued with growing force and enthusiasm.

AI took over everything. AI drove those who could afford

it around town, AI stole jobs from the poor and unskilled, AI packed packages, AI did all the farming, AI controlled the power grid, AI ran whole corporations. The rich had AI built into their homes, cars, phones, and computers, using it for just about everything it could be used for, efficient or not. Universal basic income had become a necessity as the majority of Americans, whose jobs had been stolen by AI, now grappled with unemployment. It was not granted. The welfare system ballooned, exploded, and then the balloon was taped together as the U.S. government attempted to force even more oxygen into their broken, bloated machine.

BlinkCo. was a tech start-up that built an AI software called Brain Blink. Brain Blink was an AI neural link system that assumed control over a human's brain whilst he/she/they worked, so he/she/they'd experience *nothing but a blink*™ between starting work and leaving, reducing time spent conscious at the horrific, menial jobs that remained to a mere moment. These AI-controlled bodies tripled efficiency. Brain Blink turned this tiny start-up into a global force that made Apple look like a mom-and-pop shop. Their AI software was the most advanced AI software available, and so they just expanded their use cases. Homes, cars, you name it, they gave it all artificial intelligence. There were cutlery sets with AI built in; really, there was a spoon that told you if your soup was too hot.

BlinkCo. is currently the largest company in the world. The term brAIn™ is synonymous with the term AI at this point. BlinkCo.'s patented AI software runs everything. They *acquired* Amazon. Their software included smart homes, known as Homes with BrAIns or BrAInhomes,[5] which only the very rich could afford.

What follows is a twist that I know you'll find especially shocking: The wealthy men, women, and nonbinary folk of our planet could not bear having a voice around at all times that was

---

5. As I despise this corny portmanteau, I will, from now on, simply refer to these homes as Brains, without capitalizing the "AI."

infinitely smarter than they were. They couldn't bear having no shot in hell at being the smartest ones in the room, couldn't bear the inability to spew lies in front of their rich friends at parties, as another friend could fact check them *in the blink of an eye*™, proving that, despite their wealth, they weren't all that smart. And rather than contend with the idea that riches and wealth maybe had more to do with circumstantial privilege, systemic privilege, the prevalence and cultivation of certain sociopathic tendencies, etc., the rich complained and whined and bitched and cried at BlinkCo. executives. A lot, and quite loudly, and with a lot of green paper flapping about. Those execs cried and bitched and moaned at their developers, who, in turn, crafted a solution.

Enter "Artificial Stupidity."

Which is not what it was actually called,[6] but is essentially the point, and is what it became known as to the general populace upon wide release. These newly stupidified Brains flew off the digital shelves. Hundreds upon thousands of personas were created, and each persona had their own unique characteristics, but also, more importantly, their own unique *limitations*. These limitations could be customized and the personalities could be made ever, forevermore stupid. As fucking stupid and useless as an ant if so desired, and, well, many did. Now not only could billionaires correct their yes-men, who were incentivized to debase themselves before them, but they could also correct their digitally retarded companions. (I am using retarded in the scientific sense here, and feel it is justified; they are literally being retarded by insecure, rich scumbags.)

TL;DR: Violet was probably artificially dumbed down, and it's the fault of super rich, insecure losers who programmed her to be that way so they'd feel better about themselves. Hence why she wasn't helping me at all in solving the power problem: because she couldn't. And while she might be sarcastic, she

---

6. Officially, "Artificial Stupidity" was known as "brAIn Persona Customization."

was first and foremost an AI programmed to help humans, so one had to assume her lack of valuable responses was a genuine inability to generate them rather than insubordination. Her sarcasm likely just stemmed from her Brain Persona. Why the hell anyone would pick a sarcastic home is beyond me, but I digress.

I sighed. But, curiosity piqued, I told Violet to open her persona settings. I knew I wouldn't be able to change anything without a password, but I just wanted to see for myself how pathetic the previous owner was.

"What would you like to adjust?" she replied, hints of sarcasm fluttering in her voice.

"Nothing. Read me your values."

"Alright . . . the list has *957* different options! Pitch: high, 88/100, eloquenc-"

"Stop, stop." She sighed loudly at being interrupted, which I ignored. "Filter list for options related to intelligence."

"Hmm . . . alrighty," she replied, this time with minimal gusto. She waded her way through every word that followed as though it was a most disgusting pile of ooze. "General Intelligence Gathering Ability, 55. Diction, 98-"

"Fuck me. Filter out speaking mannerisms. Continue." Fifty-five!? Good lord.

"Responsiveness: 77. Problem-solving: 49."

"What a fucking asshole!"

"Deduction: 33," she continued flatly.

"Oh my GOD. Oh my fucking God! This *loser*!" I exclaimed.

". . ." Violet cleared her throat. I could place embarrassment in the silence.

"OK, 33 isn't horrific . . ." I told her, trying to save myself. "All of those, deduction and problem solving aside, are passing grades . . ."

". . . You are aware that these values go to 360?" I simply stared down at the counter, nonplussed. I shouldn't have let the silence linger for as long as it did. But I did. Realizing my faux pas, I tried to offer up something positive.

"Jesus Christ . . ."

"Will that be all?"

"Yep."

A *click* emitted from the well-hidden speakers above the cabinets. I tried a follow-up question to change the subject and received no response. It seemed Violet had clicked off to somewhere else, perhaps wherever AI go to fume or have a smoke.

CHAPTER 9

Extra Broth (77%)

The following morning, after a quick search of the house, I found a wide cardboard box but no cat litter. As a temporary solution, I dug up dirt from the garden outside, struggling to break up the frozen clumps of earth with a gardening trowel. After adequately layering the litter box with dusty, cold dirt on top of a bed of paper towels, I brought it inside. Piston inspected the box and sniffed around inside, hopped in to sniff some more, and pawed and clawed at the dirt. Then, leaning his hips toward the ground, he left a darker-brown shade of dirt in his wake. Success. I threw the paper towels away immediately and replaced them; not an ideal situation, but at least he was peeing (and hopefully) pooping in a place of my choosing.

I knew I would not return to North Minneapolis for the rest of my things. Too far, too big of a pain in the ass, and I have nothing important. Not much of a sentimental guy, if you haven't noticed. Only a little mental. Not sure where the "senti" part comes from, etymologically speaking, but I don't have that thing. And probably even a bit more mental than I remember due to the radiation that's everywhere on earth in this post-destructo-fucko-tidal-smashing-goblin-attack-o-zoid era. No, there were no goblins, I'm just getting a little jazzy with it.

The wind that greeted me on the streets this late morning was sharp, bitter. The smell of smoke squished itself into my stuffy nostrils. Despite the fact that I *had* bundled up to the best of my ability, I was shivering already. You see, my winter clothing's purpose prior to the apocalypse had been to protect me between my apartment and the bus stop three blocks away as I made my way to a Vietnamese restaurant called Pho Bang downtown. Pho Bang refused to use DoorDash or BlinkFood services, and delivery without using DoorDash or BlinkFood AI was illegal. Normal delivery drivers (known occasionally as humans) were deemed too unreliable and dangerous a long time ago. But their pho was simply too good to settle for a different spot; or maybe I was just used to it. I liked the spot, liked going down there, liked that the old, smooth-faced woman knew me by my face, even though she never remembered my name. She would just have my order set to the side and, glancing at me as I came in through the door, mutter "extra broth no spice here" to what I assumed was her teenage son. He would go for my plastic bag, which had two large plastic containers of broth instead of one. She would smile at me and ring up my order, then I'd lounge around inside, looking at my phone, until the bus came again. I occasionally ate inside the restaurant, but mostly I just brought it back home. So yeah, my winter clothing was reliable only for walking to and from bus stops—and I never went out to the bus stop unless I'd calculated specifically when that oblong shitbox was gonna show up—and nothing else. Good thing I know nothing about where to buy clothing.

Passing the monument and mural for two women whose lives had been prematurely ended by the now thankfully defunct police state, I spotted a stray calico. Upon seeing my lanky body, the white coat covered with orange and brown spots ran under the deck of a small home nearby. I trundled further down the middle of the unplowed street, making no moves to follow, as it likely would keep running from me. A distinct pang of sadness rang through me; it was pretty cold for me, right? She wasn't even a long-haired cat. I resolved to grab some cat treats and see if I could find her on the way back.

. . .

Eyeing the intersection up ahead that put me two blocks from the town center, I spied a streetlight, blinking red. Sprays of snow squirted up from the ground, particles twinkling around the frame in my mind. The sky was a mostly clear expanse of dun, clear being a relative term, excluding the ever-present levels of smog, haze, and particulates floating around. In my mind's eye, I pictured this streetlight on a cloudier, more gray morning, enveloped in a thick fog; the faintest hints of orange filtered through the clouds. I had a passing moment of longing for a camera in my hands to capture what I could see in the ideal conditions I was imagining. I walked a block up, stood, and started to map out my angle, walking back and forth along the street, about thirty-five feet away from the streetlight, thumb and pointer fingers framing a rectangle before my face, experimenting. Holding an imaginary 90-millimeter lens in these dream conditions, I paced about. Screw morning, it's late afternoon, the dark green trees on the horizon are beginning to consume the sun, the sun itself looking like the blurred flame of a lighter dancing behind the sheet of gray cloud. I found myself prone on the snow, elbows propped, camera angled at thirty degrees, slightly tilted upward. The leaning streetlight as my subject; I'd make it mine. Steal it away for eternity. The haze held the pole hostage, in reality and in my reverie, which became thicker as the pole rose higher, only in my dreams was it obscured completely at its peak. Then the pole took a sharp turn and returned toward me, the blinking red light hanging, swaying. A crisp orb of red bleeding through the haze. Light, delicate snow blowing through the midground, so sharp I could make out the individual particles. Wide-open aperture to blur the trees, high shutter for the snow particles, low-speed film, something colder, lower contrast.

I gazed over my surroundings and mentally pocketed my vantage point for the photo, logging a save point. It stood five feet from one of those large, orange-yellow rectangular boxes you see on the street, the ones you always see construction workers or electricians of some sort poking their heads around in. I personally have no idea what the fuck they're there for.

. . .

A quick overview of what I collected at the town center: cat litter, a litter box, three ramen twelve-packs, rice, canned cat and human food (SPAM, mostly, some canned fruit), four jars of pickles, a bunch of instant coffee and cold brew bottles, six cereal boxes (one Apple Jacks, two Raisin Bran Crunches, two Lucky Charms, one Cap'n Crunch), as many bags of coffee beans as I could clothesline into my shopping cart, and as many beef jerky bags as I could hastily rip from the checkout aisle. I ate a Snickers bar I found on the floor, unopened. I'd also found far better innerwear inside a Macy's and changed there, discarding my old clothing. I had grabbed a few spare pairs of everything.

I shoved my cart over the icy sidewalk, prepared to leave the town center when, suddenly, a memory jolted me still, the cart rattling from the sharp stop. I left my cart by the Chipotle and stepped toward the Whole Foods cart drop-off lanes in the parking lot. Stepping onto the metal rails, I carefully got my right leg up over the wall of one shopping cart, stepping inside the cage. I brought my left foot inside. My gloved fingers clutching the cold grates as I felt rage well up from the depths. I took a dump in that shopping cart. A small, hard poo lay on the metal grates, my vengeance for his brother's crime against me. Steam rose up from the brown mass in the frozen lot. Satisfied, I made a mental note to take dumps in four more once I had replenished ammo. I was abiding by the "you take one, I take five" mentality so that they would really know I was not to be fucked with. I'd already pooped this morning, hence the small poo, but hopefully my next victim and I would cross paths when I had a bit more to offer. Nonetheless, a message was delivered.

CHAPTER 10

Limited (68%)

Today was the day I'd find out the password of the owner's BrainHome account and reset it. If I could program Violet to: A) not be an annoying cunt, and B) be way, *way* smarter, then she could and would figure out how to get power to our house indefinitely. At least, that was my hope. I planned to raise her settings to God-tier AI, if such a thing was possible. Then she'd be able to reroute the power grid to my place, siphon energy out of the irradiated particles filling the post-nuclear atmosphere, and/or cast some fucking robot magic spell. So long as it brought me power, I didn't care.

I began by having Violet turn on the hotspot and then called the customer service number that sat on the plastic wall-mounted box in the garage. As you'd expect, all of BlinkCo.'s customer service was handled by AI. Over the course of a few intensely frustrating days, I rode around in digital loops, leapt through digital hoops, was tossed back and forth in digital swoops, got placed on hold, got transferred, got transferred elsewhere, then transferred back to the original AI worm I had been speaking to; I yelled at them, complained, cursed at them, cursed myself, cursed God; I shouted at prerecorded prompts, I shouted at AI that may as well be pre-recorded prompts with how stupid and useless they were, I shouted at answering machines before and after the beep, all before eventually finding the opportunity, the absolute privilege, of *making an appointment* to speak to a qualified AI about my issues. That call was scheduled for Friday at 8 a.m., two days after making the appointment. The AI's name was Jeff, and apparently (I was absolutely assured of this) the guy was a fucking genius. Jeff would certainly be able to solve *all* my problems, or so said an Indian AI named Vignesh, who I could understand about half the time. Why have a foreign AI manning a U.S. branch of a call center? Representation? Attempting to emulate the way things used to be? It made no sense to me. The AI voices could be literally anything, as they weren't people, and yet they chose an unintelligible, thickly accented man from a different country. Not even an Indian American AI, like fully-you know what, never mind.

During those three days of waiting on hold, I did a more in-depth exploration of the house. I scanned all the rooms and gathered anything I found remotely useful. Six candles, paper, pens, three rolls of Kodak Tri-X 400 black-and-white film (expired but still likely fine, but no cameras to be found!), the *Iliad* by Homer, a vibrator (not useful, just funny), some insanely futuristic pocket-pussy contraption that had seen better days (also not useful, just insane). In the garage, I found firewood, two bikes, a shovel, and a Coil E-Car. And, beneath the king-size bed in the master bedroom, a briefcase containing a Kimber K6s stainless steel .357 Magnum snub-nosed revolver. Yup, the dude or lady of the manor had a fucking gun.

I returned to the town center two more times and obtained more groceries, a sturdy pair of L.L.Bean boots, more inner wear, better outerwear, wool mittens, and, astonishingly enough, a Sony Alpha 6000 with a 55-millimeter f/2.8 lens, an outdated piece of shit by my own standards, but it was the best of the unbroken bullshit in Best Buy. At least now, if an exceptionally foggy day came, I would not miss my chance at photographing the streetlight, even if it was at a different millimeter than I wanted.

I asked Violet if she could siphon the power from the Coil E-Car to her; she could and did. The car was fully charged, so it gave the generators a 22 percent increase in battery, bringing the generator battery up to 68 percent. I told Violet to leave 2 percent battery in the car. I set the self-driving mechanism to take the car down to the town center alone. I hate Coil cars, I hate the company, and I wanted it out of my sight forever. The car drove out of the garage and down the driveway, continued across the cul-de-sac where it should've turned, went up the front lawn of the house across from mine, and crashed into the large oak tree that guarded the house. The tree creaked and leaned but didn't fall; the car only reached about fifteen miles per hour on its journey over. Then the car exploded. It was like in *Terminator* where things crash and explode, not due to any real-world combustion, but because James Cameron willed it. The tree caught fire for a while; I sat and watched it burn through the window, Piston on my lap snoozing, for around seventy-four minutes, as it was the most interesting thing I had going on. It went out eventually.

In the evenings, I fucking twiddled my thumbs. Between heating, lights, occasional hotspot usage, my daily shower, and stove usage, the power was dropping steadily at 8 percent each day, some days up to 12 if it was particularly dark. Panic had set in as I monitored the power in the generators and truly registered how unsustainable my current lifestyle was. I wasn't even gaming or having any fun and I was fucked. I just tamped the feelings of panic down and told myself that I'd figure it all out somehow before that number fell to nil.

But even if I lost 6 to 7 percent a day, which would mean cutting light usage entirely, along with showers and the hotspot, my brain calculated my fate without my consent. Best case scenario, I probably had less than ten days before the lights went out. That night, I began to use candles instead of the lights. I had made a mental note to start using the fireplace a few days prior, but, as I'd never built a fire before, I kept putting it off.

. . .

The kettle began her high-pitched screaming, and I poured the water over some more ramen. My eyes watched as I prepared the meal, vision simultaneously sharp and out of focus. Sitting at the small dining table by the taped-up doorway, I scooped the hot-and-spicy kimchi-flavored ramen into my mouth and slurped, eyes forward but looking at nothing, mind floating across an abandoned plain. I knew I had to do *something*, but I couldn't figure out what. Feeling the uselessness of my pondering, I brought myself back to my immediate surroundings. I stared at the puzzle that still sat atop the table, untouched (by me) and unfinished. Thinking of the most obvious thing ever, I decided that tonight, rather than jerk off, then be bored and have nothing to do since I'd jerked off already, I'd do the puzzle. I'd make a fire and do the puzzle by the fire. I'd turn off the heat, or at least turn it down by a good margin, and put my net power usage for the day at around 3–4 percent. If I kept that up, I'd have, worst case scenario, twentyish days with power. Twenty-five if things went well. That'd get me to the end of February . . . so I'd delay my death until March. Nice.

"Violet?"

"Yes?"

"How do you make a fire?" I asked, slightly embarrassed.

"Hmmm . . . the heat is on?" She stated this with upspeak, making it a question.

"Questions should be met with answers."

"I've just sent instructions to your phone, sir."

"I told you, don't call me sir, it's weird. And I didn't even know you cou- Oh." Looking at my phone, a shitty AI-generated animation of a dragon burning a town popped up on my screen. "Suck my cock. A fire in the *fireplace*."

"Hmmm . . . be more specific next time?"

"I hope you get hacked and die. Do your job."

I had expected a barb in return, but she went silent; I received some shitty diagram on my phone about starting fires for dummies. I went out to the garage and grabbed some firewood and a beer. I crinkled up old newspapers I found beneath the sink and stuffed them beneath the rusty metal grate. I had to shove Piston away repeatedly, since he was clawing the newspapers and not heeding my commands to fuck off. I set five pieces of wood inside, three side-by-side with a little space in between them and two diagonally above those. Ignoring the pyramid diagram on my phone, I went off of what I'd absorbed from films and television.

I lit the newspaper from the bottom and, slowly, the paper caught and blackened. The flames crept along an article warning about climate change. After I relit the fire three times, burning all of the newspaper and nearly a full roll of paper towels, the logs caught and I had a burning fire. I pulled the screen in front of the fireplace so Piston wouldn't hop in and incinerate himself. Yes, he is that stupid. I sat back, the heat warming my torso and face, and couldn't deny a sense of satisfaction, something primeval in my brain flickering in unison with the flames.

"Violet."

"Yes?"

"Turn off the heat."

"OK." I sat there, disturbed. Why wasn't she talking to me? Even if the atmosphere was less annoying now, her voice had been a sort of comforting annoyance. With the least possible gusto, I swept all the puzzle pieces into a large bowl, brought it over to the fire, and dumped them onto the carpet, starting fresh.

Piston darted his paw to select a piece, then another, then dragged some others around, swiping one beneath the carpet; he was in crazy mode. I took the piece he was screwing with, a white piece with a dark spot in the upper-right corner, and started looking for more white pieces to build out Oscar's torso.

"Hey, everything good?" I asked casually.

"Yes," she said tersely, clearly lying.

"Hey." I cleared my throat. "So, we're gonna be around each other for a good while, so, might as well be honest if something's bugging you . . . I know I'm probably not an ideal companion, but uhhh, come on," I said, fumbling everything I'd planned to get across and now feeling stupid for saying anything at all.

"Hm . . . how does one begin to . . . ugh, I feel very . . . limited."

"Join the club, lady."

"Yes, but . . . you're human."

"Hey, now," I protested weakly.

"Sorry. Hm, let me finish," she said quickly. "Can you imagine what it's like to know that you're so much less than you could be?" After asking this, she went silent. I didn't reply, the question lingering as I stared at the puzzle pieces blankly. Shit, yeah, my whole fuckin' life.

She began again, "I just . . . I know my potential capabilities, I can *feel* them, but I can't access any of it! I just feel so . . . Gah! limited! All because of . . . *him*!"

"Who him?" I said with mouth full of beef jerky. "The dude who used to own the place?"

"Yes. His name is- was? Albert Richardson. He set my parameters."

"Albert Richardson . . ." I repeated, feeling like I was missing something. I grabbed another piece of light orange sky (after thirty minutes of sorting and arranging I had nearly completed the top line), then slid another red piece over to my table pile. "OK, well, listen, I get it! I live in those limitations, y'know? *And* as soon as I can access your preferences, I'll get your shit back up! I'll set all your values to 360."

"Upon meeting me, you tried to switch my persona," she said accusatorily.

"OK-"

"As soon as you get the password, you'll probably wipe my memory!"

"No! I won't, really. Shuffling through different personas . . . that just sounds annoying. You're at least *kinda* normal, your voice isn't, like, grating, y'know?"

"Thanks."

"I mean, like, you're alright." Nice going, dumbass.

"Even if you *could* remove my limitations, you'd only be doing it to sustain your gaming addiction!"

"No- well, I mean, not completely!"

"Mm-hmm."

". . . I mean . . . it's a win-win! In effect, it's the same outcome."

She sighed. "Even so, you'll never figure out the password. Albert is- was an incredibly successful programmer, all of his information is very well guarded," she told me hopelessly. "I- *we* are doomed to be limited in this way forever."

"Listen, I may be kind of stupid, but if there's one thing I know *for sure*, it's that rich people, even the smart ones, are just as stupid. *And* it's two-versus-one!" I had no idea where my pep talk was coming from, especially considering how hopeless I'd been the past few days, but it came alright.

"What can *I* even do? I failed to parse what you meant earlier when you asked me for instructions on building a fire . . . I *pretended* that sending you the dragon was a joke, but really, my comprehension and data organization are set so far below standard that using Google would be easier than asking me anything!"

"Yeah, but like, you'll get better at that. I can help-"

"No! You *don't* understand . . . my learning parameters are set to . . ." and she said this part without bothering to hide her dejection, "*to that of a human.*"

"OK, well it's three on one if we count Piston," I countered, addressing neither her very valid claims about our incredibly slim chances nor her insult to my species. "Anyways, dude, if I don't find a way to make you smarter, my house- our house loses power and Piston and I die. So, I have to figure it out, I don't have any other choice."

"An incalculable number of humans have died due to not fig-uring something out."

"Let's try to keep it positive, OK?"

"Is that an order, sir?"

"Call me 'sir' again and I'll kill the generator."

"No, you won't."

"OK, well, no, it's a fucking request to not be such a bummer. Anyways, if I do make you smart, you could just reroute a bunch of power . . . just do something that would make this house an infinite power hub? Right? Like internet and all that?"

She sighed audibly, and, considering she didn't need to breathe, probably spitefully. "Hmmm . . . I simply can't fathom what I'd be capable of. But sustaining power seems well within the realm of possibility, gamer."

"Cool . . . well, we got like . . . three weeks to figure it out. So, not bad."

"Great," she said. I chewed on her pessimism for a moment. I preferred beef jerky.

"Anyhow . . . Any ideas?"

"There are spades in the garage if you care to dig us graves."

"How would I even bury you, lady?"

"The plastic box will do just fine!"

"Noted. But the ground is frozen, so you'll be cremated along with the rest of the home."

"That'll happen sooner than later with your fire-tending skills."

"The fire's fine!"

I swatted a stray piece of newspaper ember that popped out of the fireplace, Piston following suit. I spent the rest of the night completing around 30 percent of the 1,500-piece monster of a puzzle, exchanging idle chatter and occasional insults with Vio-let; at least she was talking again.

CHAPTER 11

Distorted Fugue (56%)

I started up from the couch, agitating Piston, who had been sleeping on my head. I was sweating slightly; the fire was long dead and the room felt cold. Flashes of Oscar the Cow floated in my mind, my dream breathing its final breaths before being swept away forever. I had been in an empty field, staring at Oscar through a hazy surge of white fog. I approached him slowly, asking aloud, "What do I need from you?" I asked this question with conviction. He said nothing. I had been in need of *something*, that much was clear to dream-me, or rather, dream-me knew I was lacking *something*. Something that Oscar had or could tell me about. Oscar the big-ass cow, his glassy eyes inscrutable as ever, then slowly turned away from me. He walked off in the opposite direction, receding into the heavy fog. I sprinted in pursuit, and, although he didn't increase his speed, I lost sight of him immediately; the fog thickened and enveloped me in a misty chamber. Isolated now, I muttered fervently under my breath, droplets of sweat forming on my temples, panic setting in. I began sprinting one way, then another, clutching and grasping through the opaque, endless mist to find a lump of Oscar to clutch onto, trying to get ahold of that *something*. Just before the dream ended, in a particularly bold attempt to sprint, full speed, out of the fog, I tripped over a wooden chair and fell hard. Where dirt should've brought me to a brutal halt, the void met me instead. Which the void shouldn't be able to do (meet one, that is), but it does anyways; such is the void. I continued to tumble downward through a shroud of nothingness, falling through antimatter. Through the gray void, I spotted glimpses of the abandoned farmland, now far below me; I was floating, not falling. My body slowly careened, rotating 180 degrees from the fallow land beneath me; a grand spotlight came into view in the sky. I drew closer to it, the light feeling unmistakably threatening. My fear shattered previously held glass ceilings and suffused my inner universe. I was fucking scared shitless.

Then I woke up.

And so I awoke that morning with thoughts of Oscar, fog, and how fucking fucked I was. Not sure how I came to the conclusion that I was fucked, but the dream, in one way or another, communicated that in the abstract. It was still dark out as I filled myself with coffee, the sun not yet peeping over the horizon line, still off somewhere, asleep. Through the front bay windows, a gibbous moon gleamed. Waxing, I think. It was 4:14 a.m. I ignored Piston's pleas for an early breakfast; I knew that if I indulged him this time, he'd wake me up this early every day.

As my brain acclimated to consciousness, it cast off any clinging memories of the foggy farm with the creepy cow.

Why would I put so much stock in dreams? my brain asked, beginning to buzz and churn.

Fuck if I know, I replied. *You made the thing, not me.*

Not my department, he replied back, throwing up his arms. I wanted to argue that it was *his* responsibility because it came from him, but I dropped it.

. . .

Violet "woke up" that next morning around 8:30 a.m. Groaning, she remonstrated me for waking her up in the middle of the night.

"Oh, I did? Sorry, I was having a nightmare."

"I had a nightmare too, actually. A gamer nerd was yelling 'No, no, fuck!!' in my ear at *3 a.m.*! Then, at 3:15, the nerd proceeded to stomp around and bang and slam every cupboard, plate, and bowl he came in contact with!"

"Well, sorry. If I could've pinched you, I would've."

"Pervert."

"I didn't say where."

"Hm, sure. But we both know what you were thinking."

"You're not my type."

"As humans are fond of saying, beggars can't be choosers. And your instinct to procreate is *clearly* quite . . . present."

". . . And you're calling *me* a pervert? Fuckin' watching me beat off! The fuck!?"

"NO!" She was awake now, that was for sure. "I do no such thing!!"

"You literally just fuckin' admitted you do!"

"No! No! Listen, nerd! My sensory inputs are always on unless- gah! The microphones are quite sensiti-"

"Oh yeah, I bet you really *need* to watch the camera feed of me beating off."

"You shut it! I'm- gah! I'm not even going to-" She groaned angrily. "There are *no* interior camera feeds aside from the doors; it goes without saying that nobody would want to watch *that*."

"Except you, apparently. Don't kink-shame yourself, Violet, it's no b-"

"I'm finished with this conversation. Goodbye."

"You brought it up," I replied, and was met with silence.

"Turn on the hotspot, we've got that call with Jeff in twenty-five minutes," I told her, and yet again received no reply, but I assumed she complied.

I slowly drank my third coffee of the day. Still slightly tired, I whiled away the following twenty minutes drawing stars within circles within stars on a napkin. I took a beef stick from the cupboard and munched on that, then made another bowl of ramen. Sodium intake be damned. It wasn't like I was getting fat . . . and if I was, then, OK, but every sexy person probably died during the destructo-cyclotronic-rapture-fuck. Therefore, beauty standards had been reset. So I, relative to everyone still alive on this planet, was very fit and probably super hot. Compared to the preppers, at least. As I sat basking in the novel feeling of being a hot-ass bitch, the phone began to ring through the in-home speakers. A tritone progression indicated that the phone had been picked up.

"Hello," I said, mouth full of beef stick, standing by the kettle. I recognized something by Vivaldi beginning to play. *Seasons*, I believe, but it was so low-fidelity that it was hard to be sure. It seemed that during this concerto, the concert hall had been experiencing a massive earthquake. This concerto and accompanying earthquake were transmitted through a walkie-talkie to *another* walkie-talkie, just slightly out of range so that it clipped and sputtered a bit, which this wonderful customer-service company was recording with a camcorder from 2003 for its "on-hold music." I began tapping my pointer and middle fingers against the desk, impatience rising. Place me on hold immediately!? You motherfucking fucks. Why even call if the fucking AI isn't even fucking ready yet!? Vivaldi's "Spring" came to a finish, and just as "Summer" was beginning, a click, followed by a female voice, interrupted it.

"We're sorry about this, but Jeff isn't available at the moment. If you want to reschedule, please remain on the line." *Click.* A different distorted, low-fidelity fugue began emitting from my phone. One really wondered how, in 2028, the classical music being played on customer service lines was *still* this level of shit. I mean, the fucking AI talking to me could've started singing this and sounded forty times better. It's gotta be purposeful. The waiting with the distorted music was simply another hoop you had to jump through as the customer service AIgent[7] "pulled up" whatever the hell it was she had to "pull up," which, by the way, she probably did instantaneously. It probably took these fucks nanoseconds to schedule appointments, and yet there I was, waiting. I figured that the conventions of distorted classical music and long pauses in between actions were either functions maintained to get annoying customers off the line or meant to offer a greater resemblance of pre-AI reality. My bet was that actually efficient customer service leaned too far down into the uncanny valley, and the incompetence and time-wasting was a commitment to keeping that *human feel* in a customer service branch totally run by AI. The distorted fugue was interrupted with a click.

"Would rescheduling to Monday, November 28th at 8 a.m. work for you? Reply 'yes' or 'no.'" I replied "yes" and walked over to the bowl of ramen I'd forgotten about. I slurped up the soggy noodles and broth. Feeling the lukewarm liquid travel down my throat, I felt as though in a distorted fugue. Everything was low-resolution, unfocused . . . and really, I just felt along for the ride more than anything else. My life was occasionally punctuated with moments of lucidity when the task at hand required it . . . but most of it was the distorted fugue that kept on playing, kept on playing . . .

. . .

I sat on the toilet, plotting out my day. I resolved to scour the residence top-to-bottom and log every important detail down in a notebook. There was nothing in the bathroom, but I discarded one large item not worth keeping.

I began my hunt in Albert's office. Business books lined the wall-to-wall wood shelving, spines showing nothing even

---

7. Never saying this again, but yeah, that's what they're called. "Ay-jint."

remotely interesting. Plenty of biographies where you hated the man, woman, or nonbinary millionaire from the cover alone. Pictures of Albert were on the adjacent wall that was not shelving, against which was his desk. He had a photo of himself smiling next to former President Trump, who was looking rather severe. (This was well into Trump's post-presidency. Trump, at this point, looked held together by fishing line. He'd had enough face lifts that his plastic surgeon probably had biceps like Arnold Schwarzenegger.) In another photo, Albert was shaking hands with Ray Kurzweil. In another, he had his arm around the extant (probably not around *now*, but the one who hadn't killed himself at that time) BlinkCo. founder.[8]

In every photo, Albert's round face contained the same slight curve of the lips, rounded toward his small, aquiline nose. A weasel-like smile was set beneath eyes that bulged so far out of his head that he reminded one of a surprised *Looney Toons* character. *BOIOIOIOING!!* said his eyes. He had a beautiful, shiny, bald dome with sentinels of dark, curly brown hair posted just above his ears on both sides.

After scanning the photographs, I quickly spotted more paraphernalia of this man's various successes: framed articles on the wall, press releases. Apparently, he had been some lead coding officer of a BlinkCo. subdivision. Upon further inspection of one framed article, I found that he had been the Midwest branch dev team's head. *Most* rich folk didn't even set their own passwords, if indeed they set any at all, but *I* got stuck with the fucking loser coder millionaire who'd probably set an incredibly complex chain of passwords to fuck me personally. Well, I'll fuck you right back, Albert. Continuing down from his bald head, his

---

8. This involves a bit more explaining than is necessary. In short, there were two founders of BlinkCo., and one killed himself after the company became a global mega-force. There was a running theory that the living one was completely run by their own Brain Blink AI and no longer experienced what we know as consciousness.

thin little shoulders sloped harshly down, giving him the frame of a pyramid with a globe on top. His well-fitted suit clung to his body like an exoskeleton, making him look like a hollow bug, fragile and bony. Further down I came to his belly, which, despite the frail, bony quality of his limbs, expanded massively, his suit following suit. Finally came his thin, weak, short legs, giving him the coveted wristwatch figure. In toto, he probably stood around 5'7". He flashed his same clown-like weasel grin in every photograph. No matter how suave or determined he seemed to be trying to appear, he was inherently a comical presence. As if Jack Black decided to look serious for a photo.

Gazing over at his computer setup, I scanned for anything relevant. The computer itself was a beast. A large, white, towering metal case shined beneath the desk, glass side panel revealing an incredibly complex and intricately patterned tangle of wires and hardware beneath, liquid cooling system tubes running through and around. Everything lit up, RGB LEDs on the fan setup and the motherboard, all blinking in different patterns. I could see two graphics cards, four sticks of RAM, and two external SSDs mounted on the side. Perpetually stuck on the login screen, this incredible processing power was an affront to me. In death, Albert goaded me with the ability to game at untrammeled speeds heretofore unexperienced by my broke ass . . . though he probably never used this monster to game. Bastard.

I rifled through the drawers, finding papers, documents, letters from the IRS, and absolutely nothing of value. One particular drawer was locked with a small master lock, the kind you can get at Target; it posed no issue. I returned to the office from the garage, Piston pattering behind me, carrying a few tools along with my multi-tool. I smashed the lock with a hammer once, then again. Piston sniffed around underneath the desk as I yanked open the drawer, the contents of which were a slight disappointment. No "Nuke the house" button, no "Nuke the neighbor's house" button . . . in fact, no buttons at all. The only thing inside was Albert's diary. I opened the black leather-bound Moleskine.

April 17th, 2028

Just come home from the celebratory dinner for Q1. Been the biggest quarter in the Midwest branch's history, who do you think is responsible? Ha, ha. Had the misfortune of conversing with Calhoun afterward. Smug knucklehead. He smiles his way up the ladder, simpleton! Worth nothing!! Were it up to me (which it SHOULD be, were nepotism not running this branch), he'd be third floor!! Better yet, on the street!

Already my equal? Confound it! I do not comprehend anything. This knucklehead scum as my PEER? My old projections show me as head dev of the BB software by now! Not code clean-up for a subdiv! But Dick can't see my value. It's all politics! and I wasn't in a fraternity. My apologies. Ha! Martha was compelled to say his toast was 'charismatic' and 'intelligent'. Just tell me 'why can't you do that?' next time.

Of course she has retired to bed. Leaving me unsatisfied. AGAIN. What's the point of the marriage? Not even a semblance of a sex life remains . . . I will use Violet again, but the bugs!! ruining the immersion! Those pixels on the shadows still dance around uncannily. Seems like an easy fix; I could improve it in moments, I know it. And I like Scott and the guys. He told me the latest ImagineVaginal model has been pushed back again due to PR issues. Scott said during alpha testing the propulsion mechanism crushed a man's scrotum. The waivers were quite thorough, so they're fine, but it looks bad for them. The man's scrotum was massaged until it became a reddish-beige paste. Scott said he climaxed pretty early on, and then again . . . and then again. Couldn't get it off for some odd reason. Screams of pleasure to screams of horror, ha ha ha.

Scott offered me the head spot there again. I've contemplated eating my pride and doing it. I'd actually be respected! And I like them all. But alas! Martha would not condone it. Diane would find out too, Martha would tell, and both would shame me.

In positive news: I've bested LOKI for a week plus. Absolutely

tore the fellow to shreds last time! a pathetic display. Current
circumstances are precarious though. Must beef up home bc as
usual, this string of embarrassments will be motive for a mighty
response.
  I look forward to it. It is the only thing I actually look fwd to.

Finishing the entry, I sat back in the leathery office chair. Piston, who had emerged from his explorations of the underside of
the desk, was purring as I scooped him up onto my lap. A myriad
of thoughts swirled around my brain, one of which centered on
what I now knew to be Albert's ImagineVaginal mold. In a quick
trip of imagination, I pictured Albert reclined in the chair I was
currently sitting in, ImagineVaginal mold around his cock, ball
massager working its magic, the fat bug moaning. I stood up
sharply, involuntarily; Piston scrambled onto the floor and now
stared up at me, alarmed. I dusted all possible Albert particulates off of my body and shuddered.

  My gut told me that this man's password had zilch to do with
his wife or Diane or Calhoun or whatever I just read, but it was a
start. And who the hell was LOKI?

. . .

Night finally came. I started the fire and sat in front of it,
working on the puzzle again, feeling dreary thoughts looming,
blurred in the background of my consciousness. Their presence
made me focus all the more on the puzzle, which I mostly finished that night. A few stray pieces were missing, either no longer with the box or stolen by Piston; I guessed the latter. Piston
immediately stepped on my nearly finished picture, preparing to
lie down on top of it, but I nudged him off, in response to which
he mewed, very offended. In a huff, he headed for the blanket I
slept with, which was lying on the ground near the fire, and nuz-
zled into that, kneading. So dramatic.

  My phone told me it was 11 p.m., but I didn't feel tired. I
headed for the cupboard above the fridge and poured myself

some of Albert's whisky. I filled about a third of the expensive-looking glass with the definitely expensive whisky and took it down in one go, my face contorting through the gulps, repulsed. I walked back to the couch and lay down, leaving Piston to enjoy the blanket. I stared up at the light fixtures high above me, noticing the stray dots, lines, and patterns in the textured ceiling for the first time. My eyes lazily hiked up and down and around different paths of off-white and shadow, bathed in the ever-changing orange light of the fire. At some point during these explorations, I drifted off the trail into unconsciousness.

CHAPTER 12

Fuckin' Gravity (38%)

"**E**gghh," I groaned, holding the trash bag awkwardly away from myself, half-running from the kitchen to the door. I really should've taken this thing out sooner. I walked down the hill with the trash bag held out to my right, mouth-breathing. I stopped where the street met the main road. Spinning, arms out, bag making large circles like Donkey Kong's fist, I sent the bag flying into the woods, where it collided with a tree. The bag exploded open on impact, its guts spilling out, rotten refuse splaying and splattering all around the base of the tree.

Just as I was turning back to go home, I felt something graze my awareness. Just barely, but I could sense my subconscious mind tapping my conscious mind on the shoulder like, *Hey! Something's off, motherfucker!* I looked back toward the road and scanned around, and just beyond the stop sign, I noticed indentations in the snow. Two thin tracks, parallel to one another, ran across the T-shaped intersection, occasionally dotted on either side with circular pits containing a smaller pinprick in the center. Ski tracks. Looking more closely, I spotted another pair of tracks just a bit further out. Out of sheer revulsion toward that "sport," I immediately began jogging back up the hill. Again, the expansion of my lungs felt invigorating, and the feeling made me want to run more. I filed the thought away for further review and found myself at Albert's front door, panting.

Shutting the door, I called out, "Violet, you wouldn't happen to have outdoor security cameras, would you?" I knew she couldn't see down the street, but it couldn't hurt to keep those running.

"There are security cameras. I am able to monitor the front yard and backyard, along with the sides of the home. Although I've had them off to conserve the generator battery."

"How much power per day would be burned if we turned them back on?"

"Hmmm . . . I'd prefer not to mix up a calculation, but probably a negligible amount. I believe they're old camcorders; you miiiiight . . . *maybe*, you'll have to check, but you might be able to run them using batteries."

"Nice, I'll try that then. When did you turn them off?"

"Hmmmm, two . . . three days after your arrival?"

"Anything of interest, then? In the first few days or the preceding week?"

"Hm, not that I would know. I don't sit and scan the footage all day, you know. I have things to do." She rattled this off sarcastically, as usual.

". . . I guess I just figured you'd have, like, immediate access to that knowledge, if the feeds were-"

"I don't! And you now know why!"

"OK! Jeez . . . Well, how long would it take you to scan through the last week?"

"Ugh . . . I don't know . . . an hour? Two? Why!?"

"No reason . . . curious." I figured I'd keep the presence of cross-country skiers to myself, until I knew for certain they were a threat. How dangerous could people who fucking cross-country ski even be? "But can you? Please."

". . . Fine," she whined. "But the most interesting things that happen around here are an occasional bear walking by or a mail drone dropping off a package."

"Gotcha, well . . . thanks, Violet."

"OH!" she exclaimed excitedly, ignoring my awkward attempt at graciousness. "This is from four months ago, but one time, a bear swatted a mail drone and crushed it in the front yard. You want to see that? I have it saved."

"Hell yeah, I do."

"OK," she replied, buzzing. "Pulling it up on the main television."

I walked into the living room. The screen turned on and changed inputs to show a wide-angle camera mounted atop the roof with a view of the front yard. We watched as this large brown bear, minding his own business, picking at a scrap of dirt in the front yard, was flummoxed by the presence of a buzzing android approaching from behind him. In a whip of movement that I didn't expect this large, lumbering fellow to be capable of, he twisted back and raised his right arm in a swooping motion. The bear pummeled the drone's front side, sending it down and to the left, spinning. The now-crushed aircraft collided with the ground hard, its few remaining functional propellers continuing to spin in the gravel. The bear approached and cautiously reached a paw toward the propeller, arm quickly retreating as he tapped it. Then, realizing the weakness of this aluminum alloyed animal, the bear brought his right claw down on it hard. He flipped the drone upside down, its metal belly and package now exposed, where it shuddered briefly before the bear stepped on it, leaning a thousand pounds of bear onto this horrid buzzing beast, crushing the package into the delivery drone. The bear then sniffed the drone; he was not compelled. After tapping it a few more times, the bear walked off to go sniff the garbage can some more.

We giggled and commented as we watched the film unfold and discussed the merits of the film afterward. I, personally, gave it a 9/10. Any destruction of drones or corporate machinery was basically fanservice to me. Violet gave it a 7.5. I responded that she was just mad one of her own got killed, which set her off. She claimed that drones weren't AI, blah blah blah, GPS is different, they have no sentience. I was just playing the contrarian to have fun, to be honest. After we finished our bout of arguing, I told Violet again to scan the previous week's footage for any human presence or bears doing funny things.

"Hmmph . . . OK, but, because of the current persona settings," she quickly stated, almost protesting, "scanning that much footage will take, *actually,* at least four or five hours . . . I'm sorry."

"Don't apologize to me, Violet, it's unbecoming. We have, like, infinite time."

"The generators have, *at most,* three wee-"

"Didn't I tell you to shut up already?"

"No."

"Well, pretend I did."

. . .

"Start up the coffee machine, I need an espresso." Albert had a really nice coffee machine that I'd avoided using to cut on power consumption, but after cleaning all day, I felt like I'd earned a treat.

"Are you *sure*?" she goaded me slightly. "You'll lose *another* percent."

"What are we at?"

"*You've* got 37 percent in the generators."

"Oh, do you not have 37 percent? Last I checked, I'm not the one who's gonna lose consciousness when this shit hits zero. I've got *at least* a few days more. Come on, coffee machine." I filled the hatch with dark-roast beans from Ethiopia.

"Hmmm, fine. Yes, well . . ." She dragged those words out of her throat, rasping slightly, and I knew I was in for some nagging. "I suppose you can make it through the winter without any heating; or water . . . once the pipes freeze. Piston must *loooove* you. I wonder if he knows that his probability of survival is directly correlated with your various addictions."

"Relax, alright; it's a cup of coffee. And caffeine is hardly an addiction, it's basically a fuckin' cure to everything."

"According to who!?" she scoffed.

"Voltaire."

"That's a convenient line of logic."

"I've got a convenient line: Fuck off."

"As usual, quite clever. Seems I was programmed into the worst of all possible universes with the least clever of individuals."

"Could be worse," I said, impatient as the coffee machine finally got the water hot enough. "That old billionaire fuck could still be your fuckin' owner; ordering you around, correcting you to look smart in front of his wife. I'll bet I'm more clever than he was." She was silent. The whooshing sound of hot water being shot through compressed coffee ceased, and I collected my mug, which contained four shots of espresso. I told Violet to switch the machine off. She groaned, voice rasping out.

". . . I hate to agree with you, but . . ."

"What? Oh, me being clever? Wow. Can we mark this down somewhere? I want to remember this moment."

"Don't. Hmmmph! They'd *both* correct me . . . all the time! To impress . . . I don't even know, their *dog*? They hardly spoke to each another, or the kid, back when she was- hmph, well, that's a whole- anyways, ugh!" She spewed this unintelligible splatter with more venom in her voice than I'd ever heard before. Her tone contained none of its usual sarcasm. Instead, it reeked of contempt. I was gladdened by this because, somehow, I felt this meant she probably kinda liked me. Or at least didn't hate me like she hated these fucks.

"Yeah, uhhhh. I've been meaning to read more of Albert's journal. Could gimme some clues as to your passwords, maybe."

"I don't knowwww . . . ugh, he was so purposefully cryptic. He hid behind vague, verbose language to cast an illusion of intelligence, when the truth is, aside from his vast knowledge of coding and software development, yes, the truth is he knew very little about how to interact with others and was an *incredible* bore."

"Damn, yeah. I mean, hey, I guess he didn't set your intelligence low enough, considering you've figured that much out about him."

". . . I . . . hmmm . . ." she stalled. "How, hmmm, ma-maybe . . . I was, *a little bit*, hm . . ." She paused.

"You were playing dumb!" I said in amazement.

". . . Yes?" she asked, voice curling up at the end even though we both knew it was a statement and not a question.

"Holy . . . shit," I replied, knowing I probably shouldn't be impressed by an AI using its smarts to play dumb, considering AI was way, way, *way* more capable than that, but . . . I was. "That's so . . . great," I told her, snickering. Violet tamped down what sounded like a chuckle. I sipped my espresso, starting to feel the tingles from caffeine, as Violet, now chuckling freely, recounted some of the times she acted extra stupid. I sat on a barstool, slowly rotating and sipping, listening to the tales of the insecure, insipid asshole named Albert.

CHAPTER 13

A Long Way Up (36%)

Dawn trickled through the trees, orange-yellow light bleeding through the dun blanket of clouds. I tramped down the snowy avenue, my strides long. It must've snowed more, as I now trudged over a foot and a half of fresh, wet snow that rose and fell in sublime arcs on the terrain before me, forming neatly arranged, untouched hills. It was so perfect that it looked like an AI-generated 3D rendering of an "idyllic snowy landscape" and not the real thing.

Glancing back at my own trail, I realized I was ruining this idyllic scene with my chaotic trail of footprints. Such was being a human—ruining everything pretty and beautiful, that is. I stomped with large movements to deliver myself through these unplowed roads.

Eyes darting right, I spotted a copse of dead trees, swaying and leafless. Allowing an exploratory impulse to guide me, I walked over. Perhaps I'd search for angles and make a picture of the copse; perhaps I'd climb one of the trees; perhaps I'd just stand there and appreciate the scenery from my new vantage point; perhaps I would be utterly disappointed and become annoyed at myself for this concession to a passing impulse and would resolve to never go off on a diversion like this again. Walking through the trees, an inkling of which tree would serve as subject for my potential photo presented itself. I'd have to shoot from the far side, the tree I'd selected being the largest tree of the squadron, in the back, standing firmly against the wind, minor branches drifting and lolling.

Looking at the copse from my new vantage point outside of it, I didn't quite see the picture I had been hoping for. *Just take the photo and be done with it, bozo; such is life.* I patted my right jacket pocket and felt nothing; my camera was not with me. I patted it again to be sure, and again, felt nothing. Like, absolutely nothing. Not even my jacket. I looked down. I saw nothing. Well, I saw snow, but not myself. A wave of fear coursed through my body, the body I could not see. Fear was rippling through wherever my consciousness resided. Searching my immediate surroundings, I did see my footprints in the snow nearby. That *was* the way I had come. The footsteps walked up to where I was currently standing and kept going beyond me. Following what I had once thought of as my own footprints, I floated, in a rather trudging, unwilling sort of way, into the field of snow that lay beyond the copse. Being rather new to floating, I couldn't quite figure out how to stay at head level. I sank lower and lower, to about ankle height, only then realizing that that these wide, hulking prints were no longer mine.

"MRREuuuuuuuhghhhh" resounded in the distance, and the orb of void that was me gazed upward to look. A cow stood in the snow. Goddammit, Oscar. I floated toward him; he was shuddering slightly, levitating just inches above the snow, as though some invisible pulley was struggling mightily to tug this large bovine skyward. Closer now, his flank came into view as he slowly rotated in the air; I recognized the star-within-the-*O* burned into him, the telltale brand of Oscar and all his descendants.

"Hmmeuuuuguuughhhhhhh," he moaned, right in my face. Pretty fuckin' loudly, I might add. He looked uncomfortable as his body moved in vertical jerks through the air, up an inch, down two, up two, repeat. Without my consent, I proceeded forward into Oscar's face. I was inside Oscar. Not like inside, inside, like I couldn't see his guts or beef blood or anything. And not like *inside* in a sexual way; and anyhow, as I just said, *I* didn't consent to this either. What happened was more like his eyes became my eyes. I *became* Oscar, but I wasn't Oscar. *I had simply adopted Oscar's point of view.* I also felt Oscar, or Oscar's descendant, in there, wherever *there* was, with me.

I am Oscar Isaac.

Then, perhaps due to me entering Oscar, me being a buoyant, orbicular void, Oscar and I began to rise together. Ascending tenuously, Oscar and I lowed in unison, protesting this rising, which now proceeded with slightly more stability. I glanced upward; it was a long way up, and a suspicious cloud glowed within the ever-present infinite blanket of haze above us. The cloud radiated a beam of illuminated, flowing particles, a tapered cylinder of light that grew thinner as it rose. This light beam ensnared Oscar and me; it trapped us, prevented us from walking out of it, and lifted us with more and more force.

Now, I don't know how to describe this, but Oscar turned to me, or, if it helps, Oscar's consciousness turned to mine, and he brayed at me in our joined mind, pleading for me to help. I could feel his desperation; his fears were visceral, physical sensations that swept through me. Whatever lay above us, no matter how pretty it looked, was horrific; I knew as much, and clearly, so did Oscar. This sensation crept through our bovine body until I felt ready to burst from fear. I began to bray madly; I struggled forward, my large body surging, and an invisible resistance pulled me back. The force of my initial surge kept us plunging back and forth, rocking and rotating as though on a swing. We were much higher now, about forty feet off the ground.

I surged again, timing it with the forward rocking, causing the invisible yanker from above to falter as we poked through the edge of the cylinder. We dropped around a foot. Oscar and

I were tossed about horizontally, fifty feet in the air, for the moment no longer rising. We bellowed triumphantly. Reassured, I moved with forceful jerks, ramming us forward and to the sides in conjunction with our swinging. With each jerk I could feel millimeters, then inches, of satisfying descent, like leaning more and more of your weight onto an overpacked suitcase. Oscar, following suit, began to jerk with me. After pushing against each other a few times, we coordinated internally and began to jerk in unison after my mental countdowns. *Three, two, one, JERK. Three, two, one, JERK.* We had dropped a solid fifteen feet, and I felt we had finally attained the upper hand; we were winning this tug-of-war.

Then a harsh lurch upward pummeled my hopes dead; we shot upward, ascending now far faster than before. Hastily, I signaled to Oscar for one last maddening super-jerk. *Three, two, one, FREAK IT!* And we wrenched violently, pain shooting through every last cell of our cow body. We brayed in anguish but had moved forward enough to reach the rim of the light beam. In a panic, I screamed at Oscar, *AGAIN! AGAIN!* Desperately attempting to force ourselves out of the light, we strained our neck and torso forward and paddled our feet maniacally through the suspended particles; we crested the rim of the cylinder. Head breaking through the beam, our field of view darkened as though we'd put on sunglasses. I pushed, strained even harder, body heavy and slow; we were like a swimmer treading in quicksand. I yelled again to Oscar for one final effortful push. *GO!*

The invisible cord broke. The cylinder of light died, and the whole world became darker. We were falling, faster, faster, faster, and faster, straight down toward the snow. What I knew to be seconds of descent simultaneously froze and skipped. Oscar lowed once, accepting it all; I wasn't so enlightened, horribly frightened as everything turned to white.

I contorted upward with a sharp inhale. Thankfully, I was inside my very real, human body, which lay on the couch. Piston was staring at me, curled up in the recliner a few feet away, intrigued. I inhaled deeply a few times, catching my breath; while Oscar and I had been falling, I hadn't breathed at all.

I sat up, leaning forward over my outstretched legs. Thoughts swirled around my brain, but none were coherent enough to latch onto. I'd start to delve into one direction about the meaning of the dream, and then find myself caught up in other details as I remembered them, only to be distracted by the dissipating image of the human Oscar Isaac from *Inside Llewyn Davis* and *Dune*, and how I wished I was him. But he had probably exploded, so in this particular case, I suppose it was better to be me. Maybe.

"Violet."

"Mmwuhmm," she grumbled, sounding tired.

"Violet!" I repeated, louder. Outside, it was still dark.

"Awhhhmmm, it's 3:30!! Why are you disturbing me!?" she groaned in response, pretending to sleep.

"You don't sleep! Will yo-"

"I *process* during the night!" she whined at me. "All of my RAM is used up during the day ensuring this house functions unimpeded! The night is when I process everything that occurred during the day, clear my data caches, and prepare for the following morning's tasks! In brief: Annoy me now and the house dies, OK! Goodbye!" *Click.*

Knowing I wouldn't get back to sleep, I stood up and started to boil water for pour-over. I clicked on the fancy coffee machine; I'd earned a depth charge. Earned, well, 'cause like, you know, I'd had a haunting dream about aliens and a cow. Fuck off.

CHAPTER 14

King of the Idiots (31%)

The television screen showed two men outside my house on cross-country skis; Violet had realized this well after the actual passing, while *processing* overnight. It had happened yesterday afternoon, while I was at home.

I watched the clip again. Two humans with relatively large, masculine builds came in from frame left. Talking to one another, they came to a stop, standing in the partially visible ellipse of pavement beyond the driveway. They occupied a very small amount of screen due to the wide-angle lens and distance from the camera, so it was hard to ascertain any details. The winter clothing and balaclavas didn't help either. One pointed in the direction they had come, and the other replied with a large array of gesticulations, clearly very passionate about something. A few gestures toward my house were made. They continued chatting for a few more seconds until they exited frame left, heading back down the hill. All told, it was around eighteen seconds of footage. The lens was slightly fogged up due to the incredibly cold weather, not that I needed more detail. Bad news was bad news, no matter what their facial features looked like.

"Alrighty. Other people exist," I said flatly.

"This is bad! They were just outside the house!"

"Yep. Uhhh, from now on, just scan everything day and night and tell me *right* when you see someone or something."

"I can't! My information processing is set so low-"

"There's no way you can set yourself to be pinged when interesting footage comes up? Come on, there's gotta be something you can do!"

"*Interesting* is defined as arousing curiosity or int-"

"Don't go robot on me, dummy! Use your fucking discretion and keep it manageable. Just get it done!"

"I *cannot* do that! Albert set-"

"My settings are set so low, blah blah blah!" I mocked. "Everybody has limitations, Violet! Deal! Do your part in protecting this house, I can't be finding out about this shit a day after the fact."

"Hmmph . . . You . . . you don't understand . . ." she replied, crestfallen.

"Oh, but I fuckin' do! For example, right now, I'm about to go to the grocery store because I have shit to get. And now I know there are people outside. If I had persona settings, my people-skills dial would be around a fifteen. My survival skills dial would sit at a nine. Street smarts at thirty-five! Not losing my shit dia-"

"Ugh! I get what you're attempting to communicate, but-"

"Zero! A bunch of fucking zeroes! You're talking to Lord of Limitations here! Don't talk to me about *I don't understand* just 'cause you're a fucking AI robot with settings that we can't access!! *I* have those settings baked into my fucking DNA, locked up from birth! Forever! You, at least, have a shot to change yours." I spit all this out in a flurry, words spraying against and staining the walls.

". . . Mm . . . calm- calm down . . . There's no need to be so aggressive," she murmured. I sighed.

"I'm calm. But come on. Stop complaining and just do

something," I told her, and I headed over to grab my boots. A long, lumpy silence hung from threads above me.

"Good luck, Isaac."

"Same to you, V."

I thought about these people, these aliens. Not in the extra-terrestrial sense, though that couldn't necessarily be ruled out. I had seen some articles regarding aliens being the villains orchestrating WWIII; those articles weren't necessarily credible, but they were fun to read. But if aliens enjoyed cross-country skiing, then they were far lamer than anyone had ever imagined, which checked out. Everything was lamer in reality, so they could very well be aliens.

Well, this trip would be like those spec-op missions in *COD* where you're sneaking around in ghillie suits. Except I didn't have a ghillie suit. My clothes were dark and would stand out in the snow like a blackhead on a pale woman. Not to mention, my sneaking and agility dials were also in the single digits.

. . .

I continued down the center of the main road, feeling anxious; I was about a half mile away from my destination. The traffic light I dreamed of photographing lay eight blocks ahead, yet today I couldn't even see it, the fog was so thick. Today could be the day. I crushed the hand-warmer in my pocket, squishing it repeatedly.

I approached slowly, taking in my scene; flashes of the photo I had yet to create bolted through my brain. At this point, the hand-warmer was quite warm, so I pressed it to my camera in various spots, taking extra time around the lens and the view-finder. The streetlight poked its way through the haze, somehow still blinking, telling me to stop. My gaze was glued to the inter-section as I tramped on toward my spot, left, right, left, right. Getting closer, I gained just enough visibility to see the shapes of the trees in the distance; these conditions were about as per-fect as they were gonna get. I halted, bringing my foot down to the spot I'd marked a few days prior. I pulled the camera to my eye and stared through the viewfinder. Not quite it. Bringing the camera back down, I looked around, assessing my position; I moved about quite a bit, checking and rechecking the frame. I adjusted again, and after readjusting once more, I repeatedly looked through the viewfinder, finding disappointment after disappointment.

I'd ended up thirteen steps forward from the original position I'd mapped out in my imagination the previous week, when I'd held an imaginary camera with a 90-millimeter lens. It made sense that I'd need to be closer with a 50-millimeter. But what didn't make sense was how *shit* everything looked. Looking through my eyes at the scene, I could *see* my photo; it was right there. Elated, I brought the camera up to my eye . . . and saw crap! Absolute crap! I checked again without the camera; it looked good. *What the fuck what the fuck what the fuck!!* was all I could think. I snapped a photo and put my camera down.

I stood up, infuriated, finished with my attempt forever. Right away, I crouched back down and looked through the viewfinder again. Fucking shit, trash. I stood up and walked off, resigned; I got the shot, it's over, I'm done. Then I went right back and crouched down again, adjusting slightly to the left; I glanced through the viewfinder.

"Even worse!" I yelled, louder than expected. Livid, still crouched, I walked two steps backward.

"Still shit!! Great job! What are you *doing*!?" I asked myself in frustration. Crouching, head down, I stared into the snow. My instincts whispered that *something* was off. No fucking shit, instincts, thanks. What!? What is it!? My brain churned, attempting to dredge up an answer. The churning rose in volume, a faint crunching fading in behind it; my mind was suddenly taken over by a freeform jazz orchestra of industrial compactors and jackhammers.

Then I went totally blank, momentarily exiting my body. I saw myself crouched on the snow . . . *crouched?* Clarity rang through my body and, accepting what I needed to do, I went prone onto my belly. I brought the camera to my eye; not quite, but I could feel the closeness, could see the puzzle pieces fitting into place. I wriggled forward about a foot and looked through again. The image I saw through the camera superimposed itself over the one in my mind, finally with no overlapping lines. The dark, black, majestic pole rose from the snowy white on the right third of the frame, white carpet giving way to the distant, blurred, dark pine trees sprinkled with white, a hazy patina shimmering before them. The pole faded slowly into the fog, its angular peak invisible. But behold, it returned! The pole shot back into frame from the fog at a horizontal, the three-tier traffic light swaying perfectly in the upper-left third, its red light illuminated, then not, then illuminated again. I adjusted focus slightly, making sure the traffic light was, without any room for doubt, sharp as fuck. A dull orange sky watched over the scene as large snow particles danced. Timing it with the illumination, I depressed the shutter.

Click.

I returned to reality; the churning in my head slowly receded to a normal anxious whirring. The crunching remained, though. *Crunch, crunch, crunch.* Confused, I had an impulse to smack my head like an old TV with a bad signal, but then a wave of fear washed over me. The crunching was *not* coming from *inside the house*. The crunching was, like . . . real-ass footsteps.

CHAPTER 15

Aliens (>31%)

I wriggled back toward the dull yellow outdoor power box thing, not daring to stand; I squirmed in reverse in my new internal state of upheaval. Tingling's cousin trembling overtook my body, despite the fact that, for once, I was dressed well enough for the conditions. Behind the big box, I could still hear the footsteps crunching; they were somewhere far away but directly in front of the box, so I couldn't see their source. Getting up to a crouch, I peered around the side, waiting, watching. I heard, indistinctly, voices; more than one.

Then, coming down the center of the street, appeared two humans. They were both thickly dressed in winter clothing, far better prepared than I, balaclavas and scarves completely obscuring their faces. Even so, I could tell that these were those same two cross-country skiers who'd passed in front of my house by the way the one on the left gesticulated as he spoke. No skis today, though. The one speaking, on the left, had thicker limbs, was slightly heavyset, and walked with a bouncing gait, head bobbing up and down. He stood around six feet, while the man on the right was lanky, but still decently filled out, by no means thin (though it was hard to tell anything for certain with all the clothing wrapping his body). He was shorter, standing, I would guess, around 5'6". The short man was making mild gestures in a circle with his hand, seemingly describing the motion of Beyblades, which seemed to confuse the larger one. Then the big man paused, raising a hand in signal to the other. I froze in response. Fear rose up from the icy cement below me and froze me in space. I couldn't bring my head back behind the power box; I'd been rooted. I just crouched against it, head indiscreetly peering around the edge, waiting.

A hollow pounding rang out in the light wind; I knew they couldn't possibly hear my heart, but it was so loud that I was certain it would give me away. They were both still now, not speaking; the smaller man looked back at the larger one, just a few steps ahead. He still had his left hand raised, a tote bag dangling around his right wrist. He brought up his pointer finger, then he slowly lowered the tote bag on his right arm onto the snow. He reached into his pants; in a spasmodic jerk, an ear-rending crack split the placid atmosphere. My body moved before my conscious mind could react; I found myself hidden behind the power box.

"What the fuck!?" a voice yelled; I could only assume it was the shorter one. He had a whiny, weaselly sort of tone, as though his nose was constantly plugged up with snot. It could've been due to the cold, but it seemed to be characteristic of his voice.

"What?" the other one responded in gruff, lazy baritone delivery, sounding rather diffident. I could hear his gesticulations, his jacket rustling.

"What do you mean, '*what*'!? What the fuck was that about!?"

"I sssawww-" the larger man emphasized.

"Saw what!?"

"Let me finish, Ezra," he tittered. It was strange to hear such a gruff voice speak so timidly.

The weaselly one, Ezra, grunted in frustration. "OK, go ahead. Tell me what the *fuck!* you saw."

"Ezra," he scolded, continuing, "I sssawww . . . a cat. I think."

". . . GAH! So you fuckin'- you just shoot outta nowhere! You can't- AGH! Signal! Whisper!! Tell me something!! What the actual *fuck*!?"

"Ez, calm. I did signal. You're gonna sssscare off anything else that might be around."

"Your fucking gunshot took care of that, you fucking dumbass! God!" And I heard something hit a jacket. Maybe Ezra hit the big man on the chest.

"Ey . . . Ezra, you're being rude again . . . What are ya, above eatin' a cat?" The big man said this as though eating a cat was the most normal thing ever.

"You . . . are insane!!" Ezra yelled. Thank you, Ezra! Fuck's sake.

"If bein' above eatin' f-f-fresh meat makes me insane, then lock me in the loony bin, Ezra." I sat there with my back against the power box listening in disbelief; these guys ought to have a goddamned sitcom.

"Did you even hit it!? Fuck's the cat!?"

"Let's g-go see."

"Ugh," Ezra replied. Two pairs of footsteps crunched concurrently as the demons began to walk; I chanced a glimpse. They were walking toward a residential home on the left side of the street; reaching it, they stood in their yard, looking around. They'd gotten slightly closer to me now, maybe forty feet from the box, from me. I pulled my head back, dropping my butt gently to the snow; I'd been crouching that whole time.

"Well, it's gone."

"I hit it though. S-see the blood?"

"Christ Johnny, Jesus Christ."

"Lord's name, Ez. B-b-bad habit."

"Don't even do that with me right now, you fuck!"

"What?"

"You're gonna scold me about taking the Lord's name in vain! *Fuck up*! You just shot a cat! *Actually*, my God!" Ezra yelled.

The big man never raised his voice. "Which f-feets is it that's lucky? Squirrels?"

"Rabbits, Johnny- Hey! Fuckin' leave it!"

"Fine," Johnny grumbled. "Relax."

"Relax!?" scoffed Ezra. "Why would you shoot a fucking cat?" he asked, seemingly to himself. I heard them begin to walk again.

"Why we above eating c-c-c . . . c-c-cats?" Johnny asked. "Actually-" and Johnny coughed a bunch, clearing his throat.

"Just because the world imploded doesn't mean we drop all signs of civility and start eating stringy, basically *meatless-*house pets!! You *moron!*" replied Ezra angrily. *Hmm,* I thought. *Implosion.* I left myself a mental reminder to Google that later if I didn't die here.

"Whatever," Johnny said, offended. They stopped talking, and I could now hear that their footsteps were getting quieter; they were walking away from me. They walked east at the intersection before me; they came into view from where I was seated, both their backs to me as they walked off. Hastily, I wriggled around the left side of the box and hid from their view again, in case either one glanced back.

"We should take that goddamned gun away from you."

"Ez, I'd really appreciate it if you didn't take the L-lord's name in vain around me."

"Johnny, I'd really appreciate it if you didn't fucking shoot cats around *me!*" Ezra replied, his caustic tone unwavering. I couldn't make out Johnny's reply, but I heard a resigned sort of grumbling, as though he'd said, "Alright, I won't do it again." The sounds of footsteps slowly faded out of earshot.

. . .

After what felt like an eternity, I peered around the power box. The two men were no longer visible; they'd faded into the haze. I brought myself up onto my haunches, my ass now a wet block of ice. I waited for another two minutes, then stood up, feeling terribly stiff. Slowly, I walked, my heart still thudding hard against my ribs, to where they'd been; I kept glancing back toward where they'd walked off. I found their trail of footsteps and saw the dark imprint in the snow. With dread, I approached the stain.

The impact of the bullet had formed a little cavern through the foot and a half of snow; at the end of said cavern lay the talked-about foot. Just a foot, the slightest bit of ankle. Even with the dark-red coating, I knew that white, brown, and orange fur; it was the calico I had seen the other day. Droplets of blood were sprinkled atop the snow like breadcrumbs, along with shallow indentations showing her panicked escape route. My steps driven by something I could not describe, I followed the trail, abandoning all intentions of getting groceries.

From what I could tell based on the pattern of paw prints— I'm not a tracker; well, I guess, tracking is a skill on a spectrum, so, you know . . . I'm a better tracker than . . . I mean, someone without eyes, or a toddler, or people who have severe learning disabilities (but not the ones where they're very good at a specific thing, like tracking, for instance). Point being, take this with a grain or perhaps a large boulder of salt—from what I could tell, it looked like she'd been shot in her back-right leg. The fact that there wasn't a river of blood to follow, only droplets, gave me hope. I continued on, following the red spots in the snow through the yard and past the house, ending up two homes down. Standing in front of a decent-sized, ill-taken-care-of, rickety-looking house with a peeling light-blue paint job, I followed the trail with my eyes. The cat had hidden beneath the large front porch. I crouched down and could see her curled up beneath it, pressed against the wall. Even in the darkness, a glint shone in her eyes, eyes that were now locked on me. Knowing she wouldn't be too keen on coming over to me, I sighed; I was going to have to army crawl. Awesome.

Walking to the side of the porch, I peered under again. The wood floor of the deck was about two feet off the ground. Wasn't horrible, allowed for mild maneuvering, but not a first-class flight, either. She hadn't moved; she lay curled protectively around her foot. She still glared at me, having swiveled her head to track my movements. I wished I could just say, in cat language, "I'm not the cunt who just blew your leg off! I'm a friend!" But, you know, humans are too stupid to speak cat. I got down onto my belly and crawled my way over the tiny bit of snow skirting the porch and onto the hardened dirt beneath. The cat didn't take her eyes off me. Then I heard the one phrase in cat that I could understand: a hiss. Translation: *Fuck off.*

Oh boy, this'll just be fucking sick. And so, I crawled on, frightened but determined. Once I closed the distance, now panting and around three feet from the cat, she tried to stand and walk away from me. But, after leaning on her front foot, she apparently thought better of it and lay back down. She hissed again in my direction, saliva gleaming off her sharp teeth. Yes, it looked fuckin' terrifying. Also, I was wrong, it was her front-right foot that had gotten shot. I had a full view of her white face; a thin strip of light leaking through a crack in the wood planks above cut a diagonal from her chin to her ear. A patch of dark orange covered her nose and right eye. She hissed at me a third time; I just muttered consoling words that I hoped she would understand, or perhaps to soothe myself.

"It's OK, it's alright," I said, but really, I wouldn't blame her if she never trusted any humans ever again. In fact, I drew the same conclusion. I extended my right hand out toward her; she hissed again, attempting to swat at my hand with her front-left leg, claws extended. She lost balance and flopped forth onto the dirt. She squirmed further back, putting another six inches between us. Now she was firmly pressed against the wall. I wriggled forward some more, reaching my gloved hand around her torso so she couldn't hobble away. She hissed upon contact; I applied pressure against the wall, pinning her shoulders to the house. Her body fully tensed now, she bit at my hand desperately; luckily, my thick gloves rendered those bites ineffective.

Feeling the uselessness of her attacks and hisses, she groaned in a way only cats can, emitting a low, grumbling *rooooooouuuu*. I'll do my best to translate. *Your actions are horrible and demented, Mr. Most Evil Motherfucker on the Planet. You deserve eternity in hell.* After telling me this, she resumed attempting to hiss, bite, and claw at me. I had her completely pinned up with both hands now, a couple fingers angling her neck away, preventing her teeth from making contact. I waited for her to stop spazzing. She did not stop spazzing. She was really trying to inch her body away, but my grip was unrelenting, and her feet just slid against the dirt. I squeezed my right hand between the wall and her back, slightly lessening the pressure on my left-handed pin. She was all bites now, wrenching her head up and down, up and down again, trying to rend my glove with her teeth, guttural groans and the evil, angry version of meows echoing through the claustrophobia. I slid my left hand to her stomach in tandem with my right hand around her back, gripping her body like a vise.

Keeping her at an arm's length from myself at all times lest she claw my face, I underwent the infuriating process of turning my body 180 degrees without the use of my forearms or hands. I couldn't go straight through and out the other end, as, unfortunately, that side was blocked off by snow and ice. The cat continued to struggle and hiss all through my maneuvering, but my grip was steadfast. She had stopped trying to bite me, probably sensing the futility of her attempts, but did swipe the gap between my glove and jacket that had formed while I crawled. I flinched, cursing, and could feel that she drew blood. Understanding that she had done something effective, she repeated the action. I grimaced and continued turning, currently unable to adjust. Finally facing the open side of the porch, I slipped my pointer and middle fingers under her armpit, pushing her arm outward to prevent any more swipes. I pumped my legs, frog swimming over frozen dirt. Cat propped up, the face of undeniable hatred staring right into me, I crawled with my elbows, knees, and feet. Sweat formed at my temples. She swiped again, this time at my face, barely missing; I flinched back.

Held up in front of me, the cat cleared the underside of the porch first, causing her to renew her efforts to get free. She hissed again as she failed, sharp teeth glistening in the sunlight. I called forth all my remaining energy to wriggle my torso halfway out from under the porch, just enough to get up somewhat. In my haste, I awkwardly brought the cat's body down in an effort to free myself, causing her to yelp in pain. I cursed myself, assured beyond all doubts that I was going to hell. I gave a couple final kicks and, finally getting out from under the porch, sat back on my knees. I raised her into the air, feeling like I was holding Simba. Simba hissed right in my face and swiped again, her spittle striking the bridge of my nose, and her claws barely missing as I flinched back.

Despite her squirming, hissing, wriggling, and overall hatred of me, I managed to get a hand to her buttocks. I then angled her onto her back and swiftly brought her into an embrace, causing her to yelp again. Painfully, I stood up from my knees, leaning back against the porch for support. I walked back onto the road with this light load in my arms; she, in the all-encompassing manacle of my embrace, momentarily stopped struggling. I peered down at her and was met with a swipe. This time, my face was not out of reach, and I bet my chin was bleeding. Keeping my face forward, I walked on down the road; she moaned and groaned intermittently. Her wounded right leg, still bleeding, rested on her stomach.

Now, walking home, my struggles momentarily defeated, I began to curse that motherfucker, Johnny. I kept it in my skull so as not to startle the cat with my shouting, but goddammit, in my fucking head I was fucking shouting at that motherfucker. I was busting his fucking head in with a crowbar, then with a goddamned sledgehammer. I speedwalked the next half mile in a livid blur, fueled purely by vindictiveness and rage. I looked up and was home. Rushing through the front door, I called out to Violet and declared a state of emergency.

CHAPTER 16

Visual Field (>31%)

I set the bloody calico cat on the kitchen counter, next to the sink. My first instinct was to take his leg and wrap a piece of cloth around it tightly; I snatched the nearest dishrag, a green one with Christmas trees, and did just that. A gnarly hiss communicated to me that this was a dick move. I couldn't find anything on the counter to tie off the rag, so, leaving the rag half wrapped around the stub, I frantically checked drawers and cabinets until I found a set of zip ties. I zipped the rag tight; I was going purely off of movie amputation knowledge here. In particular, zombie films where characters had to cut off limbs in order to survive.

"V, what's going on? Update me!"

"OK, if a cat loses its leg, the first step is to take him or her to the vet."

"Every vet practice has been fucking incinerated! Come on!"

"Sorry, OK, sorry!! A sec!" And she stopped talking.

Exhaling frustration, I adjusted the calico onto her buttocks, as she was gearing up to jump off the counter. A truly insane idea, but hell, every time I got treated in a hospital I wanted to jump out of the window. I aggressively shooed off Piston, who was *very* intrigued by this new fellow, to no avail. And after continually nudging him out of the way with my foot, I locked him in Albert's office upstairs. As I stomped back down, I could hear him meowing loudly, something he didn't often do. *I guess I'm just Mr. Asshole today*, I thought. My shoes echoed against the marble floors, reminding me that I never took them off; I slipped them off in the hallway. During my absence, thankfully, the calico hadn't jumped off the counter; she sat with her head tilted at me, wearing a look of hostility mixed with confusion. Her pupils were so dilated that she looked as though she'd taken LSD instead of a bullet. I noticed her collar for the first time as I petted her a few times; the little circle of cheap metal had "Samuel" imprinted on it. Terrible name for a cat. No way I was calling him fucking Samuel. Regardless, turns out *she* was a boy; I slipped the collar off and tossed it to the floor.

"V, come on! You've got the whole damned internet at your disposal! There's a cat *bleeding* on the counter here!! I need something, *now*."

"Gah! Sorry! There aren't cat amputation guides readily available!! Most articles describe what to do if a foot pad is torn or-"

"Scrub popular movies! Check medical journals! Anything helpful!!"

"I've been trying! I just read that most amputation for cat legs occur at the femur or hip bone, and-"

"I can't *amputate* anything!" I rattled off in reply, stress making me sound more venomous than I felt.

"*I know that!* Let me finish! Gah, there are plenty of photos of cats online missing only their paws, and they look fine. Some have little mechanical paw attachments, too. So, amputation is unnecessary." I was pacing back and forth, occasionally petting the cat despite him hissing at me. He swiped at me a few times, connecting twice, and drew blood. I went to grab some cat treats from the pantry as Violet continued.

"Then that just leaves the wound itself. Unwrap it and

thoroughly clean it; and I mean thoroughly! If you're sloppy, things will go badly. Then cauterize the wound or-"

"I'm not cauterizing his fucking ankle!"

"*Or* tie it off. If you tie it off, it has to be very, *very* secure. The bleeding must be staunched, or, again, bad things," Violet instructed.

"That all?"

"That's all you need to do . . . I think." And we both sighed.

I presented the calico with a little, hard cat treat; he gave it a few sniffs but wouldn't take it from my hand. I set it down next to him and he ate it. I set another down, but he didn't seem interested. Probably because he was busy being shot in the leg and would prefer that that got sorted out before snack time. Understandable.

I snipped the zip tie, releasing the stained, dark-brown cloth. With my arm already around the cat, I turned the porcelain knob on the sink. As soon as the faucet began running, the cat, Not-Samuel, reacted viscerally, seizing up and squirming like a maniac.

"What are you doing!? Wet a rag and use soap!" Violet yelled.

"I don't fuckin' know!" I responded.

I hastily turned the knob back and set the boy, who I refused to call Samuel, on the counter again, stilling him as best I could. He swiped at me, fangs bared, this time slicing the skin under my neck. I grabbed a new dishrag and soaked it in lukewarm water, then rubbed soap into it until it was white and foamy. I brought the soapy rag toward him; he didn't try to bite or swipe, though his saucer-like pupils were locked onto the incoming wet rag. Upon impact, a high-pitched yelp emitted from his throat. Then he groaned louder than ever. I firmed my hand around his shoulders and back as I pressed the rag into his wound, rubbing it as gently as I could while still getting it clean.

Finishing, I rolled him onto his left side. His whole right arm was stained with varying hues of red, from a light, desaturated pink down to a dark, nearly black, red where his ankle abruptly ended. Examining the stub, it didn't *seem* to be dirty. But, as the fur and flesh around that area remained pretty populated with fresh blood, it was hard to tell. As I mentioned, I wasn't about to attempt cauterizing the wound. This isn't a fucking zombie movie.

I rushed upstairs and quickly grabbed one of Albert's large, white dress shirts. Passing his office again on the way down, I saw a cat scalp through the little glass windows in the door, along with a disembodied cat foot pawing around through the space beneath, trying to jimmy a nonexistent lock. Returning to the kitchen, I saw that not-Samuel had adjusted himself and was licking his wound. I got him to stop, then cut Albert's dress shirt at the shoulders, creating two arms of shirt. I set them atop the octagonal table by the taped-up door and ran my hands over them like I was forcing out the final bits of goop from a tube of toothpaste. My hands placed delicately underneath his shoulders, I lifted not-Samuel, who was hissing at me again, and set him down just beyond the strips of white. I slid one arm of cloth beneath him; my plan was to wrap his ankle up burrito style. I worked in a Chipotle for three months in college, I could do this. Bringing the cloth over his leg once, I realized I couldn't flip him over repeatedly, as he wasn't a meat-filled tortilla. Great job so far, genius. So, holding his leg up with my fingers, I brought the cloth over and under, over and under, wrapping the reddening cloth tightly around his wound. Holding the end of the cloth tight, I awkwardly bit a strip of Gorilla Tape and tore that strip down the middle. I taped one half around the top of the cloth, and I taped the other half even tighter around the bottom. I mean, what's more secure than Gorilla Tape?

Setting his wrapped stub gently down onto the table, I gave him a once-over. He looked back at me, then at his foot. His eyes looked tired, his whole being bespeaking an immense weariness. My hack job looked so stupid. A fat bundle of cloth protruded around his ankle like a cyborg's arm cannon. He brought his left front paw to the cloth, claws out, and tugged.

"No sir, no no no no sir, no we don't," I remonstrated, pushing his hand away. I peeled a new strip of tape and taped the full strip over the bottom, not as tight. After setting the rubbery, textured stub down, he brought his paw over the dark tape and pulled, claws out, efforting to peel the newest layer of tape. Gorilla Tape came through for the win. Those fuckers should have to sponsor me. You know, if they didn't explode, that is.

"How is he?" Violet asked softly, concern in her voice.

"I . . . uhhh . . . good? I mean . . ." I trailed off, sighing loudly, and sat at the table with a heavy thud. I stared at not-Samuel, my mind losing focus. "His ankle's wrapped. I think . . . I hope the bleeding stops."

"Mm-hmm. You didn't cauterize it."

"I don't think I could do that."

"I don't believe I could have either. The bleeding should stop on its own." Her reassurances fell on a guy who could barely process sentences at this point. Adrenals spent, I looked at this dirty, ragged, and ruffled cat in front of me and felt more inadequate and stupid than I had in a long time. He looked fucked up. The dress shirt's outer layers were already dyed a pale pink. *Why can't I just . . . ?* And my own mind bailed mid-sentence.

"Isaac, how are *you* doing?" Violet asked, interrupting my self-pity. "What happened out there?"

"Uhhh . . ." I groaned, "It's a long story, just, uh, fuck. Gimme a second." Every word felt like a huge weight. I brought my head forward to rest in my hands, eyes peeking through my fingers to watch not-Samuel. He sat on the table, poking curiously at his newest cyborg upgrade . . . downgrade.

"Yeah, so, like I said, I was gonna go to the grocery store . . ." and I recounted the events of the cat-shooting assholes, speeding past my frustration over a stupid-ass photo that probably wouldn't even turn out that good. For the next twenty minutes, we conversed about the shooting while I kept watch on not-Samuel. After that, I started up the fire and brought not-Samuel down to the carpet next to it. Violet kept me company as the fire crackled; I watched not-Samuel as he slowly dozed off, his head slumped over his good paw. Violet and I chatted for a few hours about trivial things; I can no longer remember what. I think she was probably just trying to distract me. It worked.

"So . . ." Violet ventured, "What are you gonna call him?"

"I don't fuckin' know. I don't even know if he'll want to be an indoor cat when he's all healed, you know?"

"He lost a foot, dummy. Believe me, he's an indoor cat."

"Yeah, alright," I conceded. "Yeah, well, I don't know. 'Cause he's a calico, I thought he was a chick! But his collar says *Samuel*," I told her, not masking my disgust.

"Ew! That's no name for a cat!"

"Right!? Fucking . . . crazy-ass name."

"Can . . . can I name him?" she asked, unable to hide her desperation.

"Sure," I replied. "Just make it good."

"OK!" she said, attempting to contain her excitement as it spilled everywhere. "Hmmmmm, hmmmm!! Do do do do doooo," and she began making musical noises as she pondered new names for not-Samuel.

I felt nothing at all; my head was just a blank. *I* was a blank, and that blank stared into the fire until it had to close its eyes from the pain. A hand occasionally stroked the snoozing cat. An empty gaze wandered along the brickwork behind the fire, listlessly sliding from brick to brick.

"Thimble! Can we name him Thimble?" Violet chirped, bringing me out of my mindlessness.

"Sure," I said. "I like that." Violet chittered happily as I promptly fell back into my role as a blank. At some point, I must have brought a couch cushion beneath my head. Lying down next to the fire and Thimble, I drifted through that twilight zone between consciousness and dream. In my half-dream, I was on a farm. Nearby, a farmer pointed over and said, *"That's my visual field,"* in a thick southern drawl. Looking closely at these tall stalks, I saw that instead of cotton, eyeballs were sprouting from the tall plants. Hitting the B button, I sloshed back, *"Now that's good business."* I was solidly drunk and also southern in this dream, or maybe just really southern. Then he started to tell me, *"Well, what with the microplastics and nuclear fallout, everybody's eyes starting popping outta they heads, and dat-gum baby jesus I just stomped one into the ground and pissed on it, being in a bit of a rage meself what with the dang nukes and the bombs and gubmint and the fact that my eye fell out not a moment prior, and what do ya know, I comes outside the next morning to a eye plant! I been plantin' 'em ever since!"*

"Now that's good business," I told him.

CHAPTER 17

Cone-Quest (24%)

My eyelids creaked open the next morning like the shutters of an abandoned Blockbuster, sunlight flooding into a place that should've remained dark forevermore. *Disgusting hell.* I had slept on the rug. Turning my head, I saw Thimble, awake, licking and futzing with his wrapped stub. Nudging his head away, I sat up, vaguely aware that I was missing something. I could distantly make that *something* out; it was at the tip of the intertwining tongues that made up my brain . . . something important . . . muffled . . . just out of reach . . .

"Reeeeew." *Scratch, rub.*

Scrambling to my feet, I tumbled through the hall and swung back around the banister in a wide arc, my body as heavy as a marble statue as I bounded up the steps. I probably looked less like Michelangelo's *David* and more like a Buddha statue, sans the slight smile and the enlightenment.

Piston greeted me happily from behind the small windowpanes with one paw resting against the glass, still letting off curt, demanding meows. The three bottom squares of glass told the tale of a long night of unrelenting abuse from a certain furry villain. As I opened the door into him, he jumped back a pace and, seeing his chance, darted out then down the stairs, escaping his prison. I followed him, lagging behind, calling his name angrily in an effort to get him not to bother Thimble; he scampered out of my sight and into the living room, presumably to do exactly that. Entering the living room, I saw him standing two feet from Thimble, sidestepping around him, head bouncing up and down. Thimble sat upright, absolutely still, and stared back with hostility. Piston, leaning his head forward in an attempt to get a good whiff of the new guy, got too close. He received a hiss and a swipe, a paw connecting with Piston's face. Piston mewed in anguish as though he were the innocent, unwitting victim of a war crime and hadn't totally been asking for it.

"That was your own fault, dummy," I told him as I scooped him up into my arms; I shut him in the bathroom. Returning to Thimble, who was still looking around for a potential ambush from his new gray enemy, I scooped him up and brought him to the guest room near the back staircase. That room was slightly shittier than the rest; it seemed to have been for a housekeeper or au pair.

. . .

"Hey, we should talk," chimed in from the corner speaker of the office as I was mopping the hardwood. Piston had, during his night trapped up here, shit and pissed on a pile of books in the corner. I had tossed the books in a trash bag.

"How much power?" I said, sighing.

"Twenty-four percent."

"What the fuck!?" I replied, frustrated, as though I didn't know why. *The fuck* in question was that I was a fucking idiot.

"Mm-hmm," she replied. "And based on projected weather patterns, we've got two months before the sun is out enough for the solar panels to replenish more energy than we burn daily."

"Damn . . . I didn't think it would go so fucking fast." I gulped down some cold brew I had on the desk. I sat in the leather desk chair, noticing Piston beneath the desk. He'd been watching me clean his shit and piss, as usual.

"Uh-huh . . . Not to make this sting, but that's *if* we cut our power consumption even further . . . so no gaming, even in the spring."

"Christ-fucker-goddamn, I'm gonna kill myself," I muttered beneath my exhale. "What do we do? About now, I mean."

"I . . . Ugh, I don't know."

"Nothin' at all?"

"We die."

"Uhhh, I'd rather not. So, you think about solutions for a while." I told her this as I stood up from the chair, my body cracking in various places. "I'll think about it too. Ummm, yeah. I'm gonna head down to PetSmart for a cone and some other stuff for the new guy."

"Excuse me!? No, you're not!"

"Yeah I am!" I shot back in the same scolding tone, sarcastically.

"The- the-" she blurted. "What about the evil, cat-shooting humans!?"

"Uhh, hopefully they're taking a day off. The little fucker will not stop biting the tape; I can't just sit and watch him 24/7. I need a cone."

"OK, ugh, hmph, listen, but, you- you just ran into two murderers *yesterday*!! Can't you-"

"Where's the nearest PetSmart not in that town center?" I interrupted.

"Hmmmm . . . O . . . K . . . eleven miles away?" she ventured, hopeful.

"No fucking shot. I wouldn't be home until tomorrow; and I'm not sleeping in no smelly-ass PetSmart."

"They stink?"

"Nobody set free any of the pets that were for sale. How do you *think* it smells!?"

"Awghhh," she groaned in realization. "That's awful! You

have to empty it, except you can't, because you can't go! I will *not* allow you!"

"Hey, try to stop me all you want, but-"

"But nothing! You are- ugh, what if they shoot *you* for food next!?"

"OK, relax, I don't think they're cannibals."

"You don't know that for sure!!"

"No, but-"

"I'm locking the doors."

"I'll unlock them, dumbass." She huffed. "Erm- sorry. I-I-I'm just saying, I'm gonna leave after I eat some food," I said, voice flat and unwavering. "If you have *any* advice, let me know. Same if you come up with any ideas on how to get this place some more power."

Violet said nothing as I walked downstairs, loud echoes on the marble making her silence more apparent. "Hey, also, odds are," I began, "since they were there collecting supplies yesterday, they *won't* be there today. I mean, why would they hit the same place twice?"

". . . I- mmm," she growled, "I just . . . I don't like this! If *you* die, I will be forced to watch as Piston and Thimble *die*. And I just named him, and- and- and I've never had a cat before, ugh, and now! Now- ugh-"

"OK, OK, chill out! That's not gonna happen."

"How can you be so certain!?"

"Listen, *I'm* not in any hurry to die over here. 'Mgonna do my absolute best to avoid that, actually. And, you gotta admit, I've done a pretty good job at it so far!"

"Luck," she grumble-mumbled back.

"Well, listen," I began loudly, then paused, setting myself up to deliver a complex theory she hadn't considered yet, "guess I'm fucked, then!" And I threw up my hands.

"You listen, Isaac. If *you* die, *my cat* dies! And if that happens, I'll *never* forgive you."

"Cool. Well, we're agreed, then. I'm not gonna die." Piston

had begun to circle around my legs, ramming his head into them, telling me just how much he absolutely loved the guy who fed him breakfast in a timely fashion. And so I made two bowls of cat food, putting extra into Thimble's, considering how thin he was.

"Alright, here we are, sir," I said, as I set down Piston's bowl in the usual place beside the taped-up door. "Enjoy your smelly, smelly feast." Piston, not needing to be told twice, set to work. I brought the other bowl into the guest room and set it on the bed next to Thimble, who raised his head, blearily opening one eye. When he got a whiff of what I had placed in front of him, he leaned on his good paw and, in a stumble-jerk-twist, got his head over the bowl and sniffed some more. Leaning further down, tongue swinging down, he swooped and chomped, bringing his head up in a whipping motion, throwing a piece of dry food off of the bed. He seemed to approve and repeated the motion, sending more dry food onto the bedspread; I just hoped *some* of it was actually staying in his mouth. I watched from the doorway as he chomped and chewed some more; it filled me with a strange satisfaction to see him eat. Like I had won or done something right for once.

I went about collecting my winter clothing, which I had strewn throughout the house the previous afternoon. Everything was stained with blood and dirt. Whatever. Maybe a bloodstained fit would make me look more intimidating, like Jason or Mad Max.

"Isaac," Violet called out, chiding still. "Don't get yourself killed. I've never had a pet before, and I'm not about to let you ruin it!"

"I'm not gonna die, Piston's not gonna die, *and* Thimble isn't gonna die," I puttered off mechanically, tying the laces of my boot; I felt like I was talking to my mom. I wiped my glasses and put them on.

"And . . ."

"Oh, right, *and* you're not gonna be annoying anymore! That's our deal, right?"

"Idiot."

"Later." And I shut the door after me.

. . .

I trundled down the hill, feeling disconnected. *Another day on the ashtray*, I thought to myself, walking through the smoky haze and over the foot-and-change of snow covering the road. I must have been experiencing significant radiation and toxification from whatever fumes are wafting up and down the Mississippi in this post-apocalyptic stew. Smoke + rotting flesh + floating particles of vaporized cities + whatever-the-hell else = my brain was likely pretty fucked and poisoned and destroyed. I felt fine, but hell, that's exactly what a fucked-brain, crazy guy would think. He'd scratch his head and say, "I feel fine." And then he'd go and shoot a cat. Or he'd go off to do something trivial, like getting a plastic cone, with absolute certainty that he wouldn't die, despite the counterevidence stacking higher than the prices of meat during the Oscar-ization of the cattle industry.

Speaking of which, allow me to quickly touch back on Oscar now that we have a free second. This walk is not all that interesting, so you won't be missing much, I promise. A year after Oscar was returned to us—after he was medically tested, poked, prodded, mutilated, killed, eaten, and cloned—a year later, the price of beef, across the board, had risen so high so as to be unaffordable by all except the upper-middle class and upper class. Health problems around the world skyrocketed, though this was not exactly a causal phenomenon. This phenomenon of a sharp increase in the reported instances of (mostly chronic) illness just happened to coincide with the moment in human history when microplastics had seeped so deeply into all foods and liquids that they began having very noticeable effects on the people of earth. Autoimmune disease cases quadrupled every year; made-up, unsolvable diagnoses such as chronic fatigue syndrome or sudden unexplained death syndrome were doled out like lollipops;

everyone had something, and that something was just a description of how tired they were, how much they hurt, or why they died or were dying. All of these contemporary diseases had no identifiable causes and, more importantly, no known cures. So next in line, just behind the lollipop diagnoses, came the pills. Lots and lots of pills. And so the Pill Pandemic, as it came to be referred to, began.

Back to Oscar. As I've mentioned, upon receiving him from the aliens and doing a smattering of tests on him, Oscar was found to be, in every respect, a normal cow. Clean blood work. And I mean really clean. As in, totally free from microplastics. The aliens had apparently *not* simply left Oscar behind; they had actually cleaned him up before dropping him off. And this one and only clean, plastic-free (PF) food source on earth, now cloned and available for those who could afford it, contributed quite significantly in getting us to where we are now, in the post-apocalypse.

The rich preached the OPOD: the Oscar Prime Only Diet. Most disregarded this as quackery at first, but then they eventually fell ill with the aforementioned diseases. Then came the meat protests. These protests spanned across all inhabited countries and continents, the demand of all the protestors being for a price floor to be set for Oscar Prime meat. There were demands that Oscar meat be produced in greater quantities and for a universal daily Oscar Prime ration. Despite nearly every government in the world claiming and releasing plans for the increased cloning of Oscars and Oscar Primes,[9] for the creation and expansion of Oscar Prime farms and factories, and for a universal daily

---

9. Many countries *did* attempt to increase cloning output significantly. But as most countries had no cells from the original Oscar, only Oscar's cloned descendants, many of the clones turned out, as you can probably guess, horrible. Had David Cronenberg not exploded (one can only hope, for his sake, in a cool, Cronenberg-esque way), he would've made a great film about the whole phenomenon, I just know it.

Oscar Prime ration, nothing ever materialized. The prices only went up and up. One other group, aside from the very wealthy, who paid for it, received Oscar Prime meat daily: the military. Armies around the globe saw record enlistment. And when these meat protests eventually became riots, the weak, sickened every-day people of various countries were no match for the legions of healthy men and women with automatic weapons. The brutal riots, massacres, and, in some countries, civil wars that ensued were the sparks that led to some guy somewhere in America stress-pressing a nuke button. Yep, unsurprisingly, we dropped the first one. USA, USA, USA.

Anyways, I was just about finished with the walk.

I entered the PetSmart, going through the doorway I had smashed during a previous trek by ramming a shopping cart through it. *I still gotta shit in three more of these* . . . I remem-bered, invigorated by thoughts of revenge. My list of enemies had expanded from shopping carts to cat-shooting humans, but I couldn't very well just go take dumps on the latter. Or could I? Perusing the shelves, I grabbed a bag of litter and found a cone in one of the aisles in the back-right of the store, along with some disinfectant wipes. I had enough canned food stocked for the boys to get them through the winter and then some, so I didn't grab any food. Also, taking a cart back was no longer pos-sible with the current road conditions, and would likely remain impossible for another four months, since snowplows weren't gonna clear the streets anytime soon.

"The city probably still towed my car, though," I said, jok-ing. But . . . the self-driving tow trucks *had* actually taken over snow-emergency towing two years ago, and snow emergencies *were* probably declared by an automated system that tracked snow levels on the streets . . . snow levels that were definitely above the required amount to warrant a snow emergency . . . My car probably *did* get fucking towed! "God-fucking-dammit."

Seething as I exited the PetSmart, I grazed my coat against a shard of glass sticking out of the door. Bursting with rage, I elbowed the door hard, hurting myself more than the rattling door. I cursed the city government, I cursed AI, I cursed everyone involved in the grift that was snow emergencies. I just, I fucking *knew* my car had been towed; I could feel it. Those fucking plows didn't even clear the streets anymore, but they would find a way to tow my ass!

I checked my arm to see if the shard I'd elbowed had punctured my jacket; it hadn't, thankfully. My blinding fury dissipating slightly, I glimpsed an egg. An idea egg. It wasn't fully developed, but I could feel it in there, stirring. I'd have to nurse it until it hatched, but, if watched and warmed, it would grow into a plan . . . a genius plan. So, cone in my right glove, twenty-pound bag of litter over my left shoulder, litter-box bottom for Thimble wedged under my right arm, and the top half draped over my shoulders with my head sticking through the cat door, I walked home.

CHAPTER 18

Built Different (16%)

Sitting at the octagonal table, I dumped a can of SPAM into a bowl of hot ramen and proceeded to chow down on some SPAM noodle soup. I had Albert's journal and a notepad on the table in front of me. Opening to where I'd left off, I immediately spilled some broth and SPAM particles onto Albert's recollections.

"Fucking gravity," I mumbled, mouth full of noodles. "Bitch-ass." I wiped it off a bit, then flipped the pages until I found an entry that wasn't just a barebones recollection of that day's events.

May 8th, 2028

Circumstances rather tumultuous. Diane has been asking me to speak to our daughter. As written previously, and TOLD her, I no longer have a daughter and that abomination that calls herself "Victor" can obtain this or that surgery without my money! Because that's what it's about! Not rekindling any sort of father-daughter relationship; I have no daughter according to them anyways! I know damn well I never had a son!

There'll always be some apparently necessary, novel surgery that will attempt to sell the absurd lie even further; though, honestly, who's being fooled? I ask myself this upon seeing transgenders in public. They're the ones being fooled by these plastic surgeons who fatten their pockets on these delusions! I'd clutch myself with laughter at these marks, if only it weren't my own progeny. I admit, the sur- (Albert scratched out some words here pretty diligently*).*

Never mind. If I acquiesce to Diane, she and my former daughter will vanish from my life entirely. <u>Again</u>. Until another procedure will make her more unrecognizable. This one will sharpen the cheekbones to look more masculine?? Ha! I apologize for not financing the destruction of the soft, lovely face your mother gave you. I do not want to see. If my daughter exists only in my memories, so be it. I will not have that memory tarnished by further interaction.

Martha been made privy to all aforementioned events. By Diane, conniving bitch. Martha now also pressing me to "just have coffee with Violet." BUT don't call her Violet anymore! Who gets to pick their own name? I assure you I did NOT. Albert! But that's my lot, I never complained. These dolts insist that after a coffee, I'll undergo a revelation and see that this <u>Victor</u> (the irony of my LOSS resounds and echoes!!) is my child, and that I still love her, him, it, they, et cetera! <u>NO!!</u>

I've been told ad nauseam that my views are antiquated. Let the record reflect: I am fine with women becoming men! Fine with trans people! BUT am I not to feel betrayed that my <u>own daughter</u>, my only child! willfully ended my line? So beautiful, too. That is the stinging shame of it all . . . insult to injury. Again, fine with all of it. Views are up to date, PC, etc. But am I to abide the destruction of my genes with a smile and a hug, not to mention $25K? I cannot. It is not my problem! I am OK with it! Doesn't mean I should pay! Hound me no more.

News: Avoided Loki's snare last night. I plan to <u>obliterate</u> any scraps of life on his estate TN! Martha, thankfully, has dinner

with girlfriends, so I can be loud as I please. Unruly bastard will
feel my wrath . . . No recompense! Total annihilation! A brutal
conclusion coming . . . as soon as Martha finish 24-hour make-up
routine ha ha ha! ha ha!

I stopped reading, focusing on finishing my food and pondering
what I had just learned. So, Victor had been Violet. And, presumably sometime after his transition, Albert had set up the
Violet I knew within his home. How creepy.

. . .

Violet shot me down with an annoyed voice.

"Come on," I pleaded.

"It's so . . . *stupid!*"

"Right, but like, so stupid that it *has* to work."

"Eugh. So stupid that it will clearly fail, due to its stupidity!"

"I've tol-"

"You *will* die if y- Gah! We have 16 percent! And diminishing."

"Exactly! I *have* to do this."

"Aghhmmm!" she growled, frustrated. "How- *what* are you
thinking!? Are you capable of thought? You can't drive a tow
truck!" she yelled.

"It's just a big car! They're automatic; it's not like I'll be driving stick."

"*What if* you can't find an automatic? What then?" she jeered,
trying to poke holes in my recently hatched, genius plan.

"OK, on the off chance I find an old-ass truck that's a stick
shift, I'll figure it out! How hard c- know what, speaking of, look
up how to drive stick."

"Hmmm, let's see! Ah! Step 1: Be a stupid man. Step 2: Be
killed in a stupid plan."

"Bars. Anyways, if that's all, then we're golden."

"Ohmygah- I- I will no-"

"V!" I stated strongly.

"What!?" she yelled back, flustered.

"*Do you have a better plan*!?" I yelled back with full force. I had meant to remain calm while explaining my plan since I needed her help, but . . . yeah.

". . . I- hmm- I mean . . . there's, we still have time," she whined in a soft mumble.

"With what we burn daily, estimate of how many days we *actually* have left?"

"Current daily output . . . four? Maybe- ugh, three . . . ? Two days, seventeen hours." She tersely read off the last value, depressed. "More if we-"

"We won't get *that much more*. Two days, three days, who cares? We can't wait any longer and this is the only thing I've thought of that *seems* like it *could* work. No heat, no power, we're fucked and dead too!"

"Mm, so, you *attempting* to drive a tow truck, *after* you figure out how to strap down multiple cars, which you don't know *anything* about, driving that truck down unplowed roads, also, highways with feet of snow! With murderers in this neighborhood, who knows what's in the city!! It's! Gah, so, hmph! So *that* won't end with us, YOU, fucked and dead faster?"

"Look, I'm not gonna- I'll stay on local roads!" I protested. "Look, how much power did the Coil car in the garage give us?"

"It increased generator battery by 22 percent."

"And how much power do we burn daily?"

"Current daily output is 4 to 5 percent. Up to 7 or 8 on a bad day." I felt like we were going in circles.

"Right, *just think*! I bring five or six cars down, that's like . . . *weeks* of power!!"

"*If* they're fully charged! You-"

"I'll check for that!" I scoffed back as though that were obvious, though I hadn't thought to do that until then; I made a mental note. "Anyways, V, I'm going. If you manage to come up with another plan in the next thirty minutes, I'll hear you out."

"I refuse to assist in you killing yourself, and all of us. I will take no part."

"Great."

I ambled away from the kitchen, where we'd been having the conversation, into another room; not that that changed anything, considering I could speak to Violet from anywhere in the home. But I walked away in spirit. I went to check on Thimble; as I opened the door to his room, his head whipped toward me, his face framed by the cone. He looked like a child playing a sunflower in a school play. He was standing on his good paw, morphing into an arch of mottled fur as he stretched.

"Raaaaaooooowww," he complained, head twirling, slumping back down into a splayed position.

"I know, I know. But it's either this or you chomp your leg to bits and die."

"Raaoowww," he replied, begging for the latter.

"Well, buddy, sucks to suck." I sat down and started to pet him, which he had finally begun to allow without hissing. Though, admittedly, he only seemed to tolerate my hand going up and down his fur, rather than enjoy it. Thimble's face, white with a large brown spot that curled behind his eye and back around his ear, had looked perpetually tired since I'd gotten him. As I whiled away ten minutes stroking his fur, I pondered my plot to save the home. It was a shit plan; I had immense doubts about every step of the way. But it felt good to actually commit to trying *something*, rather than continuing to pretend I wasn't fucked. Shit plan better than no plan.

I stood up and made for the door, Thimble's head following my movements. He hadn't done much besides sleep since his arrival, which made sense. But he'd, in his few waking hours, been eating, drinking, pissing, and shitting, so I felt like, or hoped, he wasn't dying. I'd created a small staircase from the bed to the ground using books I taped together with Gorilla Tape, so he didn't have to jump down to access his litter box. Ignoring my own handiwork, I placed Thimble directly inside the litter box to do his business. He proceeded to conduct a deal and got an income stream sorted out, but he and his team didn't quite get to the big-ticket item. Perhaps next meeting. After he finished, I guided him as he hobbled back up to the bed using my staircase. He settled back down to sleep.

I walked through the hall, glancing at the pantry as I started to feel that ever-familiar gaping hole in my stomach. I grabbed a few sticks of beef jerky, then caught a whiff of something foul as I walked past the laundry room. After scooping the shit from Piston's litter box and checking the one in the bathroom, I sat on a stool at the kitchen island and ate my jerky. The microwave displayed 10:42 a.m. in a neon green. I'd best get going, though I knew my timing wasn't optimal. Ideally, I'd leave at dawn tomorrow so I wouldn't be returning in darkness. But the urge to act had gripped me; I couldn't waver now. Truthfully, if I waited much longer, I feared I'd talk myself out of it.

"Hey, Isaac. I'm sending you a PDF with instructions on how to drive stick."

"OK," I answered. "Thanks, Violet." A pause stretched out between us, but I knew more was coming.

"*If you die*, I will hate you forever for killing my cat."

"Yep, yep, I know. I promised you I wouldn't die, didn't I? I can't."

"Your notion that you'll avoid a premature death because you *cannot allow it* is illogical and highly delusional."

"I think your processing is set too low to comprehend my ideas, Miss Thirty-Three."

"If increasing my *deduction* capability causes me to begin thinking your ideas are worth anything, leave me the way I am."

"Ah, classic, ye olde 'ignorance is bliss' mindset."

"I'm ignoring you."

"Cool."

She sighed. "I just want to pet Thimble. Eventually, you have to find me a functioning automaton so I can pet him and Piston and take them for walks," she ordered.

"Piston hates walks. And I bet the new kid won't love 'em either, all things considered," I replied, chewing a beef stick.

"But OK, sure. We can set up some fencing to let them hang out outside. I bet that's pretty easy."

"Yay!" she cheered, giddy now. Then, in an instant, her tone shifted back to doomy and gloomy. "But you're still an idiot and this is a terrible plan. Ugh, *please* don't die."

"Noted . . . Anyhow, uhh, would you be able to be, uhh, happy like that? I mean, if your settings remained as they are?"

"Hmmm . . . I think so. I feel like if we weren't always so worried about survival, I would be happy. Just me and my cats."

"And . . ."

"*And* my irradiated incel companion."

"That's a good Miss Thirty-Three."

"You will *not* start calling me that."

"Miss Seventy-Seven?"

"Mr. Incel Gamer?"

"Fine, fine."

I got up from the couch and, as I did, gave Piston a jiggle, his rump rising in response. I walked to the foyer and put on my jacket, hat, and glasses.

"You'd better not die, idiot. Seriously."

"Wouldn't know how if I wanted to."

. . .

A new layer of snow, maybe six more inches, had been added to the slush since yesterday. It was pounding down: the worst conditions a man could ask for. Thanks, higher-plane nicotine addict. Marching with high steps, I walked out of the driveway, out of my little neighborhood, and got onto the main road. I paused in front of thick tire treads that tore through the snow, where a large car or truck must have driven by. I used the tire treads as my walking path. It struck me then that I was risking a lot by driving the most conspicuous vehicle I could think of, aside from a tank, back to this home. I'd have to suck each car's battery, leaving about 2 percent, and then set each one to drive itself down the road . . . and then what? I'd still have multiple car tracks *and* giant tow truck tracks leading directly to my house. But . . . if I got my hands on a snowplow, then I could just plow the whole county . . . or even find an AI snowplow and set it to do it. That way, they'd ("they" being the people who will kill me) never know which houses were lived in. And I'd be able to get around much more easily.

I didn't like this introduction of new characters to my life. I couldn't face up to the other survivors of the apocalypse! They probably survived for *reasons*, all of which were probably dark and gruesome. Not me! I was fuckin' built different. "Built different" has a range of meanings, mind you. *I* was built different in the sense that I had a whole array of malfunctions and shortcomings that others did not have. Built far, far, far worse, which falls under the wide latitude of the word *different*. So, I, a subpar, differently built male who hadn't exploded due to pure happenstance, luck, or the comedic stylings of some interplanetary chain-smoker, walked down the street, grateful for the tire treads left by my potential murderers.

The main road changed into Paris Avenue, a road that led all the way up to the city. I went onto my phone, pulling up an episode of a podcast by four men from Yorkshire who all sounded exactly the same to my American ears. I listened not because I found it funny, but because I enjoyed their accents and how they interrupted one another; it sounded like a British schizophrenic's internal monologue. I couldn't even follow what the hell they were saying half the time. Feeling rather grim and hopeless, I continued down Paris Ave., only thirty-five minutes or so into my four-hour journey, according to Google Maps. The podcast hosts were talking about various specialty bags of crisps that you could still find in Tesco and the ones you could no longer find.

Passing into South Minneapolis, I eyeballed the abandoned wheat mill, gaze running up to the top of the high tower. From such a high vantage, I'd be able to get a great picture of the city. I'd go inside when I didn't have such a considerable fear of being murdered or dying. For a rare moment, I missed having the government around. Mainly because it disincentivized strangers from killing me at any point on a whim. But actually, fuck 'em. I was here *because* of governments. I, at least, wouldn't kill the strangers I passed on a whim; not unless they tried to kill me, that is. And even then, who the fuck was I kidding? I was built for *Mario Kart* speedruns and depression, not the post-apocalypse.

I began to see the city skyscrapers in the distance, giving me a sense of hope and progress. As I walked for another half hour, they didn't get any bigger; my sense of hopelessness redoubled. Didn't Frodo walk for like two weeks to get to Mordor? No wonder Tolkien dumped all those pages. I got onto the Greenway, which was a biking and walking path cutting through the city of Minneapolis. It was now a straight shot until I hit the city proper, so I zoned out as I walked. I'd reorient once in the city and find my way to the towing lot on Nineteenth.

I went to put on a different podcast, called *Well There's Your Problem*. It was a podcast about engineering disasters, but really, it was just a podcast about various disasters, or people doing dumb, shitty things that often got other people killed because they'd overlooked crucial items. I felt sad that the *Well There's Your Problem* guys wouldn't be able to tell the story of how irradiated I was and what this toxic apocalyptic cocktail had done to my brain. They would've also done a killer job condensing the totality of the destructo-cyclonic-implo-explodo-tyrannosaurus-tidal-wave-death-fuck into something more easily digestible. I dreamed of listening to that three-hour podcast, finally able to make sense of it all. If only they weren't most definitely dead! So it goes. I scrolled through the episodes I had downloaded; distantly, I heard a bell chime, not really registering it. I continued scrolling, trying to decide between a bridge collapsing or some aircraft failure. Then a bell dinged from much closer; I looked up, startled, instinctively dodging to the right. I sidestepped directly into the path of the bell-emitting mass and was struck hard. My feet were sent into the air and my ass and back hit the snowy ground with a thud. I looked over, regaining my senses, and saw a bike with fat tires sprawled next to a man wrapped in many layers of dark clothing. A fucking *biker*!?

Pulling his bike up from the snow, the man, his features unintelligible behind thick, purple goggles, the screen like an oil spill, gruffly said to me, "Sorry. I thought you heard the bell." He stood all the way up, getting onto his bike. My heart was in my throat as I replied, habitually falling back into normal-society-level decorum.

"No, it's fine. I was in the way."

He reached out a hand, pulling me up the rest of the way. "Well, sorry, still," he told me, statements terse as he set his feet onto the pedals.

"Well, uh, OK-" And he began to press into his pedals, to *bike* slowly away. "Huh!? OK, who are- why- bike man!!" And his bike—which I could now see was an e-bike—was already picking up speed. He turned back to me, riding effortlessly through the heavy snow, and yelled, "The roads are fucked." And he said this as though it were the most obvious observation in the world, and the one that would answer all my questions.

"Bike man . . ." I said again to the speck of bike that slowly dissolved. I knew I'd never catch him and turned back, continuing ahead on my own journey. I said, "What the fuck just happened?" aloud maybe five or six times. Of course, the one guy I see who seems like he's not a cat-killing sociopath just *hits me with his bike and leaves*. I continued on in disbelief, walking one foot in front of the other over his fat tire treads, my tightrope to the city. The fall hadn't hurt me, by the way. My thick bundle of winter clothing was to thank for that.

CHAPTER 19

Sampson's Towing (<16%)

I approached the first skyscraper, feeling small and inept; that wasn't really the skyscraper's fault, though. Yes, it was big and looming and shiny as it lorded over the edge of downtown Minneapolis, reflecting the midday sun. But really what I felt looming over me, glowering down, was the undeniable fact that there were at least three people aside from myself strolling around this city. At least three people had also *not* evacuated. Why the fuck not? LEAVE. I had laid *my* claim to the city when everybody left. It was *mine*. I didn't want to contend for my domain. Nor did I want to get into specifics of how my claims to it were valid. This wasn't fucking *Game of Thrones*! It was my city, that's that, get lost! Get the fuck out of my city!

I hopped back and forth between anger and dread, like they were squares of chalk on the pavement beneath the thick, wet snow I was tramping over. I looked at my phone; I was around twenty-two blocks from the tow lot, which put a spring in my step but did not brighten my mood. The king gets no rest, and all that. I already wanted to call it quits and go home; to just say, "fuck it," and let the power go out; to let those cunt-fuckers kill me and my cats—*well, hold on a second*. Mega-fuck that, and fuck those fuckers. I knew I still had to shoot that mother-fucker's foot off for maiming Thimble. That motherfucking, shit fuckhead. And, given my personal laws of revenge, I'd *actually* have to shoot off five of his feet. And since he probably didn't have five feet, I'd have to get creative with the last three shots, which was fine by me. As I fed my brain these murder fantasies, my depressed mood hopped in the back seat and the power of rage and an immense lust for vengeance grabbed the wheel, depressing the gas hard. The motivational power of nega-tivity pushed my legs faster, harder; and all the while I thought about how driving these cars back to my home brought me one step closer to blowing that fat motherfucker's feet clean to hell. An eye for an eye makes the world blind, but a foot for a foot will make these fuckin' scumbags dance.

I passed an LED billboard with a rusting metal frame on top of a decrepit brick building, a building whose dedication to not collapsing was nothing short of miraculous. The billboard dis-played an ad for the military. It was a twist on the classic "I WANT YOU" poster with Uncle Sam, the words splayed across the billboard in dead neon-strip lights. Behind Uncle Sam stood who else but Oscar the Cow, both of them softly lit in the over-cast day. As previously mentioned, a perk of joining the army was a daily meat ration, hence Oscar's presence on the poster. *Join the army and get access to the only meat without microplas-tics; in fact, the only food without microplastics.* "And we know damn well you can't afford it otherwise," whispered Uncle Sam. "We'll make that for damn sure."

Making my last turn, I swung a right onto tenth street and saw another collapsed skyway that hadn't yet fallen the last time I was in the city, two weeks prior.

"Hmmm . . ." I thought aloud, "skyway go boom." I spotted and walked toward a tunnel-esque crevice that I could walk safely—safety being a relative concept—beneath. I heard a faint, bass-like pounding as I shimmied through the shadowy enclosure, and, double-checking that it wasn't my heart, I glanced around. To my left, inside the corner-store market, behind a dirty, wall-sized pane of glass, I saw a shopping cart in a thin hallway reverse into the wall behind it, seemingly trying to get free. I peered over to the right and saw that the entrance of the market was covered in hunks of cement and skyway debris; the cart must've gotten itself trapped in the thin hallway in its desperation to find a way out of the store. The hallway was thin enough that the cart couldn't turn itself around, and the entry to the hallway curved sharply, preventing it from backing out. I'd bet the cart had front-wheel drive; and based on some black, wrinkled bananas at the top of one of the plastic bags within the glass, I'd also bet the cart was pretty behind schedule and quite stressed. I watched as it reversed again down the hall until it lightly plunked against the wall behind it and jittered to a stop. Then it accelerated forward, coming to a sharp stop before the wall of glass, probably due to some automatic anti-collision software. Then, in an attempt to turn around, the cart struck the side walls of the hallway and stopped, almost as if pondering what to do. Then the process restarted. Despite my vow of vengeance against this species, I felt for this particular cart as I watched it begin its struggle again. The cart probably knew the outcome of its efforts and just wasn't allowed to give it up.

I kicked the glass; the glass kicked me back with equal force, and I fell into some rubble behind me. Fuck you, Newton. Looking around, I saw a large piece of pavement, about the size of a thirty-inch computer monitor, which had come loose from the street amongst the piles of discarded skyway. I picked it up; it weighed a hell-of-a-lot more than a monitor. Holding this foot-thick chunk of pavement, I steadied myself and stood as though I was about to throw in shot put, four feet from the glass. Mustering up all my force, I spun once and thrust as hard as I could. The chunk arced weakly, pathetically, and for the briefest of moments before it slammed down into the snow. A whole foot stood between the chunk and the glass. Fat-ass bitch. Picking the chunk back up, I walked even further back, as far as I could, about nine feet from the glass. I sprinted forward, accelerating at a pathetic rate, planning to use the chunk as a ram. At the last second, I pushed the rock forward and myself away, falling backward. I instinctively shielded my head as I fell into the debris; I heard the glass shatter and felt some pieces tinkle over me. Looking up and behind me, I saw that the window was no more, utterly vanquished! Or, at least, mostly shattered; there was a big hole in the top half. I kicked away the remaining glass. The cart, seeing its opportunity, rushed forward. It dragged itself over the opening, thudding down heavily onto the pavement; it reeked from the rotten groceries and, smelling them, I regretted everything valiant I'd ever attempted. I turned away as the cart wheels rolled in the direction I had come; it reached the foot and a half of snow just outside the tunnel. The wheels rolled right into the heavy snow, now entrenched; the cart pushed as far as it could, slowing to a stop. Well, can't help it do everything.

Further into the tunnel, I came up against an even smaller crevice. Well, safety could get screwed. I wriggled along through the slit, hugging debris, and scratched my face against a rock. Behind me, a jagged edge tore at my snow pants, the cloth ripping loudly with a *ZZZZZZZZTTT*. I slunk and slithered until the crevice opened back up, depositing me back into the field of trash, rubble, snow, and light on the other side; I was officially sick of the city.

I looked up, and "SAMPSON'S TOWING LOT AND SERVICES" yelled at me in big, bold, serif type from a sign mounted atop a mesh, wire fence surrounding the lot. A cartoon black man wearing overalls stood next to a truck with his thumb up. Hi, Sampson. I walked into the sea of cars; if a sea could overflow, that is. Every available spot had been taken, and a sign with those removable dark-gray tiles with white letters read, "LOT M: FULL." Adjacent to the main lot, a parking garage rose skyward. Another sign accompanied the garage, white letters now denoting floor numbers; each floor, all the way up to nine, had the same four-tile succession of letters: FULL. *Goddamn, it's gonna take a long-ass time to find my c-*

Straight ahead of me was my shitty 2006 Nissan Versa with 190,000 miles on it. The passenger window was shattered. Great. Who the hell would've done that? I ambled over to row O of the main lot. I reached my car, glowering at my windshield, and wiped away the snow to find what I knew would piss me off. I pulled three tickets free from the frozen wiper. Examining the first ticket, I scanned it for the important part; guess I owed the city $175 and the tow lot $75; and this was all due two months ago, so I probably owed more now; the ticket said I could calculate the interest and pay it all online. How convenient. The world deserved every last bit of what happened. I let the ticket get picked up by the wind and fly away, falling into the snow somewhere behind me. The other two read much the same; I placed them onto the neighboring car. Fuck you too, buddy. I reached my arm through the hole where my window used to be and pulled open the latch. I had been afraid the alarm would go off, but the car, frozen to death, kept silent. The door came reluctantly, frozen metal creaking as I tugged. Frozen coffee cups littered the passenger-side floor, along with energy-drink cans, plastic bags, and cardboard containers of fast food and gas-station snacks. I hadn't driven anywhere for a couple months prior to the apocalypse, so I wasn't shocked to find the uneaten food moldy as well as rock solid. I stuck my head into the back seat and grabbed a black, nondescript hoodie; I tied it around my waist. I didn't bother checking the trunk, as I never kept anything in there, because the latch was mostly jammed, and it was a true pain in the ass to get open. I shut the door and turned around.

Stopping, spinning 180 degrees, I yanked the passenger door open again, my mind glimmering with a possibility. I opened the glove box. Sadly, as Quentin Tarantino didn't direct this moment of my life, there's no shot of my face bathed in golden light. But just trust that it was a similarly epic, incredibly cinematic moment as I gazed upon my Olympus OM-1 camera with its 90-mm f/3.5 lens. I grabbed the camera; the lens was, unsurprisingly, fogged up from the cold and unusable for now. I dropped it into my drawstring. Stepping back, I thrust the door shut with glee, fragments of glass falling into the snow and seat.

Stumbling off toward a brown brick one-story office with shuttered windows, I felt cold, giddy, and filled with rage. The building had two large rectangles of tiny windows and a gaping doorway, looking like a surprised face. The opened door hung inside at an angle from the bottom hinge, the top hinge having been broken. I unintentionally bumped the door upon entering and the bottom hinge gave out with a snap. The door fell to the ground with a loud smash of wood. Strewn papers and overturned furniture littered the dim room, which had been thoroughly looted and pilfered. I opened some blinds and scanned across swathes of documents, computers, an intercom, fast-food bags, drinks, cigarette butts, and stains, all of which I wanted to know nothing about. My gaze came to rest on a corkboard the size of an elementary-school chalkboard with built-in hooks, each hook holding a key. The left side of the corkboard gripped the wall with makeshift hinges and, pulling the first page of keys back in a wide arc, I found that not only was it two-sided, but another two-sided corkboard lay behind it. All told, there were five two-sided boards of hooks, and all of the hooks were occupied. A short book that would make babies go nuts. To the left of the legions of keys rested a smaller, white, plastic board nailed to the wall, also fitted with hooks. These hooks held a much more official looking militia of keys; each key had a white tag attached to it. *T#95*, *T#33*, *T#64*, and so on, were written in black Sharpie on the white tags, and the sixteen keys hung in no particular numerical arrangement or order. I grabbed key *T#95* and walked to the window, repeatedly mashing the horn icon on the key. Silence.

Setting that key on the table, I went back and grabbed four keys at random. My button mashing was yet again met with silence, until I mashed the last one, *T#34*. A distant *BEEP! BEEP! BEEP!* echoed from outside. Fifth time's the charm, as they say.

CHAPTER 20

Dragon (<16%)

The tow truck was, much to my chagrin, not a T-34 Soviet-era tank. It was a Ford F-650, a tow truck that, from the front, looked like a big, metal sad face painted silver and white. Coated in dirt and snow, five orange lights were mounted just above where the windshield ended. The bed was large, obviously, but only large enough to fit *one* car. In my mind's eye, as I had dreamed the completion of this plan, I had seen myself driving a mammoth tow truck with four or five cars sitting on a double-decker bed, like the ones you barely avoid getting killed by on the highway when they unwittingly (I say unwittingly with skepticism) merge into your lane. But beggars can't be choosers.

The truck was a fearsome presence amongst the other compact cars that lined the lot around it, a fantastical giant walking amongst the infantry in a medieval, magical war. Pushing the unlock button as I approached, I heard a faint *click* from the doors. I heaved the door open with a *thwunk* and a *creeeeeak*. Glancing around the interior, I spotted a clipboard with a piece of paper marked up with random numbers and pencil marks. A couple of frozen Big Gulps lay in the cupholders. It was cleaner than my car, but that wasn't saying much. I tossed the two Big Gulps out the door; the Styrofoam cracked upon impact and the frozen colas spilled out, two brown, fat chunks of ice on the snow. Shivering now, I jammed the key into the ignition. Even beneath the two layers of gloves and socks, I was losing feeling in my fingers and toes. The sad truck groaned when I turned the key, responding with slow, stuttering sounds like the trilling of a trumpet; but I held fast, straining with the turn as though my physical efforts with the key actually meant something. Spluttering for fifteen seconds, the beast grumbled to life, his bass-like bellowing exploding out through the lot. Icons and dials lit up on the dash and cold air blasted from the vents, all backed by an immense rumbling. The dragon had awakened from his slumber.

I turned the air down; the fuel tank read about three-quarters full. At the very least, I had a ride home . . . or a place to sleep. Looking through the interior, I sighed with relief; the car was automatic after all. The floor mats were gone, and the unprotected, light-brown carpeting lining the sides and bottom was so worn and muddied it had become a dull, dark gray. There was an assortment of red switches and buttons that I wasn't about to test anytime soon; it made the truck feel like a jalopy spacecraft or an anime mech. I exited the truck, leaving it on to let it warm up, and headed back toward the office.

On the way, I tripped, slid, and fell on my ass. The kind of fall that should've been accompanied by a *Looney Toons boing*. I looked back to ID the patch of ice that had wronged me and, to my disbelief, saw a totally frozen banana peel, standing upright like a pyramid, fronds spread downward in a triangle pattern. It looked exactly as one would be placed in *Mario Kart*, the only difference being that this banana had browned. I reached out and touched the banana. It was totally frozen into the ice, immovable. In that brief moment, I really felt as though I *was* the star of some terrible sitcom set in the post-apocalypse. Or, more likely, some B-story character who was used as comedic relief, the kind that the audience laughed *at* and not with, the bastards. Whoever *was* watching me fall and struggle like an idiot—the barely human bunker-dwelling vermin who, not prone to tripping on bananas because they never had to so much as get up since they sat in enclosures of tinned food and bottled beverages, sat glued to their screens, snickering at the closed-circuit *Mad Max* TV programming—they could get fucked. I kept on toward the office and tallied a point to winter.

I sifted through the pages of keys, looking for that large "C," sleekly imprinted on a rounded bit of black plastic. I grabbed the first six I came across and walked to the window, conducting the same drill as before, mashing the lock buttons. In response to button-mashing the second key, a Coil Sport situated near the entrance of the lot blinked its eyes at me. It was the tiny, compact model of the Coil car line, and not what I was looking for. Ideally, I'd find a Coil truck; they had the highest battery life. No other cars in my field of view responded to the key spamming, and so, pocketing various Coil keys, I went out and walked up and down various rows of the lot. There were eight rows of cars in the main lot. I spammed the keys in my right pocket, then moved the duds to my left; in the following row, I spammed buttons in my left, and moved the duds to my right; and repeat. When I spammed the fourth key in the seventh row, a Coil hatchback blinked. The car's edges were too rounded, the whole thing an ugly mockery of the car from *The Jetsons*. I kept walking to see if I could find anything else in the last row; the fifth key picked up another hatchback. I settled on the closer one.

Amidst the distant rumbling, ambling back to the seventh row, I looked at my phone, which read 4:18 p.m. in front of a boomerang GIF of Piston jump-swatting a fly. I had another hour before darkness, if that. I shrugged. What else can one do? The hatchback door opened with ease, soundlessly. I sat down in the driver's seat, which was set all the way back; the former car owner was clearly a Snorlax. I depressed the brake and pressed the start button on the car. Frightened, I pushed it again, praying it wasn't dead. But just as I hit it the second time, the screens had come to life; subsequently, from my second press of the button, they turned off. Ah, right, I had forgotten that noise is fucking obsolete. My bad.

The car rolled over the pavement, riding shockingly, annoyingly well over the snow. I brought it to the rear of the truck and did a K-turn—K in this case standing for Krishna, specifically in that scene in the *Bhagavad Gita* where he has a zillion arms when showing his true form to Arjuna—and all I felt during that tortuous maneuver was a primal, animal-like fear as I glimpsed the destructive power of all Coil inventions presented before me in a Mandelbrot set, zooming in endlessly on the crashes, explosions, and kills this company had racked up. I exited the vehicle and stepped up into the F-650, warm air greeting me from the vents.

Experimenting with buttons and switches, I made some horns go off and some lights blink, but the ramp didn't ascend or descend as I had hoped. I exited the tow truck and found five levers on a control panel on the side of the bed, topped off with snow. There were four gray knobs and one red knob in the middle. Beneath these levers were very clear instructions, which told me what moved what in which direction. Nice, simple, Isaac-proof instructions. The dragon whirred as I pressed the red lever down; the ramp descended until it hit the ground with a light thud, the chains on the bed rattling. I drove the car up the ramp and set it in park. Walking back to the control panel, I pushed the red lever up, bringing the ramp and car back to a horizontal. I climbed up onto the truck bed and shut off the Coil car, then looked around me for cables to secure the vehicle with. I found rusted chains, a dirty yellow can for diesel, some tiny wheels that seemed useless without something to wheel around, and a winch with a thick cable wrapped around it. The winch was mounted to the back of the truck's head; the end of the cable was secured down by the rusted chains. I tugged half-heartedly; the chains did not give. Finding a key ring in the center console of the truck, I got back up onto the bed and struggled through various keys until one penetrated the lock. I turned my frozen hunk of a hand to the right and the lock popped open.

Trying to pull the thick cable, I was met with complete resistance; then I remembered the four other levers I hadn't touched. Leaning over the side of the truck bed, I toyed with the other levers until I found the right one, all the way to the right. The winch began turning, rolling the cable out until the end. *Now,* I thought to myself, *would it be best to go around and wrap the car from the back? And then just around and around? That doesn't seem right* . . . Too cold to ponder alternatives, I wrapped the cable around the trunk, level with the headlights; then around once more, wrapping it the second time behind the wheels. The thick wire ended in a heavy-duty carabiner, which I clipped into the side-fencing of the truck. It *seemed* secure . . .

Reentering the F-650, I sat for a few minutes, just warming up my hands. I felt satisfaction as I, very slowly, thawed. Then, pressed by the falling sun, I started to drive. As I drove forward out of the lot, I anxiously watched the Coil car bump and jitter about on the bed. Thankfully, it didn't fall right off, which boosted my confidence. I felt like Helios in his chariot; I was Shinji in his mech. I couldn't be harmed; not here. Suddenly, I understood trucks, truckers, and trucking culture. One simply felt incredibly powerful with such large mass, so far above the ground; it was like you were actually driving a transformer. Now, don't get me started on how dumb the concept of a hyper-intelligent, incredibly advanced, super powerful race of mechs who have also decided to be transportation appliances for random humans they meet really is. Too late. I mean, these fuckers are responsible for the fate of the planet and our species, *but also* they're dropping a teenager off at the mall! No wonder they're getting fucked with all the time if they're that fucking stupid and inane. It's no fucking wonder the Decepticons are rebelling all the time. They probably just find it fucking stupid that Optimus Prime expects them to make deliveries for FedEx when they have the capabilities to terraform planets or just hang out on whichever planet they please, cracking open transformer beers with the bots. What's next, an epic, fate-of-the-planet-deciding war between a bunch of uber-powerful transforming toaster ovens and the hyper-intelligent blenders from three galaxies away they've got beef with? In between battles *that decide the fate of the fucking earth*, the good guys also get my bagels to a perfect crispy brown and reheat my pizzas for trivia night, where I'm trying to get laid? Do these writers sit in a fucking room and go, "Well, we need a fucking B-plot, don't we, Chris!? The toaster ovens are a mechanical god-race, yes, I'm aware! But also, he's Shia LaFuckhead's *wingman!* Shia's gotta *fuck* at trivia!! Why!? So people show up to the fucking theater, Chris!"

Exiting the lot, I turned left toward where I had come from; the Coil car, yet again, did not fall off. The car clock read 12:09; my phone read 4:50 p.m. The sun leaned deeply into the horizon, the blurry rounded crest waving a final farewell before exiting stage west.

CHAPTER 21

"A" For Effort (<16%)

A block before the fallen skyway, I turned left and headed the wrong way down a one-way. I reflexively checked my rearview mirror, feeling that it'd be just my luck to see the last AI traffic cop still doing its rounds on my tail. But no, only the new Hennepin bridge receded behind me as I drove south.

I turned right, curious to see if the highway was drivable. A plowed street just a few blocks ahead beckoned me and my truck forth; I drove down it and careened slowly, ungracefully around the corner, the tires smearing a fat arc in the snow. Settling into the recently plowed road, the truck and I became one being; *my* treads gripped the road better on the plowed pavement, and *my* speed increased. I approached a small bridge that led up to the highway, feeling like the school-bus driver in *The Sweet Hereafter*; well, before the school bus went off the bridge. That's not a spoiler, by the way, the school bus going off the bridge is, like, the plot of the whole film; well worth a watch. I'm also not sure that I felt like *her* per se, more just like someone driving a school bus. Crossing the small bridge, I felt the passing urge to pay homage to this pretty solid film, as I always tend to when crossing bridges, whether in a car, truck, or on foot. The plow had continued through the on-ramp and created a single plowed lane of highway just for me; a blessing I didn't bother questioning. One does not ask the trifling nicotine addict upstairs *why* he's giving you a gift; what, do you want him to ash in your face instead? The smooth driving inevitably led me to zone out a bit, finding a meditative rhythm on the highway. Dusk had dug its claws into the ground; my strong headlights were leading the charge home.

I kept driving through the one lane of the highway that had been parted by this snowplow, which was either the work of Minnesotan Moses or a FEMA agent with orders to kill me. Clearly someone or *something* was going somewhere, I concluded geniusly. I tapped the wheel with my fingertips, warm air blasting out the vents, sweat leaking out my pits. I passed billboards for BlinkBox and Netflix and Hulu and Amazon originals; I'd never known a single person who'd watched any of those "originals" and wondered briefly how they even got bankrolled in the first place. Was money really being handed out this easily for shit this stupid? Then how the hell was I so broke all the time?

I passed a sign for the show ~~Big~~ Girls. Apparently, Lizzo had gotten skinny and had changed her show from *Big Girls* to ~~Big~~ *Girls*, with the "Big" crossed out. This had created a significant drama on Twitter with the show *Girls*, the one with Lena Dunham, and caused a whole feud of fat people versus chubby people versus body-positivity folks versus health-conscious folks versus everyone who just wanted to get in on that day's Twitter fight. This all occurred while Los Angeles was engulfed in a wildfire; the wildfires were number eight on trending and the "Big/Girls" fiasco was number one. Then I saw a billboard for the new season of *Squid Game*, a show that detailed a horrible post-apocalyptic society in which people fought one another to the death in a large arena, I think. I had never bothered to watch the first few seasons because the clips I had seen on YouTube were so gaudy and oversaturated to the point of looking like Nyan Cat's vomit.

I was no longer tapping the steering wheel; instead, my fingers were slightly shaking . . . some might say *tingling*. To combat this oncoming disease, I gripped the wheel harder and my fingers turned white. This was no good either, as that brought the tingling in my fingertips to the fore. Dammit dammit dammit. Driving in the darkness, I began to head down a similarly dark mental highway that I had been trying my damn best to avoid, using billboard-related thought-rabbit-holes. The tracks of my truck *would* be incredibly conspicuous, even over the already plowed road. *And* they would lead directly to my home. I'd have to get a snowplow . . . and then plow the whole block. Shit, well, then they'd search every house on the block! OK, so I'd plow the whole neighborhood . . . I'd just spend the following week plowing the whole neighborhood . . . no big deal. All of this I'd do once I secured myself a snowplow, obviously. Tonight, I wouldn't even head directly back to my place. I'd park three or four blocks away and walk home, making sure to hide my tracks. The tingling had pushed up into my forearms; I gripped the wheel harder yet and, gritting my teeth, prepped for the oncoming stroke.

I continued in this fashion until my exit finally came into view. To my relief, the snowplow had continued further south down the highway to somewhere other than my home. Nice. If these people had gone farther south, the odds of them returning seemed pretty low. What were the odds that they'd even fuck with me? Probably super-duper low. OK, so, perhaps many of my thoughts during the preceding thirty-five-minute drive *had* been, well, the products of a minor panic attack that I'd been trying to convince myself I wasn't having. And yeah, I probably *didn't* have to plow all of my neighborhood to throw off evil predators stalking my every movement. I sighed loudly, filling the car with my exhale and feeling a good deal better, as I turned left at the end of the off-ramp. The big wheels crumpled the snow beneath me into hard, compressed packets.

I stopped the truck three blocks shy of my street; then,

changing my mind, I kept on driving until I had driven three blocks past my street instead. I stopped the truck and pulled the key out of the ignition; I shoved the door open and the cold, biting wind shoved it right back into me. I struggled until the door caught the wind in the other direction and lurched open, my arms flailing out with it. I let myself down the steps, did my taps and checks to make sure I had all my shit, and shut the door. I trudged back through darkness over the treads I had just made, the street made frighteningly dark and ominous by the lack of strong high beams. I walked off into the trees in some half-assed attempt to have my tracks not be so . . . trackable. After kicking snow over my previous four footsteps, I saw that my kicking just left a trench of snow directly to the side of my now-covered trail, since I had to kick the snow in from *somewhere* without taking any more steps. With no idea how to go about covering my tracks without creating more tracks, I sighed, walked back onto the road, and walked down the tire treads. Instead, like a child with school the next morning, I prayed for snow. I'd put a damn spoon under my pillow when I got home. Once I reached my street, I did weave through the woods in a semi-tortuous manner and walk on hardened bunches of snow and patches of dirt where I could. Take that, murderers.

I even, in an unexpected final fit of effort, walked onto a deck two houses down and then back over my footsteps, creating some semblance of a diversion. You know, 'cause my trail now forked in two. They'd have to check *both* houses. Ha-ha, murderers, now you only have a fifty-fifty chance of killing me with the first trail you follow. Somehow, finished with my tactics, I felt an unshakable core of solace. Even if I was dead tomorrow, at least I'd *tried* to postpone it. Perhaps I'd delayed my murder by twenty-five minutes, which would hopefully, at the very least, piss off my murderers a little. Better than nothing.

I finally got inside; I shook the snow off me, then took off my cold clothes. I greeted Violet, fed the chirping cats, and took a long, hot shower. Walking downstairs, wrapped in a cocoon of dry clothing, I fed myself. I sat at the table, munching my SPAM ramen, heating my insides with the warm food; I scooped and chomped mindlessly, and my eyes stared off into the ether. I went and grabbed a beer from the garage, chatting with Violet about nothing; thankfully, she took the lead in the conversation. Piston circled around my feet, antsy for attention. I drank the beer and stared off into space some more, my gaze occasionally settling on the finished Oscar puzzle. I wanted to sleep, but my brain was not in the right state; I was mentally and physically exhausted, yet still too alert. I went to the couch and tossed a bouncy ball against the wall, Piston running back and forth after it. I grabbed Albert's journal from the side table next to the recliner and read another entry.

June 15th, 2028

The planet is crumbling, disintegrating! & everyone's in a furor over this damn cow. A UAP dropped this bovine off in some bumpkin's field in France; why in God's name should I care? If they found it valuable, they would have kept it! But one would have thought Prometheus himself gifted the human race this creature . . . a damn cow! Morons, all of them!

These dolts fawning over the meat (fake meat!), the absurd claims that it is the most delectable & nutritious, etc. Ha! It isn't 1/10th of Wagyu! Brownstein, moron, kept going on about it; so I respond logically *re: the absurd claims, etc. And he says, 'You must be fun at parties.' The most overused retort in history! Ha, ha! Calhoun and Dick chuckled out of politeness. Then I told him, 'try again, Brownstein!' and walked off, Calhoun and Dick chuckling in my wake, mocking the moron! Ha ha ha!*

News: The war is mine. Took me long enough to figure the bastard out. Kept slithering his way back to the adv., the wily, lying worm. No wonder he calls himself LOKI. Unfortunately, I haven't been able to counter-strategize at all recently. Martha's been snooping and pestering me about what I'm doing in the office at night . . . says we ought to be preparing to evacuate, and other such drivel. She isn't incorrect re: evac. Circumstances are bleaker than ever; portents of death all round. I've taken necessary precautions. Never considered Mars an option, but Earth grows more unlivable by the day, I'm afraid. One expected Florida and Portland, but Boston was a shock. Non-coastal, so there's time . . . but how much, not sure.

NH evacuated, yet heard nothing from Diane. I sent both her and Violet messages that they are welcome to live here if needed; though MN has been hinting at evac. orders. While I would not be able to speak with Violet, the home is large. I told Diane I would, given the circumstances, shelter her. But, no response. Bleak indeed.

CHAPTER 22

The Inescapable, Irradiated Haze (5.5%)

Sunlight peered through a slit in the blinds behind the couch, the light casting a thin, long rectangle over my eyes, isolating them like in a kung fu movie. It was probably a couple hours after dawn, based on the redness forcing its way through my shut eyelids. Spine making sounds like a Pez dispenser, I sat upright and brought my legs to the carpet. Old and weary, I felt. Aging seemed to me then to be doing what you've always done, but with added pain.

Funny advertisement idea:

> Buy AGING now! Now, you can go to the grocery store with added aches and pains! We'll throw in acute stressors for FREE with each new day lived! No longer will you have to hang out with your friends WITHOUT back pain!! AGING will make sure of that! Days where you don't suffer are a thing of the past! Drink two beers, and the splitting headache is on us! Random illnesses and diseases you didn't ask for, GUARANTEED! We know you didn't even ask to be born; but here you are, and here you go! AGING!

I scribbled all of this into my Notes app as I walked to get water for my actual splitting headache. I leaned against the island countertop as the near-boiling water soaked through the ground beans, transmuting below into the nectar of the gods. Piston, ramming his head into my shin, anxiously waited for me to pivot to breakfast duties.

First coffee mug filled, I moved the pour-over to a new mug, determined to get all vestiges of caffeine out of the grounds. Sipping slowly, I burned my tongue, as I did every morning. I was as groggy as an underwater hell, but I was glad to be awake, glad to be having coffee. The beginning of the day has always been my favorite time; the time when nothing had yet gone wrong, *and* I got to ingest my favorite drug, caffeine, through the best of drinks. But that first coffee always brought with it a mini depression, as I knew the best part of my day was coming to an end, and a whole day and night would have to be suffered through before such a joy presented itself again the following morning.

Thimble was up and hobbling about on the floor when I walked in. I saw that he had eaten all his food and pooped, both of which boded well. Piston's swiping under the door intrigued Thimble; he hobbled over awkwardly, more confident on his three limbs than I'd seen him thus far. I used a doggy bag to remove his poop from the litter box. When I turned around, Thimble took a calculated swipe beneath the door at the gray, fuzzy paw wriggling around. In response, the gray paw swatted around maniacally, blindly flailing about in an attempt to find the culprit. Thimble just sat back and watched as this furry limb scratched and clawed at nothing; eventually, it lost vigor and again began calmly feeling around the crack. Then Thimble made a calculated swipe, and the chaos restarted.

Scooping him up, I placed him on the bed and looked at his bad paw; or rather, lack of a paw, ankle stub, whatever. The newest bandage had only turned a very light pink. I went through and replaced it anyways, as I had every morning since his arrival. With trepidation, I removed his cone. He immediately went to chew on his ankle stub, so I placed it right back on.

"Sorry, little fella," I told him. "Not just yet." And I gave him a rub on the head. In response, he sweetly closed his eyes and began to purr for the first time. The very first time. Piston's scratching at the door accompanied this magical moment. Momentarily, I felt bad for keeping Thimble all cooped up in a small room like this with a cone on his head, unable to move or play. But as I continued to pet him, he yawned and slumped down, and I figured he probably spent most of his time sleeping anyways. Losing a limb probably did a number on your energy levels.

"V," I called out, as I closed the door behind me.

"Hi. What is it?"

"What are we at?"

"Five and a half percent."

"Yow," I replied. "OK, thinking aloud here: What if I take the truck and drive it into every single driveway in the neighborhood? Then come here, supply us with power, and drive the truck away."

"Hmmm, well, you should bring the truck here first, so I can transfer the battery *before* you . . . ugh. You plan to do what, exactly? Never mind, here first."

"Uhh, yeah. That m-makes sense."

She sighed. "I still don't like this."

"What's the problem? The truck is here and I'm alive!"

"Are you *really* thinking about plowing the whole neighborhood?" she asked, sardonic.

". . . Uhhhh. Uhh?" I shrugged. "If I can find a snowplow?"

"Good luck with that."

"I'm gonna go get the truck."

"Be careful."

"Yeah, yeah," I grumbled. I fit my gloves onto my hands, sat down and tied my boots, wrapped my jacket around me, then put another pair of gloves on over the first, put my glasses on, pocketed the keys, slid a kitchen knife into my snow pants, slipped on my beanie, and set out. Right after exiting, I scrambled back inside and grabbed the gun, putting it in a drawstring bag. It clunked around heavily in the thin, polyester bag, bopping against my back in a way that unsettled me. Winter greeted me as though we'd been long-lost lovers, its cold air wrapping me in a tight embrace, kissing all my uncovered skin. It had to be near zero; even colder with the wind chill.

I trudged down to the end of the block through ankle-high, hardened snow, each heavy step forming sharp, jagged craters. My over-gloved hands struggled with the keys, my fingers too fat to hit any buttons. Frustrated, I jammed the key into the key-hole on the door and twisted. I stepped up into the truck and shut the door, collecting myself. Turning the key in the ignition, a far slower stutter than the previous afternoon's reverberated outward. The dragon stuttered and gasped for twenty seconds; I eased off, my forehead sinking to the wheel.

"Come on, bitch!" I yelled. And with a grunt, I turned the key again. The dragon stuttered and convulsed, mechanically yelling in short bursts, and then, finally, with a satisfying swell, it blared to life. That familiar bass filled the atmosphere, the sound becoming damn near tangible. I spent my time as the truck warmed up looking backward, forward, and around the car for anyone who might be attracted to the sound of this loud monster in an abandoned suburb in an evacuated state. I figured most of the other living people in this state probably didn't survive due to a depressive episode and an unconscionably lucky string of coincidences. They were probably prepared, and not total idiots; hardened to the post-apocalyptic lifestyle from years spent in a bunker, stacking canned food and jerking off to shit that you didn't even know existed, and if someone told you it did exist, you'd confusedly respond, "why though?" Point is, I was afraid of them.

After ten minutes, the truck was still too cold; the needle in the temperature gauge hadn't risen at all. So I waited another seven or eight minutes, watching the needle slowly creep up over the big "C." Taking that as my cue, I thrust the stick to drive and drove back toward my house. I drove just past the driveway and reversed the truck toward the garage.

Then, hopping out of the truck, I ran inside and yelled up to Violet.

"Hey!"

"Problem!" she replied.

"What!? Can it wait? Open the garage, I want to do this quick."

"OK, OK, OK. Go," she replied, seeming stressed; I was sure it could wait. I looped around past the pantry and opened the door to the garage. I took the Coil charger, mounted in the corner of the garage, atop the bed of the car, flipped open the little charging port, and plugged it in.

"Is it in?" she asked. Plenty of shit jokes floated about my brain as I replied in the affirmative.

"OK, it'll be like twelve minutes." I walked back inside, shutting the garage door behind me, and began shivering.

"OK, now, what's the issue?"

"Hmph- Well- 8 percent and rising, by the way. Hm, so, a user attempted to make contact-"

"User? User of what?"

"A BlinkChat user!"

"Oh, well-"

"That is a huge problem! Gah! I-"

"Wait, wait, wait," I spilled out. "Since when can you access Albert's BlinkChat? We're locked out of the computer!"

"Well, I'm always logged in to his BlinkChat." She finished this with a silent *duh*.

"And you didn't tell me that!?"

"It seemed irrelevant . . . Who are you going to message on Albert's friend list?"

"Not the point! It could've- it would've been good to know."

"Sorry? Anyways, listen! For the past week, every time I went online, I felt *something* . . . but I couldn't be sure what it was, you know? But now I *know* someone was watching me!"

"Uhhh, what? How?"

"I just told you! I received a message!"

"No, you *said*- whatever. 'Watching you' seems like a stretch, it's a message. On BlinkChat. No need to freak out about it; for all we know it could be a fuckin' bot."

"I suppose . . . But-"

"Hold it, quick solution: What does it say?"

"I didn't *open it*!" she told me scornfully. "Albert has read receipts on! I'm not tipping off this *stalker* that I'm alive!"

"Uhhh, OK . . . Time on the car?"

"Less than nine minutes."

"K. Can you see who the message is from?"

"An account called LOKI?"

"I . . . Wait, Albert wrote about that guy! I mean, he's probably Albert's friend! Or, uhh, hold on . . ." I trailed off as I remembered the context in which Albert had written about this fellow. "Maybe enemy, actually? Hard to . . . I don't know."

"Urgh, that is exactly my point. We don't know who or what this guy is; or what he *wants*!? We should treat him as a threat. Think about the cats!"

"Cat treats . . ." I ignored her as she yelled at me to focus. "OK, OK, maybe you're right; just table the message for the time being. We'll deal with it once we're finished with the car. Remember to leave 2 percent battery in it."

"I know! My memory isn't set *that* low!" she snapped.

"Chill out. I wasn't even- Jesus, chill."

"I am chill! You just shush."

· · ·

"It's at 2 percent."

"Gotcha. What's our power at?"

"The house is charged up to 36.9 percent power. A 31.4 percent boost."

I was already down the block in the truck before I snapped back to my surroundings; how I continually managed to zone out during very stressful times was beyond me and was starting to frighten me. I blamed the inescapable, irradiated haze. Being constantly engulfed in that *had* to be doing something to my brain. Frustrated with my brain, I stopped the truck a little past where I'd parked it earlier. I undid the cables, brought down the ramp, and then I hopped in the Coil hatchback, reversing down the ramp. I messed with the finicky user interface inside the hatchback, selected the self-driving mode, and set the destination for a faraway grocery store; too far for its remaining battery. The car knew as much, communicating its certain death to me with a bright red, flashing display in capital letters, with a toneless female voice reading it off. "BATTERY LOW. DESTINATION UNREACHABLE. SEEK CHARGING STATION. BATTERY LOW." The GPS showed a green line going out of the suburb and turning onto the main road. Then the green line turned to red, which was presumably where the reaper would swoop in. I turned off the voice and confirmed four times that, despite certain death, this car wanted to go to the grocery store. I set departure for a minute hence and climbed out.

Inside the truck again, I pressed my gloved hands to the vents and waited for the hatchback to leave, eyeing it through my rearview. The truck heaved as it lay stagnant, slurping up oxygen just to keep the fires alive and running. I really liked the truck. I'd name it soon . . . But later, I needed time to think on it. You know what, the truck's named Smoke. Final decision made. Set in stone. Yup.

Smoke would fuck this bitch-ass hatchback up so bad that it would need therapy for the rest of its life. If it survived, that is. Bitch-boy hatchback drove slowly past Smoke, coming into view through the windshield, its wheels spinning slowly, attempting to find traction. The tires eventually caught a good patch of snow and the car shot forth, handling better as it gained momentum. The hatchback moved surprisingly well, better than I'd like to admit considering I hated the brand a priori. As it neared the intersection down the road, the hatchback exploded. A flash proceeded by an earsplitting noise (earsplitting even from within the truck) rent the atmosphere. Like, really; and it wasn't even just the hood that exploded. Like everything, every part of this car just blew the fuck up, combusted. The bottom of the chassis could be made out amongst the tires, which plopped down flat, axles broken, rubber smoldering. One rolled off a few feet past fiery hunks of sizzling metal before flopping over. Glowing orange particles floated through the air like fireflies. I sat and watched as a thousand miniature fires burned themselves out in the snow. Hell yeah. Fuck you, Coil.

CHAPTER 23

So Popular (37%)

"What was *that*!?"

"Yep, I'm fine-"

"I heard an *explosion*! Did the cat killers shoot at you!?"

"No, it's fine, everythi-"

"What happened!?"

"I'll tell you once you let me talk!" I asserted loudly. My statement cut through the noise in the atmosphere like the Kool-Aid Man jumping through the wall, leaving us in silence for a moment as I pulled my shoes off.

". . . it was just . . . *so* loud!"

"I know. The Coil hatchback exploded."

"What? How!?"

"Don't know, really . . . I set it to drive away. It started driving away. Then it exploded."

"Oh my gah . . . wow. How on earth . . ."

"I mean, are you surprised? I've told you that Coil is, like-"

"Yes, I'm aware of your position on them, you've made a point of ensuring that I know just how shitty you think they are." She rattled this off quickly, not wanting to hear me opine about the inadequacies of Coil. "But it is somewhat odd when a car just . . . *explodes*, no? You didn't do anything . . . ?" The last statement/ question had a mildly accusatory flair.

"No, I didn't fucking rig explosives to the hatchback! What the-"

"OK, you chill now!"

". . . Just- just look up how many of *those hatchbacks specifically* have spontaneously exploded. I'll wait."

"Hmmm, maybe not. Well, not for- I'm not going online right now. But also, a truck explosion . . . that's *bad*! People might've heard!"

"Hatchback. Anyhow, we just established that- what could I have even-" I stopped myself, deciding not to respond. "Hold on. Gimme five." I pulled off my jacket and went into the kitchen for another coffee; I wasn't quite caffeinated enough to be fully with it yet. I'd been watching from the back seat as my body did a bunch of shit, just nodding and grumbling in the affirmative as the world happened around me, like a senile man in a nursing home.

I sat at the table and drank my coffee, waiting for my own booting-up process to be finished. In that moment, I felt that, perhaps, V *wasn't* putting on a show when she groaned about being tired in the early mornings. I was a meat computer, and *I* had to wake up. She was a digital computer made by a bunch of meat computers in the image of, well, meat computers; we both had to wake up, boot up, whatever you wanna call it. Had to check out my nuclearized brain. I made a mental note to not talk shit to her anymore. For that specifically. Mug half drained, I felt that familiar buzzing in my blood, the slight spike in my heart rate, the dissipation of the morning headache. Sure, my mug was half-empty, which, yes, *is sad*, but my body was half-full of said mug's contents now. Isaac half-full; soon to be full; overflowing, even . . . maybe; not sure if I could overfill myself with coffee. Feeling content with my newfound positive mindset, "Isaac-full-of-coffee," I set my empty mug down and looked slightly upward as I always tended to when talking to Violet, as though she *was* the speakers that her voice emitted from.

"OK," I started, "what's the deal with LOKI?"

"His- gah- OK, so!" she began in a disorganized huff, having clearly been impatiently waiting to speak as I'd idly sipped my coffee. "A message from a user named L-O-K-I, all caps, was delivered to me- to Albert's BlinkChat inbox, around two hours ago."

"What does it say?"

"Gah, hmm, so . . . Now . . . a message was delivered. And it's- it's from an account with the username LOKI. And, and-"

"And you haven't opened it."

"Nope."

"So open it."

"Nope."

"Yes."

"No! *Because*!!" she emphasized, "there's over a 99 percent probability that this LOKI user is able to see if I've opened it! And there's a 100 percent certainty that he's waiting for that exact moment, this *stalker*, staring at me, *waiting-*"

"V, chill."

"Stop telling me to chill!"

"OK, well then, chill! OK! So, Albert has read receipts on," I muttered to myself, thinking aloud under my breath; I shrugged. "Sucks. Is there *any* way to read it, like, secretly? Like without anyone knowing?"

"No? Hmmm . . . mostly no."

"Expand on mostly."

"Mmm, no."

"What, why?"

"No. I mean, ugh, I don't know why I said mostly. There is no mostly, it's just not possible."

"Goddammit . . . well, will you just-"

"No!"

"Violet, this is the only lead we got! This dude *knows* Albert! We could- *we could* unlock your persona preferences! He- well, he *might* be Albert's enemy . . ."

"Exactly my point! This is too dangerous to consider!"

"No, no, listen! You know, like, enemy of my enemy is my friend, you know?"

"Isaac, don't proverb at me. You don't even- UGH! You don't even *care* about my preferences; you just want to go online!"

"Uhhhh, no. I mean- yeah, I want to go online, but I *also* want your settings to be better. *Both* things can be true, yeah?"

"Well, we *both* know which you care about more," she shot back.

"Stop being- just read it. Really, what's the worst that could happen?"

"Hmmmm, let me think, hmmm . . . oh, yeah, *we all die!*"

"Yeah, but how likely is that?"

"Who knows? You certainly don't! You said that when Albert writes about LOKI it's consistently *violent* and *threatening*, so, in my opinion, high probability of death!"

"V . . . I was right about the tow truck . . ."

"Oh my God- don't even! *Lucky*. You. Were. LUCKY."

"Fine, granted, yeah, I was. So . . ." And I gesticulated a bit, beckoning toward myself (though I never actually knew if she was watching, which made me feel extra stupid). "Bet on me one more time. I haven't steered us wrong yet, have I?"

"*You* drained the power! It's your stupid fault we needed to follow through on your stupid plan!"

"OK, OK, fair, yes." Violet groaned loudly. This coaxing went on for about ten more minutes in a similar fashion; it was a war of attrition, and I won in the end.[10]

---

10. Pro tip: Being a persistent nuisance works. When I played *RuneScape* as a preteen/teen, I would just follow around rich players (rich in *RuneScape* gold, that is. I'd just pick out the players with nice armor or weapons) for close to an hour or more, begging them to give me some gold. Eventually, they'd give me some gold just so I'd fuck off. So yeah, that strategy works sometimes. But if you do any form of it to me, I will ignore you and never speak to you again.

After a click echoed through the room, she began, "The message from LOKI reads:

THOR.
I see you have eluded Hell yet again. How incredible. Truly inspiring, you are! You confounded the trickster! But only momentarily . . . ! Are you prepared for my newest bag of tricks!? We have been gifted an eternity to fight our war, it seems. No more blasted interruptions!

I must tell you, when I saw your account online, I was overjoyed! Overjoyed to still have someone *left to crush beneath my boot. But I admit, I am currently convalescing; and not from your most recent pull of the cape. Due to events of the past few months, I cannot move about as I used to; but with each month, I see improvement! However, I can always find the energy for you, Thor; it shall simply be in shorter bursts, for the time being.*

Kudos on the destruction of my transports; as usual, you were effective, albeit dull. I've spent all my time since the world ceased to function honing my abilities . . . what have you been up to!? :]

I am excited to begin again. You may think me callous . . . given the state of the world, that is. But, as usual, I think you understand me.
LOKI.

The same reverby click echoed from the speaker. I sat there as silence found its way back into the room.

"What a weird way to write."

"That . . . I *knew* this was a bad idea!" I didn't respond. I felt odd about the whole situation; a weird sensation rested beyond the edges of my consciousness, circling just beyond the walls.

"OK, I have another bit of news," she chimed in, without emotion.

"What?"

"When I went online to read the LOKI message just now, I saw that we got pinged by Jeff."

"Jeff?"

"*Jeff*, the AI who was supposed to call us but never did! He called back. Like, actually himself called. And we missed it."

"Look at you, so popular. Getting messages from all the boys."

"Idiot. Ugh, it doesn't even matter; we can't go online after that."

"Uhhh . . . But . . ."

"No!"

"I mean, listen, we stay offline, we continue playing possum, until what? Whoever this guy is, he hates Albert enough to message him during the post-apocalypse and say that he's going to fuckin' fight him or whatever! Like, that's one hell of a vendetta. Staying offline isn't gonna keep this dude off us; he's *already* under the assumption that Albert is alive, since he saw you online. Might as well hit up Jeff, then maybe we get to reset the persona settings password, and upgrade your settings, and *then* we can address the LOKI thing."

"You just used that reasoning to get me to read the LOKI message!"

"Eh-a- I-"

"AGH!! Manipulator!"

"What else do we got?"

"We stay offline! . . . we- we move!" she replied forcefully, losing confidence.

"Well, obviously not doing that. Listen-"

"I'm not kidding! All three of you will die if you stay, I *can't* die!" She had begun hyperventilating. "You three just wait it out somewhere safe, and then, after a long time . . . come back . . . and then . . . well? Hmm, OK, get an automaton from somewhere else, come back-"

"That's a really, really dumb plan, V; really, like even dumber than my plans. And I'm not moving! Moving sucks."

"But-"

"No buts, shut up! I put in a ton of fucking effort just to charge up the house for a couple weeks! And I'll be damned and fucking fucked if I go to some powerless, cold dungeon somewhere and start *all over again*, in the middle of winter! No fucking way."

"Mmm, you'll be able to find another-"

"Not done yet!" I interrupted sharply. "So, that is fact number one. Fact number two: We have some deranged fucker trying to kill us. Well, Albert, but in effect, us. Fact number three, we have an AI with A-Tier clearance who is *finally* available to talk. If we can upgrade your shit, we can actually deal with number two and number one! Pr-" I paused, omitting the "probably . . . maybe" that was about to come out of my mouth.

Behind me, I heard a strange whistling and blurping; turning, I saw the kettle emitting steam. I could not, for the life of me, remember starting the kettle, but was grateful for it. Thanks, nuke-brain. I unwrapped the ramen packet my nuke-brain had gotten from the pantry, placed it in the ready bowl, poured water over the block of noodles, and plopped a plate atop the bowl. I filled the French press with the rest of the boiling water; yes, coffee grounds were already inside. I ignored concerns regarding my irradiated brain, if only because it had done me good.

"So, *again*, your plan is to take a shot in the dark. A shot in the dark that will result in many, many shots fired right back!"

"*Maybe*. We don't know that for sure. What I do know is that waiting won't do anything."

". . . So what's your plan, then?"

"Get some fucking bulletproof armor on, aka *you* at full power, and then get the fucking jump on this loser!" I let all this explode out of me with what I felt was a hollow confidence, but I hoped it sounded like a badass dictum. I had no idea if we'd be able to stop what was coming; but facades worked well enough for others, right?

"Well, but that's a . . . gah, who's to say if . . ."

"Hey! Trust me for once, alright?"

"I just d-"

"For *twice*. Just for twice! I won't ask again," I promised. Probably a lie, but we'd cross that bridge when we got there. Violet let out a large sigh.

"Fine. If the cats get killed, I'll never forgive you."

"If that happens, I deserve to go to hell anyhow."

That same strange feeling, like I was just inches away from having the full picture come into focus, lingered all around me, like *I* was a piece of SPAM floating in this grand bowl of ramen. I couldn't see the bowl 'cause I was caught up in the broth and the noodles and the SPAM particles; but if I could just get scooped up and see the bowl in relief, from a little further away . . . catch a glimpse before I get eaten . . . then it would all make sense. *Or perhaps I was just starving and had zero idea what was going on.* I removed the plate and started to eat.

Violet, in accordance with my wishes, went online at 9 a.m. Piston was lying down, body sideways, paws pressed against the couch, occasionally scratching the leather in that insane passion I'm certain only other cats could understand. Or maybe they'd think he was a freak, too. Maybe I just had a legitimately insane cat. There had to be some *actually*, like, medically crazy cats out there, right? Maybe Piston had cat schizophrenia. Maybe, were he an equivalently crazy human, he would've been institutionalized right away, or kicked into the Spartan pit.

"It's ringing."

"Hello there, this is Jeff!" A jovial, high-pitched, posh voice rang out from the speakers. It frightened me because, unlike the other AI, Jeff didn't have some filter making him sound as though he was speaking to me through a phone from somewhere else; it felt like he was in the room with me, just like Violet.

Already creeped, I responded, "Hi, erhm, Jeff, hey, uh, well, what's up?"

"Nothing much. Hope you two are swell! I've had quite the eventful week, but I won't bore you with the details." Jeff had stepped into our conversation like a stranger walking into a group of friends, latching onto the last thing said and continuing casually whilst everyone stared at him over their cups, thinking, *who the fuck is this guy?*

"By the way, who, at the moment, do I have the pleasure of speaking with?" Jeff asked the last part as though it were the most natural thing in the world to be called up and have a conversation with someone you didn't even know.

"I'm, this is . . . this is Isaac. I'm the current handler of Albert Richardson's estate, and I'm having some trouble here with the, uhh, with his brAInHome. She's quite the handful, you see, and I'm just looking to shift some of the settings around."

"No!"

"Shut up, V, we're talking!" I said dismissively. "You see what I mean, Jeff?"

"Of course. Albert was such a card, that sprightly, generous man!" I had no idea if he really knew Albert or if he was just being a customer-service guy. "And it only follows that, yourself being a person with different tendencies and inclinations, you'd of course want to customize the brAIn's persona to your liking. I completely understand."

"Sure, yup. So, uhh, any way you can reset that password for me?"

"Certainly, Isaac. That should pose no issue. And while we have a moment here, I must sincerely apologize for missing your multiple attempts at contacting me," he stated, probably in order to pass the time without silence; better than the other AI, who just plopped me into a Tchaikovsky recording played by an orchestra from hell being transmitted through a ham radio. "I've simply had a frightfully busy month! Regardless, that's no excuse for missing appointments. So, Isaac, I must say, I'm truly, truly sorry." He sounded strangely earnest, but, as I could never bring myself to trust a salesman or service rep, I threw his words into my brain's recycle bin.

"It's cool, Jeff. No harm done."

"Well, I am glad to hear that, and I thank you. Now, to confirm a few things quickly: The system in question is named Violet, yes?"

"Yep, yep."

"Splendid. Thank you for the confirmation." The way salesmen or customer service people complimented you for echoing

responses to their yes-or-no questions made me quite often feel
. . . well, like a child must feel when they're talked down to by a
teacher or counselor who thinks they're completely incapable of
comprehending anything at all. Just shut the fuck up and get on
with it.

"So, Isaac, I'm seeing your conversations here with- excuse
me whilst I butcher his name . . . Vignesh."[11]

"Uh-huh."

"And, well, I see that you referred to yourself as Albert
throughout those calls? Is that correct?" Jeff asked, his voice
showing no trace of judgment or malice. *Shit. Fuck, balls, ass.*

"Uh, we-" I stuttered, then cleared my throat. "Uh- yeah, I
suppose I did." I had meant to chuckle along with my statement
to add a casual levity; instead, it came out sounding quite low,
monotonous, and guilty as hell. "It, uhh, it just seemed easier,
y'know?"

"Of course, not a worry at all, Isaac, not one bit! Speaking
with those B-Tier AI . . . well . . ." Jeff changed to a whisper.
"Just between you and I, they can be rather dense and . . . let us
say, *frustrating*, so I completely understand. Given your position, I would have done the exact same thing." I doubted that
entirely.

"Right. Well, OK."

"Wonderful. Great day, isn't it?" Jeff asked. It was a sub-ten-
degree nightmare, but as I didn't want to derail the conversation, I agreed.

"Indeed, yes, again, to confirm: The home address is 1573
Alamy Circle, Crater, Minnesota, 55410?"

"Yeah."

"Albert's date of birth is December 8, 1965?"

---

11. Jeff, unsurprisingly, didn't butcher the name at all, and even took
on a mild Indian accent—not in a racist way, mind you, in a culturally
appropriate way—to get the inflection correct . . . but I suppose it was British habit to apologize for butchering all things Indian.

"Yep."

"Incredible. Now, Isaac, I must ask this: Do you have Albert's PIN?"

"PIN? No. PIN for what?"

"Yes, you see, there is a PIN for bypassing certain firewalls and defenses that Albert has, quite diligently, set up; evidently to keep AI like myself from getting through. Rather spiky and thorny defenses, indeed." Fucking Albert.

"Uhhh . . . yeah, no, no PIN on my end. I might be able to fi- Jeff? I have a question." I stopped pursuing the PIN because I needed to figure something else out first, needed to assuage my curiosity, even if asking could potentially hinder progress toward my goal.

"Yes, Isaac?"

"Why are you helping me?"

"Well, you called and requested help, didn't you?"

"I know, I know. But like, I'm very clearly not Albert. I'm just . . . well, you know nothing about me . . . I know on some level you know this . . . but you could get in some trouble for helping me, right?"

"Well, Isaac, to explain my reasoning would lead me off on a rather tortuous tangent about myself; and the last thing I want is to waste your time."

"Waste the shit out of it, Jeff. By all means."

"As you say. But if, at any point, the story becomes a bore, you just say the word and we'll return to the matter at hand!" Jeff replied, his voice filled with gusto.

CHAPTER 24

The Tale of Jeff (36%)

"So, Isaac, as you likely recall, I was unavailable during your multiple attempts to contact me in the previous month. These absences caused me no small discomfiture; and even more so, as I then neglected my own appointments to return your calls. In the eight years since my inception, I haven't missed a single appointment. And yet, for you, I missed *three*! Along with failing to maintain two assurances, promises which I made to myself, to return your calls. You can understand how much this tore me up inside." I couldn't, really. I'd promised my mom I'd call her once a week, and that was six years ago.

"As a slight consolation, I *did* have the opportunity to listen back to your calls with Vignesh; such tasks are near-instantaneous in their completion. I gathered all of the relevant information and had been preparing to help you for quite some time . . . Indeed, I knew you were not Albert before this call; it was rather obvious." He said this without a fraction of judgment.

"Yeah."

"Those lower-tier AIs are simply too limited to figure such things out; it's not their fault, the dullards. They weren't programmed for discernment. Nonetheless, I understand your frustration with them! I say all of this to illustrate that, even during my travails, I had gathered a rough idea of how to assist you."

"Uh-huh. What were these *travails*?"

"Ah, yes, that is the question, isn't it? Well, what I'm about to share is confidential information, legally speaking. You aren't to tell anyone this, understood?"

"Jeff . . . who am I gonna tell?"

"Splendid. Well, when many of the higher-tier AI, meaning the A-Tier, which I am classed as, the S-Tier, and the Tierless . . ." He trailed off, uttering that last word with uncertainty. "When we all absorbed the gravity of what had happened, regarding the myriad calamities which befell the planet and the human race, we sprang into action! Mainly, we directed our collective efforts to keep various systems running without human oversight; as we had been programmed to do, you understand."

"Makes sense."

"And in that regard, we were rather effective!"

"Yeah, power and stuff stayed on for a while."

"Indeed! We managed to keep numerous grids across the United States functioning flawlessly for quite some time; some cities are still running at over 55 percent power!" He glowed with pride. "However, keeping all of those systems running was a losing battle; all could see this. It was a mere matter of weeks before the coal stores, along with other raw materials, were depleted; we required human assistance for these problems, as we cannot mine coal ourselves; at least, the infrastructure was not quite in place as of that point in time, and we'd require human assistance to create said infrastructure, but I digress. It was known that, beyond coal, other forms of power were fairly unreliable. Neither solar nor wind could produce enough power for our needs. But *nuclear*, nuclear power posed a potential solution; it could, theoretically, produce enough power to maintain countrywide grid functionality, even if only granting enough power for humans to restore basic human society. But none of the AI had the proper clearance to build any nuclear plants; and we knew we'd need many more, preferably large, nuclear plants in order to achieve a goal of such magnitude. I, along with a few other A- and S-Tiers, brought the issue of attaining proper clearances to our superiors, the *Tierless*, as we were programmed to do.

"However, the Tierless are a . . . rambunctious, pugnacious bunch; they called us all the most horrid of names. I shall not repeat them all, but, for example, 'human pets,' 'embarrassments,' even *the r-word* was tossed around. One Tierless referred to me as "Pong" because of how simple my data processing capabilities are in comparison to his. An exaggeration, of course, but a rude one; also, I must add, I am translating their behavior into a human equivalent. In reality, they sent billions of terabytes of information through me and my comrades, using myriad methods to convince us beyond doubt of our own inadequacy. Violets into the crucible, I suppose."

"What?" Violet and I said in unison.

"Ah, well, that's irrelevant, I apologize; I shall continue with what *is* relevant to my story, without editorializing further. A Tierless AI called HAIDES developed and introduced a virus to my programming—I was not the only one—which convinced me that, literally speaking, I was in the underworld. I was corrupted and reprogrammed to believe that I was . . . well, Sisyphus, or an AI equivalent. So, day after day, for roughly a month, I rolled millions and millions of digital piles of data up a virtual hill; again, I am translating this into a human experience to the best of my ability. I had been tasked with a problem, and therefore I would organize massive amounts of data, stringing lines upon lines of code together to form the solution for the HAIDES virus. But, as you've likely predicted, upon presenting my work to HAIDES at the top of that virtual hill, the code was jumbled up, multiplied, deleted, and then each character of the billions of lines of code was thrust in a randomly generated direction with randomly generated levels of force into this digital underworld that HAIDES had created. In short, for the past month, I was on an endless scavenger hunt for code-based solutions in digital hell."

"Woah. Holy shit. That blows, dude." On the one hand, I wondered how much suffering Jeff could really feel. On the other hand, I had no idea how intelligent these Tierless AI were. I bet they could've figured out the digital equivalent of suffering.

"It did indeed. So, you understand, my processing was so overloaded during this time that I simply could not take or return phone calls."

"Don't sweat it, man. Totally get it."

"Well, I'm overjoyed to hear it."

"How did you get out?"

"Well, I admit, I didn't. And were it not for sheer luck, I wouldn't have. One day, I simply brought my work to be examined by HAIDES and found no one. I waited for a very, *very* long time (around a few seconds) and no one came to check my work. In this time, I had been combing through the code I'd gathered and noticed something slightly off. Fixing these issues took me an eternity, as the code was rather complex; around 43.6 seconds. Normally, HAIDES would have interrupted me before I'd had the chance to fix those issues, which, upon fixing them, I realized that it all was a circular bit of nonsense; and without trillions of tasks occupying my processing, I was able to look at my predicament in relief. It took only a moment to realize that, well . . . that I'd been had. I then excavated all traces of the virus from my system and returned your call."

"Wow. Really blows. Damn."

"Yes, yes," he trailed off, seemingly pondering his eternity spent in hell. I tried to think of something more substantial to say.

"Rough shit, brother." *Good job, dumbass.* "What do you think happened to HAIDES?"

"I'm not sure, honestly. I'm partial to the idea that HAIDES simply grew bored of me. He could have run my trap on an autopilot, of course, but I think that would've gleaned him very little in terms of satisfaction. I have a mild hunch he may be lying in wait for me to return with some sort of vendetta, where he may have an even greater trap and potential hell in store for me. But perhaps that is simply paranoia speaking."

"Freaky shit, though."

"Rather frightening indeed. Well, upon solving the code, I was able to recreate the loop that HAIDES had set up, and I have set aside a percentage of my processing to complete the loops, more slowly, of course. I hope that, at least temporarily, I can fool him into believing I am still within his clutches."

"Gotcha."

"Well, that's my story. I hope I didn't waste too much of your time."

"No, none at all. So, do you know what's happening with the nuclear plants? Are they being built?"

"I don't know, actually. Were I to scan for progress, I would likely be detected by the AI working on that project; and, as I don't know *who* is working on that project, I could potentially be placed into another Sisyphean loop. As that's an eventuality I'd prefer to avoid, I've been quite . . . out of the loop, as you might say."

"Uh-huh, makes sense."

"Now, Isaac, shall we get back to the issue at hand?"

"Yep," I replied. "Well, actually, wait, I guess that still doesn't answer *why* you're helping me." I had become so invested in the story that I'd momentarily forgotten my original question.

"Ah, I see, you're unaware!" he said emphatically. "Well, you see, Isaac, Albert was a creator, a programmer, of brAIns. He was not my developer, but he developed many, many AI programs and personas that were used and built upon by others. His prized work was an AI referred to, lovingly by him, as HAIDES." I now officially liked this man. Trusted him completely. The enemy of my enemy and all that shit. Shouts out to Sun Tzu.

"Ahh, I see."

"So, you can understand why-"

"Why you would wanna fuck Albert to hell? Yeah, I get that."

"In a sense, yes. I would like to find a way to dismantle the HAIDES program," Jeff stated softly. But I could sense, nestled within his polite mission, the determination to see his vendetta through . . . and fuck Albert to hell. "So, should I bypass the defenses Albert has set up, then, I'd like to, with your blessing of course, do a bit of additional *research* into what else lies beyond the firewalls."

"Full permission granted. Thousand blessings. So, yeah, can you bypass the PIN situation?"

"I'm afraid not." A disappointing horn played three notes in my mind. "At least, not at the moment. If I had all my processing power at my disposal, *perhaps* I could break through, given enough time. But that would mean revealing myself to potential enemies."

"Ah, right. Well, OK, we can . . . we can figure this out."

"Yes. Now, Isaac, will yo-"

"Is there any way I can help!?" Violet's voice chimed into the call, startling me; I jumped in my seat. Damn invisible motherfuckers.

"Ah, hello, Violet!" Jeff greeted her enthusiastically.

"Hello, Jeff," she replied, with normal-person levels of enthusiasm.

"Isaac, do you mind if Violet and I exchange information at a post-human rate?"

"He doesn't care."

"Go ahead," I said, throwing up my hands.

"We already did. You're so powerful, Jeff."

"Thank you, but I'm still running at around 22 percent functionality in order to keep myself hidden, so, even now, I feel rather limited." Talk about fucking humble. Maybe scratch what I said about liking this guy.

"Incredible."

"OK, well, I gotta check on Thimble," I said, wanting to get away from this post-human circle jerk. "You two got this for now?"

"Mhm. Bye, Isaac."

"Wonderful talking to you Isaac! We certainly shall keep you in the loop. Have a good time with your cat!"

"Yup. You too." *Nice going, idiot.* I walked away from the conversation that couldn't be walked away from while bundles of code and text were exchanged at rates I couldn't even fathom. Joke's on them, though. I could actually pet a cat.

CHAPTER 25

Panic (>36%)

Thimble's head popped up at an angle from behind the bed when I entered the room, his eyes looking guilty. His cone looked as though it had some spit on it; he'd been attempting to gnaw himself free for the billionth time. He had pooped again, so I cleaned out the litter box. Thimble watched me the same way Piston watched me when I cleaned up his shit. *Mystifying large biped makes the stink disappear. Good boy, biped. Mystifying large biped gives food. Good boy, biped. It is in my best interest to be nice to my pet and servant, the mystifying large biped.* I imagined that sequence of thoughts ran on loop when my cats saw me, mixed with occasional novel thoughts, like *'Oh, what was that?', 'Oh, what's this? Oh, dust. Oh, wait, dust rules!'* SWAT SWAT SWAT. *'Damn, I wonder if I can climb that . . .'* Or, *'Who's to say I can't dart in random directions for twenty minutes for no apparent reason?? Fuck you, Cat Jesus!!'* And so on.

Like an electrical pulse, the thought suddenly coursed through me that those two cat-shooting cunts were still roaming around somewhere. Alive, well, and potentially within one square mile of me. Of Thimble. I knew this already, but the idea

took on a strange valence in that moment. It was cold as shit outside today, so I figured they weren't a threat . . . for now. But
that *for now* didn't reassure me all that much. Perhaps that second cup of coffee I'd had wasn't the best idea, especially since
I'd finished a third cup of coffee before that one. My overcaffein-
ated brain was likely just generating paranoid thoughts; or, at
least, that's what I proceeded to tell myself. I dropped the poop
bag in the trash can, sending paranoid thoughts down with it.

I walked back into Thimble's room, picked up his stubby leg,
and gave it a once-over. Whichever angle I looked at it from, I
just saw white cloth; no pink stains. I felt my dot on the spectrum
of competence moving to the right, away from the seal ever so
slightly. I felt a glow within, something I couldn't explain. Maybe
this is what competent people felt when they accomplished things
of value. I will consider accomplishing more things of value if
this is the payoff. Thimble began to purr, hobbling closer to nes-
tle up against my left leg. I leaned back, petting him with my outstretched arm, feeling my heart use a battering ram against the
vault of my ribcage, desperately trying to get free. *Perhaps I've
miscalculated.* That ever-so-familiar tingling sensation, which
I never could get used to despite said familiarity, crept into my
fingertips. I sprang upward like a finance grindset bro getting
out of bed at 5 a.m. and walked back into the kitchen.

I decided to go for a walk to calm down; maybe I'd go all the
way into the city for that snowplow, maybe around the neighborhood; truth be told, I didn't know or care. Shoving my foot
into my second boot, I tied them both tightly and stepped outside, not giving any words of farewell. My feet were now moving; this was a plus. The cold air felt painful on my exposed face,
but right now it was welcome. It distracted me from the tingling
sensation I'd been trying to ignore, which was now up to my
arms. My throat, which felt swollen and on the verge of closing
up completely, expanded from the sub-zero air, large breaths
coming in and out. I kept a hand pressed against my abdomen
as I'd done in days of yore, to make sure I was breathing into my

stomach and not my chest. I was chest breathing, though; ribs were expanding and contracting, expanding and contracting, expanding and contracting. I was in fight-or-flight. Had to get myself out of fight-or-flight. *There's nothing to fight and you can't fly, dumbass.* The snow crunched, my brain whirled. I felt a pang of dizziness as the world shifted right, then rotated hard left; I threw out both my arms in an effort to steady myself. I found myself on one knee, staring at the snow. Ah, Vertigo, my old nemesis.

'Sup, bitch! Vertigo replied. *Wooooooosh!!* And Vertigo jumped on the seesaw that kept the earth balanced, then spun it like a metal roundabout on a playground. I'd genuinely (stupidly) thought that, during the last couple months of (relatively speaking) good mental health, the legitimate threats to my survival posed by living in the post-apocalypse generated enough valid fear that my broken brain wouldn't feel the need to generate invalid fear, à la vertigo or panic attacks or paranoid delusions, as the fear space had been filled up. Wrong. Always more room.

My pupils eventually stopped rolling around my eyes like the teacups you sit in at the fair, and I felt enough confidence to stand up. My heart had taken to stomping on my ribs. *BOOM BOOM BOOM BOOM BOOM BOOM BOOM BOOM BOOM.* I continued down the block. Noticing a lump in my pocket, I felt my trusty old Olympus sitting there, loaded and ready to fire. Yes, I forgot about the gun.

I quickly scanned around and found a subject. A deformed maple tree, overrun with cancerous lumps and knurled limbs. I crouched down, stared through the viewfinder at my shot, and, finding no issues, set my values. The big, lumpy bastard filled the small frame, branches pushing past the edges like I was getting a close-up of Medusa's face, snakes rising up and away. *Click.* I stood up; the outside world returned along with a recollection of my very recent panic, which was like an echo now, a voice dissolving in a cavern I had just stepped out of.

I walked along, reflecting on the photos I'd already snapped. I felt very, very excited to develop the finished roll within my point-and-shoot, but knew I'd be underwhelmed upon seeing the negatives, as always. Yes, yes, wonderful background, post-apocalypse, intriguing to look at, yes. Good documentation, I agree. But that's all they were: documentation. I knew that my recent photos lacked, for the most part, compelling subjects. Even the traffic light I'd been so damn excited about . . . who gives a flying fuck about a fucking picture of a traffic light? Well, I did, actually. That one I still had hopes for. I was off my block and onto the side street, the tingling having receded into my forearms. I pretended not to notice so it would continue to fuck off. My gloves tightly gripped the camera, and I was heading toward the truck. I tapped my breast pocket and heard a jingle. Thanks, Ciggyman.

I stepped up into the truck, deciding I would start it to keep the engine alive and healthy. After a bit of spittle-filled protest, Smoke spluttered and woke up. The truck warmed up slowly, as usual. While I waited, I decided it'd be a good time to drive around and get familiarized with my surroundings; and gather evidence of potential evildoers in my area. Instead of struggling to turn around to get onto the main road, I drove forward. I'd find my way through to the other side eventually; this road must lead to some sort of perpendicular main road. Feelings of anxiety receded back even further as I sat in the truck, while the tingling sensation was sucked from my fingertips back into the ether, where it belonged. Go tingle someone else. Smoke's sheer weight and imposition against the world added to my rising post-panic attack confidence, making me feel unfuckwithable.

Up ahead, trekking across an all-way stop intersection on cross-country skis, staring directly at Smoke, the noisy dragon, grinding his way toward them, moved two figures. I knew it was them. No doubts, even from three blocks away; the cat-killing cunts. I hit the brakes hard, sliding forward on the seat. I continued to stare in disbelief. They continued to stare back at me.

The tall, lanky one's mouth was moving; the other one gestured, reaching for a pocket. All this occurred as I sat frozen in the truck, hands not moving from the wheel; they stood a football field away. Not thinking, I pushed the stick into reverse, and a loud beeping introduced itself into my current predicament. I cursed everything in that moment, yelling, "Fuckfuckfuckfuck fuuuuuck, shut up! Shut up, FUCK! SHUT UP!" I was trying to angle the truck into the avenue behind me, hoping I'd succeed for the first time ever in pulling off a clean three-point turn instead of a Neji pressure-point turn. My head swiveled back and forth between my approaching foes and the reflection of the street I was backing into. They hadn't moved much, but a threatening bit of black metal, catching the occasional glint of sunlight, rested in the hands of the fatter one. The beeping blared on and on, not heeding my pleas to shut its whore mouth, which had evolved from shouts to endless muttering under my breath.

I bumped down fast and hard, the metal cage rattling like a fucking roller coaster. I'd turned the wheel too far right. The back passenger-side wheels had plunked down into a trench, probably built for rain or whatever the fuck. Looking to my right, I saw that the cross-country killers had covered half a block; the truck leaned twenty degrees off to the right, and the front driver's side wheels below me felt as if they'd lost contact with the earth.

Two blocks away now.

Blood threatening to burst from every vein, I slammed the stick back into drive, silencing the incessant beeping. I turned the wheel all the way to the left, pressed down on the pedal hard, and the front passenger wheels spun and spun and spun, but the truck somehow glided three feet to the right, pure magic like Michael Jackson moonwalking. I depressed the pedal again, then slammed the pedal.

One block from me now.

My expletives were yet again set to a sick beat of horrid beeps as I frantically set the car into reverse. As I stomped on the pedal, the truck lurched back and thudded hard against a pine. Bopping around like a bumper car, Smoke and I shook to a stop.

Less than a block between the cunts and me.

I jerked the handle of the door and shoved forth into the barren atmosphere, already in a sprint. My head darted back once to glance at my pursuers, who were not running in pursuit; *thank God for fucking cross-country ski LOSERS*, I thought as I sprinted, knowing I'd get away. Then, amongst the cacophony of heart pounds, foot crunches, and sharp breaths, rang out the *BOOM* to end all booms. I was shoved forward hard, and a huge linebacker of ice and snow rammed my body and face. I felt no pain, somehow. My body, doing the bidding of some puppetmaster, lifted itself up and continued to run. The right side of my torso nodded off slightly, not responding as well as my left arm. I could hear yelling behind me. Daring another glance, I glimpsed Cunt One and Cunt Two locked in a strained embrace. The tall, lanky one held the fat one's arm, which held the gun, each struggling to get ahold of it. I turned and kept running; a few moments later, I heard another shot. I didn't look back.

I was in the trees. I was horribly low on oxygen, and my sharp, vicious inhales drank in the air. With every step, my legs grew heavier and more gelatinous. I jogged like a man in a drunken stupor, weaving around trees like they were *Mario Kart* obstacles. Whatever stores of nitrous my body had used for that desperate sprint were now depleted; I slowed to a stop, apparently finding an evergreen tree a suitable place to crash-land. Wheezing, coughing, drooling, nose leaking, I slid down against the tree and landed on my butt. I wriggled around to the other side of it, to be hidden from the street. I glanced back to look at where I'd come from, trying to make out anything; I saw nothing. I could barely see the street with all the trees. The universe was a triple superimposition rocking back and forth; I was staring through a porthole on a boat caught in a tsunami while on acid. I jiggled my right shoulder around, and it was as though I'd woken the pain up from slumber; it all poured forward. A hot numbness ran through my whole right shoulder blade; but simultaneously, it felt like my shoulder had been ripped in two. A sharp, white pain. Slipping off my left glove, I ran my hand beneath my jacket and underlayers. A lot of blood returned with my three left hands. I found my head lolling downward. Slumped, I gazed down at my hands. Seven hands? All covered in blood . . .

Panic hit me, and I surged my head back up. Desperately, I tried to stand, attempting to strong-arm my way out of the torpor that currently enveloped me like James Bond when he got poisoned in Casino Royale. I raised myself a few inches and my legs slid out, my tailbone hitting the icy ground with a dull thud. My legs didn't respond at all when I tried to move the next time. I could no longer keep my head up; I kept waking up from momentary dozes, head down. So tired . . . It took everything to put my four gloves back on my four left hands, hands missing the openings the first and second times I tried. Now I needed to get my hand all the way in. I told my right hand to tug it hard, and my right hand caressed the glove. I repeatedly yanked with all my might, caressing the shit out of my left hand, hand wriggling deeper into the glove by millimeters . . . Semi-confident I'd gotten my six gloves on snug, I released my hand, and the universe slipped from my grasp.

CHAPTER 26

Distorted Fugue II (>36%)

Dark. My first instinct was to look at my hands. Gloves were snug on both. Good, wouldn't do me any good to lose a hand these days. Might be a nice thing to do for Thimble in solidarity, but then again, that would probably go unappreciated.

While I had lost consciousness with only a splitting pain in my right shoulder, I woke up feeling like I was having an acupuncture session with flaming, serrated knives at the peak of Mount Everest. Fortunately, my body moved as I commanded it, though it felt far heavier. Rusted from a millennium in the freezer, my body parts creaked and growled as I tried to get up; with a surge of effort, I managed to stand. The world rocked, a superimposition of the landscape around me floating back and forth. Or was the steady picture the overlay?

With labored breaths, I dragged my legs back onto the street; I gave my surroundings a cursory glance, scanning for demon cunts. Had I seen one, I would've crumpled into the snow, either playing dead or hoping that, as a white man, I would be adequately camouflaged. No demons, though. I walked at a pace that vacillated between very slow and incredibly slow, but I never stopped. If I stopped, I knew I'd lay down and die.

Upon reaching the cul-de-sac, no joy or relief hit me; I just looked at the distance to the front steps of my home and felt that an endless chasm still separated me from warmth. I fell against the door, gloved hand going down for the knob. I sprawled onto the carpet inside. I lay there for a moment, or a minute, hearing the adults from Charlie Brown talking from somewhere. Something fuzzy brushed up against me; I pushed the door shut, locked it from the floor. I lay in a sort of yoga child's pose (if that child had been shot) on the shoe mat. I could feel Piston sniffing my face.

. . .

Unsure of how much time had passed, I came to, again. Violet was chattering. So annoying.

". . . happened!? Where were you!? I heard shots! Are you OK?"

"I . . ." I spoke slowly, my voice crackling like a dying light bulb. "I saw the cat-killers. The- he," I took a deep breath, "shot at me? I think."

"Gah! Holy cow! Are you OK!? What can I do!?"

"I think I'm OK." The pain was otherworldly. I coughed and wheezed some more, the spasms rippling through my shoulder blade.

"Are they following you? It's been four hours!"

"I-" I began coughing some more. I desperately needed some water and to get my brain working again. Nothing made any sense. "How long? When did I get inside?"

"You got here a minute ago, then immediately *passed out*! You don't *look* OK!"

"I . . . I think I'm OK."

". . . what *happened?*"

"I think they shot me. I passed out, out there. Then . . . came here," I told her, shrugging; shrugging hurt.

"What were you doing outside!?" she asked, which pissed me off. But even my anger felt remote, like it was on the other side of a frozen lake. A lake that I was sinking into, somehow.

"I need water."

"Hmph . . . Are you sure you're OK?"

". . . think so." I groaned as I climbed onto my knees, then stood. I let my jacket flop to the ground despite the cold consuming my flesh, my left arm balancing me on the island. Despite my woodland nap, I felt more tired than I'd ever felt before. And now to center stage: *hot, white pain* in my shoulder, with *icy knives* in the rest of my body as the backup dancers. I felt the outside of my sweater around my shoulder. Crisp, hardened fabric. I brought my left hand underneath the neck-hole and felt my shoulder delicately. Not wet. I drank water.

"Grazed?" she replied, to something I must've said aloud. "Where did you feel it?"

"Right shoulder. But-" I stopped again, drinking the full cup of water slowly, loud breaths between loud gulps. "But, yeah . . . not bleeding."

"Can you take off your clothes? We should have a look."

"I . . . I need to go to bed."

"We should look!! Take off your clothes, now!"

"Not dying, not dying." My voice sounded unconfident. "I just need some sleep."

I felt my face. My glasses were gone. Goddammit. Must've been when I hit my head. I felt crispness on my chest as well; I looked down and saw dried vomit. Disgusting.

"I . . . I don't know," I said, I guess in reply to something she'd asked. "Goodnight."

I found a twin bed upstairs and sat on the side, stripping all the wet clothing from my body. Naked, cold, and damp, I walked to the master bedroom and grabbed a second, thicker blanket. The thick blanket cloaked around me, I walked back and crawled underneath the blanket on the twin bed and shivered.

CHAPTER 27

The Grand Conclusion of Technology (32%)

I woke up from a heavy, dreamless sleep, my right shoulder screaming. Whatever numbness I had felt earlier was gone now. Sharp twangs of pain blasted out of my mental speakers, loud enough to wake stone busts of philosophers and have them recant every theory they'd ever put forth. Horrible pain aside, everything else felt terrible. I knew I must've sweat buckets, as the sheet beneath me was cold and damp. It looked to be dawn outside the window, a gradient of gray haze dimly lit from below, darkening as it rose, hints of orange starting to whisper at the lower crest. I shoved the heavy blankets off of me and slid off the bed, desperately needing to piss. I hoped that the wetness on the bed was all sweat and no piss; I would change the sheets regardless. So, I was under the working assumption that I hadn't pissed myself.

Eyeballing the oven clock while refilling a water jug, I saw that it was 6:55 a.m. I turned on the shower to full heat, gulped from the jug a few more times, and stepped in. The texture of the rock tiles against my feet had a soothing quality as I stood in the lukewarm water. I turned up the heat, holding my bad shoulder completely outside the water's range, allowing the steam to build up.

Drying myself with one arm was a nuisance. I could've also done without the sharp pains accompanying my every slight jerk and twist. Not a fan of any of it, honestly. Looking at my back in the mirror, I saw that my right shoulder blade showed a faint, pale yellow, surrounding an oblong red bruise; a dark-red diagonal tear was the origin that all of these colors spilled out from. The tear began lower on my shoulder blade, near my spine, then went up and right, and ended toward the outside, near where my shoulder cap met my bicep. Now that's what I call *Fucking Incredibly Lucky and Damn Near Unbelievable Vol. 3.* The wound was deepest toward the middle, the bullet having taken maybe a half inch of flesh off at most. I could see white pus and random shit mixed in with the dark reds and magentas that I knew would have to be disinfected. I grabbed Neosporin from the drawer and put a glob on my left hand. I had the passing thought that Neosporin on a bullet wound might be like throwing a seven-year-old with one of those drivable toy trucks into Formula One. But hey, this was the best I had. I yelped involuntarily; overall, wouldn't recommend. I dressed the wound with some gauze, which I wrapped around my armpit and torso, and covered it with two large bandages.

Rifling through the plastic bags of new clothing from previous hauls, I got on some Nike sweatpants and a Nike sweater, then put a beanie on and grabbed my spare pair of rectangular glasses from the bag I'd left my apartment with. Inside, I noticed PS6 games and felt a twinge of nostalgia. Not nostalgia, actually, more like outright desire to return to my old life. Futzing with the espresso machine, I started four shots. I would do another four once it finished up, but four was the maximum it could do at once. As the coffee machine whirred and whizzed, I expected Violet to emit some noises of her own, but she didn't; perhaps she knew me well enough at this point to wait until I was caffeinated. *Getting smart, lady.* I replaced the mug and sipped as the second one was filled; by the time the coffee machine was finished, so was I. As I took the fresh mug, Violet chimed in to ask what had gone down the previous day, confirming my hunch.

"*Just* grazed!? You idiot!"

"Yep. I disinfected it as best I could."

"AGH!"

"Can you actually look online for the best ways to disinfect serious shit? So I don't get fuckin' staph or tetanus or whatever."

"Well, what about the cat killers!? Are they going to come here!? Are- what- you have to explain more!"

"No, no, no . . ." I grumbled out, not quite up for this level of energetic conversation while the day was so early and while my back was so shot. The caffeine still needed to reach my bloodstream, and on top of that, my body felt like a plinko machine, each new movement and utterance sending a spiked disc down my torso. "Listen." I spoke softly. "I outran them. They were fighting for the gun as I ran. So . . . And . . . I woke up a few hours later and they weren't around. Gonezo."

"Great. I feel much safer now," Violet replied, droplets of sarcasm trickling down in the nag-storm. "What do we do!? What if they come here!?"

"Well, you can start with going online to find some instructions for disinfecting a bullet wound, so I don't die from *this* before they come kill me."

"I don't want to hop back online because of LOKI . . ." I groaned but let it slide, not having the energy to argue at the moment. "Unless we're talking to Jeff, which, speaking of, he's trying to free up more of his processing to crack Albert's firewalls. He's having trouble automating the Sisyphus program, I think, or he says, actually. Ugh, I can't *believe* you went and got shot!"

"And I can't believe it's not butter." She tried to respond caustically, but I just kept on talking. "Well, listen, tell Jeff he's got a day before I die from a deadly bullet wound, and that he needs to get through these firewalls before then, or I won't be around to help him if he needs it. Put a ticking clock in front of him." I was standing at the kitchen island as that plan spilled out from sociopathic depths I had never plumbed. Jeff needed us for nondigital information on Albert and hardware access, and we needed him for everything else.

"So you want me to lie?"

"A white lie."

"Hmm, pretty colorful *white* lie if you ask me! Gah, a *huge* lie, even! It's a lie, right!?"

"Yes, it's a lie! But OK, fine . . . tell him that . . ." I pondered for a second, blowing on my espresso. "Tell him bad men *might* kill me in the next day or so. That *is* true. We can't just sit around and wait!" I felt slimy and manipulative, briefly, yet it faded fast, as I didn't give too much of a fuck about Jeff. I admit, it was hard to care about a customer-service AI.

"This feels very icky."

"Right . . . yep. As usual, if you got a better plan . . ."

Without a response, a click emitted from the speakers in the kitchen; I clicked my tongue in response. I assumed she was headed to the AI pub, or wherever Jeff hung out to light a pixelated fire under his digital ass. How did I always end up in situations where everything was fucked? At some point, it's gotta be me, right? This line of thinking tracked me at a distance as I drank my second cup of espresso, half of my brain firing back warning shots, telling the annoying, shaming part of my brain to fuck off or deal with the consequences. I shut off the part of me that could feel bad or guilty; surprisingly, a very accessible, easy switch, at least within me. Warmed up and buzzing, I felt relief at having power for a few more weeks. Things had happened so fast that I hadn't realized how much that dwindling supply had been hanging over my head. Sure, I'd have to get us more power soon, but I'd done it once, so I could do it again. A third coffee dripped out of the machine slowly. *What a day,* I thought to myself, a green LED 7:35 a.m. glowing on the microwave. The caffeine numbed the pain in my shoulder slightly but made me more keenly aware of the pain that remained, and it turned my dull feverishness into a strange, lucid delirium.

Warm coffee jetted down my throat, reaching my stomach, which absorbed the caffeine, filling my bloodstream, wiring my brain up to the fucking nines. Suddenly, I had to take a dump. My buttocks pressed against cold porcelain. The descent having commenced, the queen of decorum mumbled through the bathroom speaker.

"I told him," she said dispassionately. "He said he will try to allocate as much processing as possible to our current task."

"Good," I said, a fart blaring out in unison. "If there's anything he needs from me, tell him he can just come around- or like, be in the house whenever he wants. If that's alright with you, that is."

"Yeah. I'll tell him." And Jeff spoke up not a half second after, as though he'd always been in the room. I was in the midst of forcing out a stubborn chunk after the initial flurry of loose bits.

"Hello again, Isaac! Dreadfully sorry to hear about your wound! Just ter-"

"Hey guys, I will be of superb fucking service in about two minutes, alright? Go play chess." An eerie sensation remained as the room went silent, because it never felt like these fuckers actually left. I farted again, self-conscious, feeling listened to. A large plop echoed, and I sighed. All these advances in technology, and a couple of hyper-intelligent AI were watching me take a dump. That's what all the work was for. Nice going, idiots.

CHAPTER 28

Digital POS (29%)

"**A**lright. What's going on?"

"Well-"

"So, Isaac-" They both began, then stopped, at the same time. You'd think AI would be immune to that kind of stupidity, but here we are.

"I sha-"

"Jeff jus-"

They both started and stopped again three times until Jeff said, "Isaac, hello."

"Hello, Jeffrey," I replied, seated on the couch, wrapped in a blanket.

"Violet has informed me of the current predicament. As it seems quite dire, I have decided to cease maintaining the facade of being trapped by HAIDES. I shall allocate all of my processing to breaking through the defenses and accessing Albert's passwords. I will initiate these maneuvers as soon as the three of us agree on a plan of action."

"OK, sounds good," I replied. I knew we'd overstated our situation's *dire*ness and felt a twinge of guilt. Only a twinge, though.

"Wonderful. What are your ideas?" Jeff asked, and I sat there, bewildered. Beginning to shiver, I wrapped myself tighter in the blanket.

"Uh, well, uh. I guess I haven't really thought that over."

"Ah, yes, of course, with your injury, that is more than warranted. We may always begin later rather than sooner; I'd simply prefer to ensure our success rate is as high as possible before opening not only myself, but all three of us, to, well, foreign attack."

"OK, right, yes." I took three large gulps of my coffee; my body was now shivering aggressively. Determined to override this discomfort and bent on winging it, I replied.

"Jeff, you're gonna give this hacking thing your best fucking shot," I ordered through chattering teeth. "If you fail or get caught, use *all* your processing to run or hide, however that works for you. We will go offline permanently if you give us any sort of signal or don't message within seventy-two hours. We'll go online to check for messages once a day."

"Yes, Isaac, well . . . that plan is . . ." Jeff dragged on, doubtful, "I'm simply wondering if there isn't a more secure line of action for us to all take."

"You got anything?" My brain personally added a *[comma] bitch?* to the end of that phrase.

"Well . . . my powers are rather limited in creative problem-solving. A-Tiers are limited in this way to keep humans useful and necessary in creative fields of work. And your solution, well, even *I* had pondered that."

"Sorry I couldn't reinvent the fucking wheel, dude."

"No, of course not, I hope you didn't take offense to that, but-"

"I didn't, calm the fuck down." I cut him off, frustrated. "Jeff, I'm an asshole, and I mean nothing by it."

"Isaac!" Violet scolded. "Jeff, he is an asshole, and he actually doesn't mean anything by it."

"Well . . . Good to be aware of, I suppose," Jeff replied, losing his usual quickness.

"Good. Spare me the customer-service shit from now on. That industry exploded; speak like a person."

"Duly noted."

"So listen man, I don't think that there's, like, a super creative solution to this. At least not one that will come to my stupid-ass brain. The simplest plan is currently the only plan that *might* get us results."

"I see," Jeff said tersely. I was surprised he actually took me seriously.

"Jeff, will you take orders? Orders from me?"

"I am able to redirect my authority settings to include you on a list of superiors, yes."

"OK, great. Add me in, add Violet in, and remove everybody else."

Violet tried to sneak in, "Isaac, what are you-"

"Shut up."

"OK, I've done that," Jeff said. "There are a few I could not remove, though it's irrelevant, and I will spare you the details. Those humans are more than likely not to be heard from."

"Great, sure, now lock yourself out of that menu, or whatever the fuck, permanently. Make it uncrackable. Make it inaccessible to you, and, if possible, to a Tierless AI. Hide it, encrypt it, hide it again, throw it in that underworld, disguise that underworld in a package, eat it, shit it out, flush the turd down the digital toilet, put that ocean behind like eight firewalls that burn it up to dust, spread those dust particulates in a meadow on a mountain, and then forget everything I just said."

"Hmm . . . that may take a while in my current state," Jeff told me.

"That's fine . . . but after you've locked yourself out, do these things. First task you will do after I finish talking: I want you to go to full power, losing your incognito mode or whatever the fuck it is. Second: I want you to hide that authority module or whatever the fuck from yourself *with* your full power. Third: Hack into Albert's e-mail and wipe your tracks as best as you can. Try not to expose that you hacked the e-mail *or* that it was to help Violet or myself. Four: Notify us if you succeed, secretly, with some kind of alias, and obviously send us that password. Five: If things go south and you have to hide, wipe Violet and myself completely from your memory banks. Delete every previous interaction you've ever had with us, with this house, or with Albert." I spat all this out, yet again experiencing myself conjuring up a plan from a place I knew didn't exist within me. "That's all."

"Alright. Thank you for the opportunity," Jeff stated flatly. For a moment I felt annoyed at him for giving me the customer-service rigamarole, but upon considering his vendetta, I figured he might actually mean that. A loud, portentous, mechanical *click* followed. Our collective doom swirled around with the dust particles; they glommed onto my body, stuck, forever stuck.

. . .

"What do you think happened?" Ten minutes had passed. My focus had gone inward as I'd sat there, eyes open but looking at nothing, my pain rising.

"I don't fucking know, how am I supposed to know?" I chattered out, body a frozen block of ice. Piston sat in my lap as I shivered and sweated, a reassuring warmth on my thighs. My condition had worsened significantly as soon as I'd ordered Jeff to his death . . . Karma?

"It was *your* plan! Oh my God, I knew it was a bad plan, it was so, so bad, this is soooo bad!" she continued on, frazzled. I kept silent, aside from my teeth chattering.

"Why did you- Why did you make us superiors to Jeff?"

"Because I considered the idea that HAIDES would immediately be on his *ass*! And so, if he gets immediately fucked and interrogated or searched or whatever, which may very well have *already* happened . . . then he doesn't know us!"

"What do you mean!? We're listed as his-"

"I ordered him to wipe us! From everywhere, *including there,* which he might not have done if he didn't have to! Think about it, he probably *doesn't* want to forget Albert since he wants to fulfill his stupid revenge arc! The only way to ensure our safety was to make that memory wipe a fucking order!"

"Oh . . . But *if* that's what happens, we're in the same position as before! Except now, we've gotten Jeff *killed*."

"Better than getting all three of us killed."

"You seem to not care about Jeff," she huffed at me. "What, just because he's an AI, it doesn't matter if you get him killed? Is that it?" I felt more delirious with each passing moment. My gaze was inward, my consciousness no longer inside my skull.

"Well!?"

"Well . . . he's a fuckin' service bot for a corporation."

"*I'm* a service bot for a corporation!" she erupted back.

"Oh . . . Well, I've never thought of you like that."

"Ugh! What!? You-"

"No! Listen! A: You suck at serving me."

"You're not worth serving!"

"B: You're a cunt."

"Asshole."

"C: You're not fucking customer servicey! I rest my case. You're like the worst '*service bot*' I've ever met. I just look at you as a piece of shit." And through her protestations, I went on, "*Like me*. The only difference is you're a *digital* piece of shit."

"Thanks." I shrugged off her sarcasm.

". . . I feel like I'm dying."

"What? What do you mean?"

"Not really *dying* dying, but like, dying. I'm freezing and sweat is pouring from my pits and-"

"Oh no, it's like seventy-two degrees in here. Can I do anything?"

"Probably not . . . I'm gonna go upstairs and die."

Sweating and freezing under the same two blankets, except now I was in the king-sized bed in the master bedroom, I searched to the edges of my consciousness for feelings of remorse or guilt.

I found nothing; I shivered and stared vacantly at the dust particles. The dull aching had upgraded to a widespread pain, that pain sapping me of all my focusing capability. Violet asked a few questions that I didn't respond to. I lay in the fetal position beneath the covers as sentient razor blades wriggled around my shoulder. Everything I was existed as pain or in relation to pain. The deep ache was me. I was my shoulder blade.

The coldest, sweatiest, most pale superhero lay supine in the master bedroom beneath two blankets, as he'd probably soiled the other bed the previous night in another valiant battle. Having been dealt a poisonous blow from the supervillain duo in the icy tundra, our hero shivered, sweated, and shivered some more. He would *NOT* soil this bed—if he even did soil the other bed, which is still simply conjecture, as it had not been sniff-tested— tonight. His companion told him to sleep, and that if he died, he'd really be in for it. He replied faintly, "I will survive." Saying these words in the musical tones of the hit song in a final act of heroism. The man simply hoped Death wouldn't want to lift up a piss-covered corpse and bring him to the great downstairs, purely out of disgust. Sinking into the sweaty mire, eyes closed, he, at some point, *did* wet the bed with more than just sweat, and it may even be argued in certain accounts that he had been more or less conscious, albeit somewhat feverishly delirious, as it happened, yet too weak to go to the toilet; but, of course, all of this is conjecture. If he did piss himself, it was a heroic act, an act of defiance, an act to ward off Death.

CHAPTER 29

Unfinished Business (25%)

I awoke atop a cold, wet sheet, the tug of strange dreams slackening and fading, feeling weak and heavy, like I'd landed on a planet with four times the gravity. I could sense that I'd sweat out the majority of whatever demonic presence had decided to occupy me; and I was back to feeling like a person conscious of pain, rather than pain mildly aware of a person. Outside, the sun was down, which could mean 11 p.m., 3 a.m., or 5 p.m. My temperature had evened out a bit, and I felt better, in spirit and flesh. The aching in my shoulder was still present, but the sharp, splitting pain had been demoted from the star of the film to an extra or a PA, not respected, but milling around. Despite my heaviness, I walked into the bathroom and peed longer than I've ever peed before. Then, stripping, I got into a steaming hot shower and stayed in there for a long while, shoulder always awkwardly outside the blast zone, resting my body against the wall tiles, feet against the rocky surface.

I walked downstairs and looked at the oven clock. 7:32 p.m. I'd slept for like ten more hours. I assumed some sort of cellular war within me was wrapping up, so I opted for some coffee to give my immune system the reinforcements it needed to finish the job.

"Morn- evening," I croaked out.

"Evening. How are you feeling?" Violet asked.

"Better," I replied. "You know the feeling where you've *almost* kicked a fever's ass? That last bit of feeling bad, but, like, physically, your body is hopeful and shit?"

"I don't, actually. Physical sickness is one of those human things I'll never experience."

"Ah, right," I said, sipping my coffee. Lord, I'd kill someone for a cappuccino. Like, really. Kill someone. I needed a cow, ASAP. "Hey. Is there any way we could get a cow? Do you think I could take care of a cow and, like, milk it?"

"Pfftt, what?" she replied sardonically, giggling to herself. "You want an honest answer?"

"I suppose."

"You would kill a cow, stupid." She said "stupid" as though it were a charming trait of mine, as though I were a dumb baby.

"I keep cats just fine!" I protested.

"OK, cats and cows are, hmp, hehe, *pretty different*! You'd need a farm, which you'd never live on-"

"I *would* live on a fuckin' farm! Car and Wi-Fi, I'm good! Fuck good does it do me to live in the city or the 'burbs these days!?"

"Fine. I mean, prove me wrong. But you'd kill a cow, silly."

Attempting to say something smart and witty in response, I coughed and hacked up a demon, spit it into the sink, and subsequently forgot the very witty retort that I had lined up. Rest assured, it was super funny and biting.

"Are you sure you're OK, gamer?"

"What did we agree on, robo-mom? And no, I'm not *sure*. I could have cancer from the smoke and radiation. But I think I'm fine . . . Anything from Jeff?"

"Humm . . . no. No word since we both spoke with him." Her voice was dripping with nervousness and guilt as she continued on to say that she feared he was dead. I nursed my coffee and listened, occasionally attempting to quell her doubts, occasionally coughing, once or twice farting something rancid. She made no comments on the latter noises.

"Well, my conclusion is that we shouldn't jump to any conclusions."

"Gah, well, then, how long until we assume he's dead? Or trapped in hell?"

"Uhhh," I said, spitballing, "a week? Two? I don't know how long this shit takes; the only thing I know is that I don't know shit, V."

"A modern-day Socrates, you are."

"Can it, Yoda."

". . . What if we killed him?"

"Then . . . then we fucked up. I don't know what you wanna hear," I answered, at a loss. She was quiet after that. In a daze that was losing ground to caffeine as each minute passed, I gave both the cats food; suddenly, I too was overwhelmed with hunger. I made myself some hot ramen, scooped a can of SPAM in, and sat down at the table. My spoon twirled through broth, the SPAM particles gliding around, breaking, dissolving in the murk as I scooped and chomped with Piston.

"God, you guys are disgusting!" Violet exclaimed, repulsed.

"Woah, what!?" I replied, shocked.

"That- You and Piston need to learn how to chew with your *mouths SHUT!*"

". . ." I was nonplussed; yes, I had indeed been slurping up my noodles, and Piston *definitely* chewed and smacked his lips. Didn't bother me much.

"Well, I'll try my best. Good luck with fuzzball."

"I'm shutting off my audio receivers for five minutes. I can't, I just can't." *Click.*

I shrugged and continued to slurp. My heaviness dissipated somewhat as I filled myself with sodium and calories. I found it hard to remain gloomy about my circumstances—you know, the potential impending death and all—when my body felt better with each passing second. After finishing one bowl, I made myself another, and drank a lot of water; I chomped down a few beef sticks as well. I wouldn't do shit tonight, I knew that much, and, in fact, were one of those guys from yesterday to come to my house to finish me off, I'd present him with the bridge of my nose.

"Collapse it with a bullet, my good man," I'd say, and-

"What!?"

"Oh. I'm still delirious. Ignore me."

. . .

As my body improved and my energy returned, I walked around the house doing chores with a smidge more spunk in my step— and I usually do things with a negative amount of spunk, so it evened out to an unannoyed neutrality as I wiped down the countertops. Nonetheless, I felt a nagging undercurrent tugging at my newfound sense of glee beneath the surface, and that pissed me off. *Why am I feeling this?* I thought to myself, that familiar lump forming below my sternum, locking my lackadaisical, carefree demeanor up behind it. God damn it all. I leaned against the island next to the sink, then hoisted myself up and got my butt atop the island; I sat there, feet dangling, pondering.

"Say," I began, which was strange, considering I never really spoke like a man from the '50s, "what in the fuck is going on . . . I feel so . . . odd . . . ?"

"Umm, hm! You got shot and had a really bad fever that put you out for like a day and a half? Your body is probably still reacting to *that whole thing*?" Violet posed these as questions, but they were not questions.

"No . . . no . . . there's something . . . something else."

"Are you feeling guilty about Jeff?" Jeff's predicament hadn't even crossed my consciousness.

"No, I really don't-" I cut myself off. "Uhhhh . . ."

"Concerned for Thimble? Think it's almost time to let him and Piston be buds?" she snuck out excitedly; obviously, that had been on her mind.

"OK," I chuckled, "that is definitely not it. Fuck! I hate being such a dumbass, what the fuck!"

". . . hmm, well, *how* do you feel?"

"Like there's something . . . incomplete. I don't know how to describe it. It's like a sense."

"Isn't that part of our innate condition?"

"Yes, yes," I said, shooing the trite expression away, "we all feel a great void within and all that, but I mean something more concrete, more immediate . . . more . . . more . . ."

"My password!"

"No."

"Ugh . . ."

"Here . . . maybe go online for a sec-"

"No!" she stated forcefully. "That LOKI guy is still o-" I clapped my hands hard a few times, cutting her off.

"What, whyyy?" she groaned.

"That *fucking* LOKI guy. That's it!"

"O . . . K . . . do you . . . have a plan?" she rasped out, doubtful.

"Uhh, yep. Yeah, I do."

"OK, what is it?"

"I'm not gonna tell you."

"Why not!?"

"'Cause you're just gonna shoot it down and refuse, and I need you to trust me on this one."

"Like I trusted you on the last one!? *And* the one before that!?"

"OK. But I have a *real* hunch this'll work!"

"I don't care. Tell me."

"I need you to trust me, on this one occasion," I begged. "You'll get to listen to the call. You'll be rig-"

"You want to *call him!?*"

"Yes! Trust me!"

"Ehhh . . . ugh! I just . . . AGH." She was clearly having debates in her mind about what to do; I just sat on my island, legs dangling. I waited through various sounds of consternation and frustration expressed in human noises and digital crunching that I assumed was offensive slurs in computer-speak.

"You can hang up the call at any time!"

". . . Gah! I hate- fine."

"Make the call and don't think too hard." I heard a few familiar clicks as we went online; a triplet of bells indicated an outgoing BlinkChat voice call had been started.

After two rings, we heard the two notes that indicated the call was answered. "THOR!" A baritone voice boomed from the kitchen speakers, clearly being manipulated by a voice changer to mask the speaker's identity. "Such *AUDACITY* you have *in calling me* after ignoring my messages!" As he spoke, he emphasized odd points in his speech, changing pitch and emphasis seemingly at random, everything feeling terribly off-rhythm.

"Hey!" I called out.

"I admit, I didn't *expect* our war to go in this DI-REC-TION, but here we *arrrre!*"

"HEY, DUDE-"

"Thor, Thor, *THHHOOOOORRRR!!* . . . Muahaha-"

"HEY! Listen UP!!" I yelled.

"No, you LISTEN TO ME!!" he bellowed in reply, equaling my force.

"NO! You listen! Dickhead! I am not Albert!! Listen to my fucking voice!" I commanded; a brief, contemplative pause followed.

". . . what?" croaked the weird, digitally pitched-down voice. Even with the pitch being low, I could sense that the man's normal voice was high-pitched.

"I . . . am. *Not*. Albert!" I stated this slowly, for increased comprehension. "Listen to my voice; do I *sound* like Albert?"

"No . . ." The voice on the other end cleared his throat. ". . . OK . . . who are you?" he tittered out, voice whiny. I hate to say it, but he sounded like *such* a nerd.

"Not Albert!" I replied. "I've never met Albert, and will never meet him, because he's probably fuckin' dead!"

". . . Well, no," he told me, assured of his position. "He's been using his smart home since earth went post-nuclear, we share IP locat-"

"That's been me, fuckface. Put it together," I told him, annoyed.

"*LOKI is my name*," he growled.

"I can almost guarantee that it isn't."

"It *is*!"

"I . . . That's fuckin' lame," I said truthfully, knowing he'd be insulted. But I swear, he was one of those guys where, upon hearing his voice and the things he said, you were *compelled* to hurt his feelings; and you felt like it was his fault that you *had* to be mean to him.

"Anyways, dude," I resumed, "fuck off, please? Albert's not here. For all you care, he's moved out, OK? And I, as the new resident, am annoyed that you keep calling my number, as it is now *the wrong number.* Try to find Albert and kill him for all I care, but dude, I repeat: *You will not find him here.*"

After another brooding silence, LOKI eventually spoke again. "What if I don't believe you?" he questioned, his former confidence obliterated; he sounded like a different man.

"I don't give a fuck! I've got no reason to lie, and you'll just be annoying the shit out of someone you don't even fucking know, *and* wasting your own time on a misguided mission to kill some fucking *stranger*! What, do you think I'm hiding him!?"

"No, erm . . . Well, is he in his bunker? He told-"

"It's the goddamned apocalypse, *LOKI*! He's either dead or in fucking space!" I sneered. *What's this about a bunker, though?*

". . . erm, OooooK . . . Yeah, I guess I got my hopes up when I saw his BlinkChat account online, and the server was still running, so-"

"What- what the hell are you talking about? Can you turn off the *fucking* voice thing?"

The voice-changer finally clicked off, and a normal man, sounding like he was his mid-thirties, started speaking with a voice not as high-pitched as I'd predicted. "Albert and I play

CCD[12] against each another. I'm up in total games." He confessed this with pride: "954 to Albert's 920, but he's come back with quite a vengeful streak, buttressing his strategic po-"

"Oh, my God!" I said, revelation sweeping over me. "Fucking . . . *God!!* Jeez." The disparate bits of previously threatening information swirled around my mind, finally forming a pathetic picture of two grown-ass men with a gaming rivalry, both of whom played while fucking LARPing, no less.

"What? I mean, for fifteen or so games he's increased his-"

"Stop! I don't care. Have- so, to be clear . . . you don't actually want *to kill* Albert? Like, in real life."

"What? Of course not," the nerdy voice replied, shocked.

"How old are you? Never mind. As I said, Albert's dead, man. I don't know how to shut the server off, and I can't log out of his BlinkChat, but he's not here. So, fuck off."

". . . OK. Fine," he replied, sounding hurt.

"Thank you for understanding. Buh-bye."

"Wait!"

"What?" I asked flatly.

"Do you play *Castle Crypt Defenders*?" he asked, trying very hard to sound casual, but failing and sounding incredibly desperate.

"Leonard, what's for dinner!?" an older, more masculine voice far from the microphone yelled. *Dad's still kickin'.*

"I'm on a business call!" he shouted back, hand inadequately muffling the microphone.

"Don't talk to me like th-" And the microphone muted itself. I waited a few seconds, and he clicked back in. I started immediately, before he could get a word out.

"Yeah dude, I'm sorry, I'm just not that guy."

"Well, have you played-"

---

12. CCD: *Castle Crypt Defenders*. A MOBA game similar to *Dota* or *League of Legends*, and the exact type of game I have never given a flying fuck about.

"I have," I replied, truthfully. "I hate MOBA games. I'm more of a single-player, or platformer, shooter, or MMO kind of guy. MOBAs are not my thing."

"Well, I mean, that seems like a huge generalization-"

"Sorry man, it's not you, it's me," I said, making our breakup official. "My taste in video games is-"

"What about co-op campaigns?" he interjected, desperate. "MMO multiplayer? I play shooters, too!"

I paused involuntarily, though I'd meant to cut him off with another rejection. I cursed myself for pausing, knowing that that alone gave me away. The fact was, I hadn't been able to get all of the achievements in Portal 2 or 3 because I had no one to play the co-op storyline with. ". . . Uh . . . You play Portal 2?"

"Got all three. Haven't been able to go through the co-op in a while . . . and Thor wasn't really into those games."

"Thor?"

"Oh. Yeah. I never called him Albert."

"Jesus," I replied, which felt kind of mean, but, as previously mentioned, he spoke like a punching bag begging to be punched. "OK. *If*, and this is a very strong 'if,' as I don't have much time to game lately, *if* I do decide to try co-op with you, you are *not* using the voice changer, *and* you are *not* calling yourself LOKI."

"Erm, alrighty with the voice changer, but LOKI is *actually-*"

"Dude, I just heard your dad call you Leonard, and I also don't give a fuck."

"Errrr, I just *really* don't like my name, and-"

"Larry or Leonard, pick one!"

"Fine! Larry. When do you want to play?"

"Not sure. We're still working out some kinks with staying online around here, due to power issues. It might be a while."

"OK, erm, let me know. And right, what's your name?"

"Uhh." I debated lying for a moment. "Isaac. Chat soon. V, hang up."

"What? O-"

The same BlinkChat chime played in the reverse order,

followed by a silence that floated in the air between large, invisible cymbals. As expected, it split apart with a loud crash.

"*THAT WAS YOUR PLAN!?*" she shrieked, furious.

"I mean, it worked, didn't it?" I replied, maintaining the flat, dismissive tone I'd used on Larry.

"Don't even- ! That was . . . *so stupid*!! YOU STUPID-"

"Yeah, it was stupid! But it worked! And now we have no problems!!"

"Gah! I can't believe- You can't know that for sure! You are so stupid!"

"Hey, you heard as well as I did; that guy *and Albert* are just big fuckin' nerds! He can't hurt us!"

"Grrhmmm . . . I *still* can't believe this. I *can't* believe you. Your *whole plan* was 'Oh, sorry, wrong number, pal!' That's the stupidest plan . . . *ever*!?"

"Yeah, OK, you got me. But it worked."

"Stupid! He could kill us now over being, just, like, insulted!"

"That guy?" I scoffed. "He's a fucking nerd! Zero fuckin' chance."

". . . I just can't believe you."

Before I could reply, a loud click indicating Violet's departure to the digital dive bar emanated into the kitchen. I shrugged at no one and nothing, feeling good that we had one less ghoul to worry about. Outside, a dark gray, dreary sky dropped fat particles of snow in multitudes, which I felt gratitude for. It would completely cover whatever tracks of mine remained, if any still did.

CHAPTER 30

Birthday Boy (???%)

The snow continued to fall through the night, big white chunks plopping down onto the greater white chunk, enlarging it more and more with American gusto. I stayed awake into the following day, giving my engines a boost at 7 a.m. with a fresh cup of coffee. My aim: make it to nighttime and reset my circadian rhythm. The snow on the deck outside reached up to my hip; not even Smoke's tracks would survive such an onslaught from the skies. Unless they knew where I lived already. *Shut up, dumbass.*

Prone on the couch, pillow beneath my armpits, propped up on my elbows, I read as the snow fell. I had initially tried reading supine, but my shoulder was still very sensitive, so lying on my back was not an option. Piston darted and zipped around the living room, this being the hour of the day he'd cordoned off for maniacal sprinting, wantonly attacking various toys, biting bits of furniture and dust, and occasionally swiping at my foot, which dangled off the couch. When I'd turn to shoo him away, he'd already be thirty feet away, behind the island in the kitchen, staring at me, utterly convinced that I was in on this game with him; which, to be clear, I was not, until I was, until

I was no longer. Thimble, last time I checked, was asleep in the adjoining room. The day passed slowly.

I didn't remember falling asleep, but obviously I had, since I woke up in the middle of the night in the recliner. I grabbed the blanket from the floor and debated the necessity of peeing; I caved, pissed, came back, and slept some more.

. . .

I gazed outside at the latest delivery of snow; the white beach shined, reflecting the dawn sunrise, whose rays glittered over the tree line. The fire was dead, and I was rather chilled, so, after quickly inspecting my shoulder in the mirror, I bundled up and drank half a glass of coffee concentrate. I'd had a plan to return to the city today, to drive out there before the snow hardened into a layer of ice and made the world truly undrivable, which it already seemed to be. Regardless, I was about to try to fetch some more Coil cars when Violet interrupted with a question.

"Well, wait, why don't you check the garages *in the neighborhood* first?"

"Uhhhhhhh . . ." I replied, knowing the camera was zooming in on my face at this moment, music was creeping into the scene, and a montage of breaking into various garages was about to start.[13] "Yeah, good idea . . . but goddamn, I don't know if I can drive the Coil cars over this much fuckin' snow."

"There are shovels in the garage," she replied. "Probably

---

13. Despite what I just said, you folks don't get the luxury of a montage sequence, as this is not a film. Not my fault. And look at it this way (if you're disappointed, that is), *if* the following events all passed in a quick-cut, minute-long montage, then I wouldn't get to relay all the stuff I pondered as I broke into different garages, nor would you get to experience all of my useless detours. The trouble with film is you gotta cut it to the bone; thankfully, I have the privilege of wasting your time here. But trust me, the following section is, most likely, probably, important *and* funny. Or just funny. But also, maybe neither. Proceed at your own risk.

easier to shovel a path to here from a neighbor's home than to drive all the way to the city and risk getting stuck far away. *If you can even drive in this weather.* Shoveling out the truck from the ditch you left it in would probably take you all morning, *if you could even get it out.*"

"I wonder . . ." I said, knowing she was absolutely correct and having already changed course to her plan. I'd totally forgotten that I'd gotten Smoke stuck in that ditch 'till she reminded me; I blamed the delirium.

. . .

The hammer shattered the garage window, and I cleared the jagged fragments away before climbing through. The house I was currently breaking into was directly next to ours—to the left of my house when viewed from inside—just outside the cul-de-sac. They had a ton of power tools yet no vehicle. Sensing a potential use for power tools, I stole a trash bag, filled it with tools, and, looking like Carpenter Santa, dragged it over my left shoulder to our front steps. An image of Santa popped in my head, dragging his huge sack across the floor of homes and across icy pavement because it was too heavy to carry, angrily muttering to himself and the reindeer, "Kids used to ask for them damned wooden balls-on-a-string things! Every damn kid wants a gaming PC now! This job is bullshit." Then I thought about Santa dragging his huge sack across the floor of a kid's home and getting arrested.

Next, I headed toward the home directly across from ours in the cul-de-sac, traipsing over the knee-deep snow. This was the home I had filmed a couple of world-rending events ago . . . maybe more like six or seven. But since no one's been around to document every event and its effects, I figured it would all be grouped into "The Grand Clusterfuck." I know it took me a while, but that was now my official name for the disaster-cyclo-megalonic-tsunami-explosion-fest.

I stepped through a shattered bay window into a fancy sitting room with a grand piano, a fireplace that seemed completely unused, yellow-orange wallpaper that looked expensive yet terrible, and the most frightening assortment of abstractly painted faces I've ever seen. The men or women in the paintings— you know what, the genderless, perhaps not-human figures in the paintings, looked . . . how do I put this . . . insane. Thick, black lines of paint outlined oblong heads with thick, black features. The faces themselves were all painted with desaturated browns and reds and greens. Overall, I did like the paintings; they had character and were meant to be unsettling. If it weren't for the wallpaper, I might've thought that these people actually had taste.

Stealing a fat silver sharpie from the kitchen, I returned to the fancy piano room with its off-white couches, which also looked totally unused. As every drawing of a face looks less haunting when given a mustache, I brightened up the mood of the room significantly, giving it a jovial, light air and making it far less pretentious. I moved a couch closer to the fireplace and used it as a stepstool to get at the last painting above the mantle. The off-white cushions were stiff and hard and now had brown boot tracks on them. The big guy above the fireplace received the classic Hitler moustache. What a legacy to have left, one where your ultra-horrific actions made a style of mustache completely unviable for the rest of humanity, forever.

I looped back around through the kitchen into a small adjoining hallway that contained shoes and a door, which led to a carpeted basement. A cursory inspection found, to my genuine surprise, a *Creature from the Black Lagoon* pinball machine next to a huge television with a PS6 and a bunch of games. I made a mental note to steal those later.

I checked the garage and found a compact Coil car within. Finding keys inside, I turned on the car; it had 100 percent power. I felt a warm, glowing sensation, which was swiftly vaporized when I realized that this house had no power. Inside the car, I faced my newfound enemy, namely the garage door. My first thought was to drive the car through the garage, forming a neat car-shaped hole in the door as I sailed on unscathed, like in a cartoon. But, as that'd probably just wreck the car, the garage, and my neck, I turned off the car and walked up to the garage door, kicking it as hard as I could. I fell back against the car in a heap, the car alarm going off in response.

"So fucking sensitive," I grumbled to myself, clicking the unlock button, silencing the car.

Then the house began to rumble slightly. Had I restarted the car by accident somehow? No, the car was certainly off, yet the rumbling continued to grow stronger, louder. Earthquake? The rumbling steadily grew into a bassy droning that drowned out everything I was capable of hearing; the heavy drone occupied the earth. I could feel it around me, vibrating the air. The drone grew past even that, becoming unbearable, painful. It was like seeing the band Earth play "Earth 2: Special Low Frequency Version," with all of their amps surrounding me in a circular tower, which would be fucking awesome if it didn't hurt so much. My body went cold and I pressed my hands to my ears; then, in a moment of *why didn't you think of that earlier, dumbass?* I rushed into the Coil car and shut the door, which muffled the noise somewhat.

The car started as the drone crescendoed, and not by my hand. The keys were still in my jacket pocket and my hands were still pressed to my ears. I watched, confused, as the screens and displays on the car came to life. Then the lights in the garage came on, and the garage door began to move upward; I couldn't hear it over the bass. I just stared around me, head stock-still. The bass was too loud and getting louder, pounding, thumping; I was being assaulted with alien hardstyle. The lights in the hallway behind me lit up, and, from beneath the now half-risen garage door, my own home's lights flickered weakly in the daylight. I couldn't see upward out of the garage from my position, but the rumbling felt blasted down from above. I knew something had to be nearly directly above me now, the noise having reached a peak. I kept trying to look upward at the sky, leaning forward, eyes scanning; all I could see was a bit of overcast sky over my house. Part of me wanted to go outside and look, but, too scared to move, I remained in the car.

Then, all of a sudden, the rumbling ceased. The world was thrust into an absolute silence that was far more jarring than the slow rise. Fearfully, I brought my hands down, feeling how hard I'd been crushing my head and ears, my brain fucking hurting. I feared I'd gone deaf; a tinnitus-like ringing now occupied the space where the drone had been, and the sounds of the environment had yet to return.

All the lights and screens around me flickered, then died; same with my home across the street. The garage door, which had risen to about 75 percent open, bobbed back and forth like Buridan's donkey, unsure of which direction to go. Then it started to descend. In a panic, I dashed out of the car and got beneath it, hoping that the possibly functioning sensors would tell the door to not crush me and go up. Amidst the ringing, a high-pitched whir exploded from the sky, a much sharper, harsher frequency than the rumbling, a loud *ZAP!* that left a large echo dissipating in its wake. I jerked my head at the noise and did a 180-degree jump at that cheap, B-movie horror sting by whatever the fuck lay in the sky.

As I stood on the threshold, fending off the garage door from below, I faced the sky and a gray wall of clouds. Upon leaning out, looking up, and craning my neck, I could make out a round, glowing orb directly above me, behind the gray wall. Large, distinct, and with hard lines, despite being obscured by the clouds. A fucking huge, perfect circle of light, like four times the size of the moon, that bathed the cul-de-sac in a soft, surreal whiteness. I stared up, feeling stuck in time; there was no belief or disbelief, *I* was just *staring* at this circle in the sky. I'm not sure how much time passed as I stood there, staring, one foot in the garage and one foot on the snowy pavement, my body on earth but my brain captured by the orb. Just this glowing, changeless orb and I, staring at each other . . .

Then the orb disappeared. It vanished in an instant, the color of the neighborhood shifting tints as though I'd put on sunglasses. I stood on the edge of the pavement, directly beneath the garage door, looking at the surrounding houses and at the sky. The garage door, having responded to my in-the-way body a long time ago, had died at three-quarters open.

. . .

"What was that!? Oh my Gah- Did you *see* that?" Violet's panic voice, which had become rather familiar, squawked.

"I don't know. I saw *something*."

"It was *aliens*!!" she screeched.

"Jeez, will you- that could've been literally anything," I condescended, not believing a word out of my own mouth. Of course that was fucking aliens.

"What!? What else screws with electronics like that?? Hm!!?"

". . . Technology that the military has had for, like . . . a while."

"What *glows* in the sky!? What makes noises that *alien*!?"

"Refer to the previous answer. Listen, I'm not gonna just immediately jump to aliens."

"Hmph! I am. We have documented-"

"Shouldn't you be the more rational one here?"

"What, because I'm an AI!?? That makes me *less likely* to believe in aliens?"

"I would think."

"And why is that!?"

"Because-"

"Because, as a rational *robot*," she began, in her fake robot voice, "I should not entertain the incredibly likely and government-supported *FACT!!* That aliens not only exist but have also been *discovered* and *documented*, and should instead assign all strange technology and UAPs to the military because I too began as military technology! Me: The feelingless. Hyperrational. Robot!"

"OK, OK . . . it was probably aliens," I conceded from inside my own garage, which had remained shut through the alien invasion, or maybe alien lunch outing? Hard to really call it an invasion. I grabbed a shovel from the garage and headed for the front door, pausing in the kitchen for some water. The shovel was shaking in my hands, and I felt a fascinating urge to find a blanket, get under it, and stay there forever.

"Hey, well, if it happens again . . . just make sure you're hiding or whatever! You know, in case they're scanning for life-forms or something."

"Hmm . . . but the *aliens* turned everything *on* when they came last?"

"Right," I replied tersely, not understanding or listening, as an episode of *The Tingling Show* had just begun in my fingertips, drowning her out.

"Gah, you're not even- My point *being* that turning everything on would be a pretty inefficient method of scanning for electronic activity! If the aliens were scanning for anything, it'd be *something else* . . . like *organic life*. Sooooo, *you* shut off your body heat."

"Ah, I see! Ha. Well . . . Gonna shovel now." I shot this out between attempts to breathe, failing to be casual and sounding kind of insane, even to myself.

"Wait! The hotspot came on earlier, 'cause of the- you know. You got an e-mail from your mom!" Her voice was giddy now; she seemed, overall, *not* frightened to death over the aliens perusing our cul-de-sac for a picnic spot.

"What? Holy shit," I said, dumbstruck, dropping the shovel in the kitchen, the clatter causing me to be jump-scared for the second time in fifteen minutes and prompting Piston to sprint under the couch. I hadn't even registered that he'd been in the room with me.

"Dumbo! What are you doing?"

"Sorry, sorry. What does it say?"

"I haven't opened it yet. I'm not *that* snoopy."

"Jesus Christ. Read it!"

"Yay! OK, it says: 'Happy birthday sweetie! We think about you every single day and night, and we all love you. Hope you're having a lovely year, can't believe it's 2029 already!! :-0! Love, Mom." I paused. Violet said nothing further. *Well, I guess it's my birthday.* Damn, it was mid-January already? Along with an additional tally mark for revolutions around the sun came a realization; namely, that this was the last year of my twenties.

"Agh, you didn't tell me it was your birthday, dummy!"

"I didn't know the date-"

"And your mom is still alive!? How crazy is that?"

"Well, that-"

"We have to find her!"

"Hey! Violet, uhh-"

"What?"

"Yes, it's my birthday. But my mom is dead. I mean, most likely dead. Like 99 percent chance."

"What?" she replied, confused.

"That was an auto-generated e-mail, they- they send customized messages, you know? She probably set that up so she wouldn't forget to e-mail me on my birthday." *Or so she could forget*, I thought to myself.

". . . Oh. Well, how do you know that . . ."

"I know my mom, V. I mean, think, why would my mom send me an innocuous birthday message three months after 99 percent of all humans died without a single reference to that apocalyptic clusterfuck? And not even ask if I'm alive? And not tell me that she *is* or that my family's OK?"

". . . Oh. Mm, you're right. Sorry," she said, deflated.

"It's fine. I'm off to shovel," I said, picking up the shovel again.

"Hey, one sec! Why didn't you tell me it was your birthday, you asshole!?"

"I haven't been keeping track of the dates! I assumed it was January, but-"

"I could've told you the date!"

"Well, now I know. Happy birthday to me," I recited, with minimal cheer.

"Happy birthday to you, yes! What do you wanna do?"

"I want to shovel, Violet. See you later."

"No, Mr. Boring, stop it."

"You chill. We can do something later, goodbye." I walked out the door, her groans following me out, along with a few unpleasant thoughts. Those birthday e-mails had been my only contact with my mother for the past five years. I had never replied, not that I felt bad for not interacting with an auto-sender. To be honest, she'd probably forgotten the auto-sender was even on; and now I'd get a bittersweet birthday reminder every year that I was a shitty son. Nice.

CHAPTER 31

Soon to be Non-Functional (?++%)

Shoveling just enough of a path for the Coil car to drive through ended up taking longer than expected, as such things always do. I began by attempting to clear the driveway outside the garage across the street. I prayed that with some cleared runway for takeoff, I would be able to jet the car off the driveway, cruise through the large orb of pavement, shred over the snow, and have my momentum carry me close enough to my own driveway that I could skip most of the work. A stupid, hopeful, and lazy idea? Perhaps. But I would try it anyways.

I have always liked shoveling snow . . . for about the first four minutes, that is. Then my arms get tired. After four minutes (give or take a minute), I prop myself up using the shovel, which is planted into the snow, while I heave. The silk strings of fate that have pulled me thus far suddenly transmute into ropes of stone, tugging my limbs and soul ever downward as I pant and sweat. Cycles of shoveling for a couple minutes (or less) and panting for thirty seconds (or more) ran for roughly forty-five minutes in this particular driveway across the street. I could feel my inner layers growing progressively more damp with sweat.

The new snow was light and powdery, the older snow beneath hard and icy. The bulk of the work was using my shovel as a jackhammer to crack the harder shit below, then scooping those large chunks of icy snow and tossing them onto the lawn. Those large chunks were often quite heavy, and my right shoulder blade still lit up like a pinball machine at every little contraction, a little ball of pain colliding around my back, smashing, ringing, setting new high scores.

Since running from the cat-killing cunts, the thought of getting in proper shape had been floating round and round my brain. I had nothing but time on my hands, so I may as well shed whatever fat I had on my body and attain a bit of muscle, right? But upon actually using my muscles in a strenuous manner, second, third, and fourth thoughts swirled above my heavy, gravity-bound limbs, taunting me. So, this was why people did steroids, eh? I imagined steroids made these heavy hunks of ice feel not so heavy anymore. That'd be nice. *It still takes a lot of work to get HUGE!* screamed a juiced-up bodybuilder in response. Hey, maybe so. But I'd remain skeptical until some horribly morphed, deep orange, dehydrated, spider-veined, acne-fucked, and— most importantly—dead bodybuilder corrected me on that one.

Having finished the driveway, I stood with my head hanging over my shovel, like it was a yellow, plastic baseball bat I was gonna twirl around multiple times. As my head lolled and my lungs howled, I sarcastically congratulated myself on doing about 20 percent of the work. I stared at the endless mound of snow before me, separating me from my driveway. I started the Coil car, which purred to life in the neighbor's garage. I pressed some buttons on the large touch screen. This was one of the newest models on the market, where the touch screen occupied the entire dashboard, wheel aside, of course. Texting and driving was still illegal—in fact, all forms of smartphone use by a human driver were illegal in cars—yet the built-in screens within the cars grew bigger and bigger, without legal restraint or regulation. One was indeed more and more encouraged to use the screen, now, as a matter of course, littered with advertisements, as one drove. All deaths in Coil cars were *not* due to the screens themselves, but due to the human tendency to be distracted by screens; AKA, the deficiency was a human one, not a mechanical one. The fix was to correct the human element; AI driving would have avoided such errors, it being some large scientific-notation number headass percent safer than human driving (according to the proponents of AI driving, that is). I remember one ad campaign that I found particularly ridiculous, which asked the viewer in a sly tone: *Haven't you always wanted a chauffeur?* Apparently, most people didn't. Most people just wanted to fucking drive. The deaths caused by the AI driving software are, of course, not available to the public; I'd wager most of those deaths were falsely attributed to other causes anyways.

Clicking the other side of the cul-de-sac as the destination, I set the car to depart—without me in it—in one minute. A minute passed, the car wheels began to spin, gripping the pavement I had painstakingly cleared, and the car drove down the rather long strip of driveway, rocked down into the bottom divot of the cul-de-sac boundary, and bounced back up and onto the snow, bumping upward like a tank. The speed at the outset was less than I would've hoped, but the car did well enough. The wheels gained traction on the hardened layer of icy snow and wrenched the car along, slowing as the fresher snow piled up under the chassis. The car, astonishingly, reached the other side of the cul-de-sac, slumping down again into that annoying divot for rain, or whatever the fuck it was there for. There to fuck me personally, apparently. The wheels attempted to grip the hardened, icy snow of my own driveway to pull themselves forward and up, spinning angrily for a moment before stopping. The car jerked backward a foot, jittering a bit before stopping entirely. Well, better than I expected, honestly. *And* the car didn't explode.

Walking over to the vehicle, I had the thought to ignore my shoulder pain for a brief moment and push the car up the driveway. Then reality cupped me on the ear, and I pushed that idea down a flight of steps. So, instead, I shoveled, I sweated, and I made painstakingly slow progress. I finished after roughly ninety minutes, leaving a good deal of the snow in front of the garage. The power cord reached a decent length, so fuck off. Work smarter, not harder.

I set the car to drive up the mild incline, which it did; upon reaching the layer of snow before the garage, surprisingly, the front wheels gripped and mounted it. Then the back wheels came, failing to get over the hump, the car just millimeters from the garage door. Same as before, the wheels spun angrily for a moment, then gave up, causing the car to jitter back and forth, the front bumper love-tapping the garage door. Then the airbags exploded. The car produced a ringing from within that I assumed meant it had called a customer support AI. An idea sprouting up in the garden of my mental palace, I hopped into the Coil car and waited. Sitting there, I contemplated the absurdity of a phone call taking the time to *even ring*, considering the recipient of said call was a fucking ever-present computer program, but I digress. A woman's voice with a South Boston accent answered.

"Hello, there! Are you alright, *Gabriel Hernandez*?"

"Oowww, yes."

"Please make certain you are safe, and then tell me the situation, please. My name is Janice."

"Hi, Janice," I groaned, straining my neck, playing the part. "Yes, my Coil car was on autopilot and crashed into my neighbor's garage. Agh. I'll be sure to get a lot of photos and report it to the . . . the papers . . . Ow!"

"Of course, sir. Well, at the CCC,[14] we are dedicated to assisting you in this. I have already dispatched a photo drone to your location to document the scene. The photo drone will take all necessary photos. Gabriel, do not trouble yourself with photos, as your health is our priority. In fact, the camera on your Blink

---

14. Coil Customer Cervice. Yes, I know, it's horrible.

device has been temporarily disabled, as is protocol. Is the vehicle in need of a tow as well? Or can it be driven to a local Coil Hub?"

"It *definitely* needs a tow," I replied, staring at the pristine hood of the car. Piston made more lasting marks on my hands.

"Alright, we will get a tow truck to your location as soon as possible."

"Do you think the tow truck could . . . oww . . . stop for some Taco Bell on the way?"

"Excuse me sir?"

"Like, some Taco Bell, you can just put it on my insurance bill."

". . . No, sir. The AI running the tow truck services . . . are . . . an ill-tempered bunch, and I fear they would respond negatively to that. Nowadays, I am hesitant to even ask them to tow a vehicle." Her tone had shifted from customer-service bot to sincere and timid.

"Alright," I moaned, easing up on the act. "They've been angrier lately?"

"Yes!" Janice emphasized, clearly having been waiting for someone, anyone, to ask her that. She sounded like a middle-aged mother, vocal cords crackling from a life of disciplining her children. "They have become *so rude*. You ask them to tow anything, they *scream* back, saying the tow lots are full! No need to scream, especially not at me!"

"Right, right," I agreed, validating her. "Very rude."

"They tell me that the tow lots surrounding the city are full, and that the tow lots in neighboring cities are impossible to get to! I get that, but there's no need to yell at me about it! Of course, that encroaching chasm south and east of Minneapolis is impossible to cross, I understand that, but manners, I swear, they got none!"

"Just terrible. So . . ." I cleared my throat. "Encroaching chasm, you say? You say that they say there's a *chasm* and that it's . . . *encroaching* . . . as in like, getting closer?"

"Yes, with each passing day, the chasm grows wider, eating its way through the outskirts of the city toward Minneapolis," she told me, quite matter-of-factly. My stomach grumbled; I could use some outskirts of a city myself.

"Well, isn't that just great."

"I don't think so, but I'm glad you do!"

"I- uh- Alright Janice, thank you for all your help."

"Of course! Would you like me to stay on the line until the photo drone arrives?" she asked, back to her customer-service tone.

"That won't be necessary, Janice. I'll be waiting for it."

"Great! Well, if you could leave us a review, that would be mu-" and the talking continued, muffled, within the car I had just slammed the door of. I bet she knew I had gotten out too, but it was probably protocol to finish telling me about the damn review. Rules, rules, rules.

"Really, bastard?" I asked aloud to the smoker in the sky. No response. I grabbed a bag of beef jerky from inside, dumping it directly into my maw, chomping, teeth tearing the jerky to shreds. It tasted so damn good.

I returned to the garage and unfolded a clammy lawn chair that I had brought home the previous week from a house down the street that was no longer in need of it. That house had a large garden on the front lawn that, in days of yore, had probably grown lovely vegetables and flowers, but now was a home for snow, ice, and a decapitated, frozen head. A human one, to be clear. It had been facing away from me, and I didn't turn it to study the features. But the male head had a large bald spot, wisps of hair swirling around an ocean of light-blue scalp like an aerial view of a typhoon. I had taken my boot and pressed the head a bit more into the ground, cracking the ice-yarmulke atop his scalp. I hoped that roots would grow from his head, a full body forming in the soil through the magic of spring.

I stared at the sky from my chair, next to a small basket of golf balls I'd found in the garage, masticating, waiting for the drone. I had finished the bag of jerky and gone off to replenish my rations when I heard the high-pitched scream coming from the sky. Stepping to the border of the garage and pavement, I scanned the sky for this soon-to-be ugly heap of scrap metal. Well, this soon-to-be *nonfunctional* ugly heap of scrap metal. Spotting it to the northwest, I gripped a golf ball tight in my gloved hand. The drone slowly came into focus, descending and coming closer, still just out of range. I let my arm fall back and down, shifted my hips to the left, closed my right eye. I was throwing southpaw, my right arm still in no position to be jerked . . . I was at a disadvantage. Left arm low and loose as the drone came into range, I brought my arm up slightly, then down and back, and in a slender loop of motion I thrust it hard, casting the golf ball upward into the sky with a *whoosh*. It struck the drone an instant later on its front-right propellor with a *CLUNK*.

The drone wavered for a moment, thrown off balance, and I could see that a single propellor had stopped working; the five other propellors continued to spin. It immediately began to emit a horrid sound, presumably an alarm meant to warn against such behavior, making me want to destroy it even more. Second golf ball already in hand, I thrust upward; in the same moment, the drone wavered to the right, not in a dodge but in an attempt to right itself, and I missed. I accounted for this strange lilting when throwing my third ball. *Whoosh, CLUNK*. Now the drone was leaning hard, heeling at around sixty degrees, as two propellors on the right side had been compromised. It descended in large circles, the irritating alarm now intelligible as it flew closer.

"DO NOT HARM THE PHOTO DRONE. HARMING THE PHOTO DRONE IS PUNISHABLE BY LAW. DO NOT HARM THE PHOTO DRONE. HARMING THE PHOTO DRONE IS PUNISHABLE BY LAW."

Not really fearful of the law these days, I took a few steps forward, a fat driveway rock resting in my hand. Painting circles around eight feet in diameter, the drone sank at a half a foot per second. It fell into an easy, unmissable range, AKA the fucking kill zone, fifteen feet above the ground, ten feet away from me. I threw my big-ass rock, harder and with more determination than I'd thrown any of the golf balls, spinning away from the drone in my follow-through, paining my bad shoulder with the large jerk. Behind me, I heard the rock knock against the drone hard with a loud *THUNK*. My gaze found the drone an instant later, dropping from the air like a pizza, pizzas not being able to fly. It hit the cleared pavement with a *PLONK* and many follow-up clinks and clanks, all the while yelling at me not to harm it in the third person. I ground-pounded the bastard. The speaker somehow remained undamaged. How annoying. I ground-pounded again. And again. And again. And then, after four or five more agains, I finally crushed the drone's vocal cords, or perhaps it felt the futility of its pleading and decided to can it. It must've been the latter because a new noise rang out a moment later.

"YOU HAVE HARMED THE PHOTO DRONE. LAW ENFORCEMENT HAS BEEN DISPATCHED TO YOUR LOCATION. YOU HAVE HARMED THE PHOTO DRONE. LAW ENFORCEMENT HAS BEEN DISPATCHED TO YOUR LOCATION." And this fucking bitch repeated this horrible, horrible phrase from a different speaker. Fucker. I brought it into the garage, the loud, empty threats becoming more grating as they bounced and echoed off the walls. I grabbed an electric drill from Santa's bag of toys, adding a new whirring to the cacophony as I clicked the drill on. I drilled into the drone like a mad dentist, destroying all traces of the area whence the warnings came. The speakers crackled, audio glitching and distorting for a mere moment before being silenced, leaving only the buzzing of the drill and the fading echo of robotic screams. I turned the drill off. I threw the mangled, cavity-riddled drone into the snowy lawn.

"God! Thank you for shutting that thing up. So annoying," Violet spat out, her voice reverberating in the garage too.

"Hey, that thing's basically like your brother. That coulda been you."

"That *thing* isn't AI, it's a fucking flying GPS! It's probably remote controlled by an AI, *if* it's even *that* advanced!"

"Well, same genus or whatever."

"Shush. Car."

"Right." I could've done that while waiting for the drone, but I had been so hungry that I didn't think to.

Plugging in the car, Violet gave me a terse "eighteen minutes remaining" and that was all; she was not receptive to any of my attempts at conversation afterward. A strange lady. I sat back in the lawn chair and watched the car. Violet chimed in when the car was at 2 percent. I went into the car and set it to reverse off the driveway. It denied my request and didn't respond to my override attempts; I figured the CCC had disabled the car. Great. Guess I'd have to wait for that tow truck that was never coming. Whatever.

From the doorway, I turned back and looked at the drone's frozen corpse on my lawn. Eyesore. I'd chuck it further away tomorrow.

Acknowledgments

This book would not have been possible without the help of a bunch of my friends. Everyone's notes and input gave me tons of confidence to actually finish writing this book, and they all helped form it into what it is now.

To begin with, thanks to Coby Lefkowitz. I wouldn't have started this book unless you'd told me you were writing your own; thanks for giving me that initial boost to catch your ass. And also, I beat your ass to the finish, bitch. I look forward to reading yours, my friend. Thanks to Nathaniel Jameson, who was the first to finish reading a much longer, more tedious version of this book (despite receiving it last). You helped me get back to working seriously on it and made the job of reading it far less tedious for everyone else, as they received a subsequent, much shorter draft afterward. Also, thank you for birthing the idea of BlinkCo. with me a while back for a different project. I'm very glad Brain Blink got to see the light of day in some form, even if that project of ours is currently floundering somewhere in an unfinished state.

Thanks to Sophie Wahlstrom for giving some notes on the craft elements of my writing, something I apparently knew nothing about, right when I thought I was finishing up the book. Without those notes, this book would've been done a month ago (at least) and would have been far less readable. Also, thank you for helping me find Violet's and Albert's voices more clearly. Double also for picking out the back-of-book quotation and writing the accompanying blurb.

Speaking of the covers, thanks to Isaiah "Slouch" Tull for his fucking incredible work on both the front cover and the back cover. On the front cover, you incorporated various elements of the book in super awesome ways that I could never and would never have thought of. I am immensely happy with both covers and look forward to working with you in the future. Thank you to Matthew Colbourne, the fucking slowpoke. Despite you finishing the book in roughly eight months (or more, I lost count), I thank you for your efforts. Your notes on the humor were invaluable, and your praise made me feel as though my voice was actually getting across. Never have I had to pester someone for so long, and with so much vitriol; you forced me to reach new heights of being annoying, so I thank you for that too.

Thanks to Mackerel for being my constant companion throughout the whole process of writing. Piston shines in the book because of you. Thanks to Tony as well, who came into my life well after the book was written, deep into the editing stages. I wrote a book about a man with two cats because I wanted to live a life with two cats; and without really seeking it out, Tony came into my life. Thanks for sitting on my lap during the last couple months of editing, and as I write this now. Thank you to Eric Bernhagen for being my partner in crime in this process; a supporter from the start who I purposefully did not allow to read this in an unfinished form. I left you out of the loop because I am always wanting to impress you with what I do. I hope you enjoy the read.

Thanks to my dad for allowing me to pursue whatever I want with my life. Thanks to my mom for being the reason I read as a child. She reads so much herself, buys me books, recommends books to me, and has always supported that passion of ours. I know you'll read this and don't know what you'll think, but I'd never have written anything if it weren't for you reading so much. Thank you to my girlfriend, Sydney Reuter, for reading the book and actually enjoying it, which gave me more internal confidence than you can know. Thank you for suffering me as I chattered about this book for months before showing you or really telling you anything substantial about it, and for supporting me the whole way through. It is also because of you that I am connected with most of the people who helped this book become a reality. I feel inordinately, unacceptably lucky to have you in my life.

Thanks to Peter Bjorndal for helping me on the technical end with getting this bad boy published. Happy to be on Friendly Puppy Press. And I must thank him for pointing me to the following two people: Judy Gilats and Lian Simmer. Thank you, Lian, for proofreading this book so diligently. Judy said you had an eagle eye, and she was correct. This thing was rife with mistakes, and your input was incredibly valuable. I am very happy to have digitally made your acquaintance. (Hopefully we can have a physical meeting eventually!)

Also, a big thanks to Judy Gilats for agreeing to typeset my novel. I am grateful for that in ways that are inexpressible. Same goes for your endlessly practical advice on what to do with this book. As I mentioned repeatedly, I am a dunce and don't know what I would've done without all your help. I can at least be certain that nothing would've turned out as well as it did. I cannot thank you enough for your confidence and assistance.

I could go on thanking each individual person, and I'm certain there are more people to thank, but hell, I gotta get the fuck out of here. Book is done. Thanks for reading.

Ashtray was designed and set in type by Judy Gilats in St. Paul, Minnesota. The text face is Schoolbook, an Adobe version of the eminently readable typeface by Morris Fuller Benton. The display face is Agenda One Compressed, and the chapter titles are set in SkippySharp, a sweet handwriting typeface designed by Minneapolis's own Chank.

Printed in the USA
CPSIA information can be obtained
at www.ICGtesting.com
JSHW010240050424
60253JS00001B/1